1

Nightingale Woods

Kathryn Brown

etting away from the past was the only way forward. Yet my journey into the promising future I had planned would eventually remind me that my past was something I could never get away from.

Part One
1996-1997

Monday 11th March

Steve Harris asked me out. I've had a massive crush on him since I started working at Winterson's Plastics and I never thought this day would come. He wants to take me for a drink on Wednesday night. The problem is he's married.

Anyway, I've agreed to go. Maybe he'll start telling me how much his wife doesn't understand him. I guess one drink and a listening ear won't hurt.

Wednesday 13th March

I looked in my wardrobe before leaving for work and realised the top I was going to wear for tonight's big night out has a button missing. That's just typical of me; always last minute. Can't believe I didn't sew that button back on. I decided on a black blouse and jeans instead, probably a bit casual but we're only having a drink. Plus, he sees me dressed up at work all day. The casual look will be a nice change.

(Note to self: don't forget to look for the button; could be under the bed.)

Thursday 14th March

Well, last night was eventful. Steve turned up fifteen minutes late, apologising profusely, saying his wife came in late from work and had lots of stuff to tell him. We found a little table in the corner of the Crown Green pub, nicely tucked away from prying eyes but luckily it was quiet anyway so we were able to chat. He looked completely gorgeous in a white shirt underneath a black V neck jumper. For a man in his mid forties, he looks so much younger. I think he noticed that I kept looking at the hairs protruding from his collar so now he probably thinks I'm a pervert. He had lots to say, especially about his wife, Olivia, to whom he's been married for eighteen years. I felt quite guilty knowing I was having a night out with a married man but told myself it was just a drink, nothing more. I expected him to start telling me how his marriage is on the rocks, but he didn't. He complimented her for being hard working and said how much he admired her. Felt a bit inadequate at one point and wondered why he'd bothered asking me out in the first place. He wouldn't let me pay for any drinks and came back on one of his trips to the bar with a packet of cheese and onion crisps, but I felt too nervous to eat them; I'm not the most refined crisp eater, and didn't fancy onion breath just in case he wanted a goodnight kiss.

I told him about all the jobs I've had previously and how I haven't been out with many guys. Looking back, I imagine he thinks my life is pretty boring compared to his. I let him do most of the talking, guys like that don't they, it makes them feel important. But with Steve, he didn't come across as being arrogant; maybe he just wanted to see if he could still pull after all those years of marriage.

When he walked me to my car and leaned in for a kiss, I thought I'd died and gone to heaven. He has to be the best kisser ever. I didn't want it to end. Drove home feeling elated at the fact the man I've had a crush on for twelve months has finally made a move on me, but as I turned into the cul-de-sac I suddenly realised that I'd just kissed a married man. Did that mean I was having an affair? Damn it, something I vowed never to do.

Friday 15ᵗʰ March

Steve came into reception this morning and I thought he was going to kiss me as he stood so close to me. I could smell his aftershave and thought how nice it was, and couldn't help thinking of that heavenly kiss last night. But I've been tossing and turning all night after worrying myself sick about the thought of getting involved with a married man. I need to put a stop to it before it goes any further.

****

I noticed Steve hanging around in the car park when I was walking to my car at home time but I decided to ignore him. Bugger, wish I'd gone over now, after all, we're not *really* having an affair are we.

Monday 18ᵗʰ March

I couldn't wait to get into the office today. I've missed Steve over the weekend and I'm a bit worried about these sudden feelings that seem to have crept up on me. It was just a crush a few days ago and now I'm concerned it might be something more. Think we need to talk about our 'date' last week.

****

It was Steve's suggestion that we meet up one evening this week as it's difficult to talk at work. I reluctantly agreed and invited him to mine. Bit concerned about the butterflies taking flight in my stomach but once we've had a chat maybe we can be friends. Just friends.

Tuesday 19th March

Steve came round to my flat last night. I think he was oblivious to the reason why I wanted to talk (must work on my facial expressions in the mirror). I put my new Celine Dion cassette on and poured him a glass of wine. We sat on the sofa and it felt a bit awkward at first, but then he kissed me and I melted again. The night of talking and making him see that I couldn't be his mistress turned into a fumble on my Chesterfield and him knocking his glass of red wine over my cream carpet. He said he'd get it cleaned for me, but I've been thinking of replacing it so this could be the excuse I needed. He left at ten as he wanted to be home before his wife came in from work at eleven.

Thursday 21st March

I only saw Steve in passing yesterday as he was in meetings all day. But his wife phoned to speak to him at lunch time and it felt really strange having to be professional with her when I have a raging crush on her husband. Not sure I can cope with the guilt of it all. She seems like a really nice woman.

****

Steve came into reception just before I was ready to leave at five. He wants us to meet up tomorrow night and has suggested the Plough and Horses in Lipton. It's quite a drive for him but not too bad for me so I've agreed. Actually, I've wanted to go there for a while. There's no harm in going if only to see what the pub's like. Maybe this time we can put an end to what could be the start of something. Something that shouldn't be happening.

Saturday 23rd March

It turned out to be a really pleasant evening with Steve last night. I managed to find a replacement button and sew it onto the blouse I wanted to wear on our first 'date' and Steve seemed quite taken with it, though I think it could have been the fact I had my push-up bra on and a bit too much cleavage on show. He kept holding my hand in the pub and I have to admit, it felt lovely. I managed to explain to him how I felt about our 'relationship' but he reckons we aren't doing anything wrong; he said it's just a close friendship and I shouldn't worry about it. I asked if his wife would ever suspect and he said never. Though I do think my cleavage was turning him on a little so he probably would have said anything. I half wish I'd not bothered with that damn blouse now. Think I might stick it in the charity bag.

He gave me a long and lingering kiss before we parted in the pub car park. I almost asked him if he wanted to come back to my place but it was ten o'clock and I had a feeling he'd have to get back. Plus, I wasn't sure I really wanted it; bit early days yet.

For heaven's sake, what am I saying? I can't have a relationship with this man, he's married. Get a grip, Rachel.

Friday 29th March

I haven't seen much of Steve all week and I'm worried he might be avoiding me. I'm going out with Kelly tonight and thinking of telling her about Steve, but a bit unsure as to how she'll react. After Greasy Graham shit on her a few months back she vowed she'd never trust another man. I feel really sorry for her, Graham was such a bastard. I'll be surprised if she speaks to me again once I tell her about Steve but I need to talk to someone. I keep thinking if he wasn't married would we see a lot more of each other. I still don't know if that's what I want. But I know I like him, a lot. This is going to get complicated and I need to be ready to deal with it.

Monday 1ˢᵗ April

Good news; Kelly's over the moon for me. Not sure if that's what I need or not really. Thought she'd at least talk me out of seeing Steve and make me realise once and for all that what we're doing is wrong. But no, she squealed in the pub, made everyone turn round then she hugged me. Is my love life so sad that my best mate, whose boyfriend was shagging the town bike, is glad I'm seeing a married man?

(Wondering if having Kelly as a best mate is a good idea. Will sleep on it.)

Tuesday 2ⁿᵈ April

I've decided that Kelly is the best mate ever. She's happy that I'm happy and that's a good thing, isn't it?

****

Steve's wife rang the office today. When I heard her voice I nearly dropped the phone. She must think I'm totally incompetent as a receptionist when I barked, 'you want to speak to Steve Harris?' God, that was so rude. I'll get the sack at this rate. I must make a point of being really professional next time she answers; would hate for old battleaxe Brenda to come storming in the office telling me someone's complained about my attitude.

I put her through to Steve and I'm ashamed to say I felt jealous. Is this what being 'the other woman' is like? Feeling jealous and inadequate? I really did think it would be more fun than that.

****

Steve came into the office just before home time. He told me that Olivia asked if I was new because I didn't seem to know what I was doing, the cheeky cow. He was laughing. I wasn't. We've arranged for him to come to my flat on Thursday night. I'm not sure if I'm nervous, excited or just plain bloody stupid.

Friday 5th April – Good Friday

Steve came round last night and we really did have a lovely night. We got a Chinese takeaway and a bottle of wine that I drank most of as he was driving home. We talked about all sorts of stuff, from his job to his family, and from my non-existent love life to the jobs I've had before the one at Winterson's. But the icing on the cake was when he followed me into the kitchen to help me wash up the plates. I was just squirting Fairy liquid into the bowl when he placed his arms around me then pulled me into him. He twisted me round, put his huge hands either side of my face, and kissed me. I was instantly turned on and couldn't resist leading him to my bedroom. He gently pushed me onto the bed then lay by my side before he started to undo the buttons on my blouse. I could feel his erection pressing against my leg which only added more fuel to my already ignited fire. By the time he got round to removing my jeans, I was literally tugging at his own jeans, desperate to get in them.

We made love on top of the duvet and I'm not sure if it was the thought of forbidden fruit or that he made me feel stupendously sexy, but I've never had sex as wonderful in my life, ever. He was so gentle whilst I just wanted to get on with it. But he wanted all the foreplay, from both of us, which made the whole experience so much more intense. It got a bit embarrassing when he couldn't open the wrapper on the condom but I used my strong teeth and ripped it open for him.

****

I guess I'm now having an affair with a married man.

Tuesday 9th April

I haven't seen Steve since last Thursday night as it's been the Easter weekend. My mum bought me a huge Dairy Milk chocolate egg which I polished off on Saturday night. Felt lonely sitting in the flat on my own with only a bottle of white wine and an Easter egg for company, but I need to accept that being 'the other woman' is a lonely business.

I was really excited about going to work this morning, definitely not like me after a long weekend off that's usually been spent on the lash doing a pub crawl round Manchester. Steve had a glow about him as he walked into reception and he winked and smiled at me parading his pearly white teeth. I noticed Claire and Yvonne were watching so I disguised my smile into a good morning nod, probably blushing like a beetroot at the same time. I have a feeling they're starting to suss.

(Note to self: be more discreet.)

Wednesday 10th April

Not good; Claire approached me this morning with a smug look on her face and asked if there's something going on between me and Steve. Obviously I denied it but I could tell she wasn't convinced.

I went to find Steve at lunch time and told him what Claire had asked me and he says we need to lay low for a while. I was hoping he'd come round one night this week. It looks like that's out of the question now. I could kill Claire, I really could.

Friday 12th April

Steve's idea of lying low seems to have gone out of the window as he's invited me to the driving range tonight. I've never played golf in my life and never thought I would but guess it's worth a try if it means spending a bit of time with him. Mum's always saying I need a hobby other than my job, though why she thinks sitting behind reception in a plastics factory is a hobby I've no idea.

****

I got home at half past nine after making a complete tit of myself at the driving range. I can't hit a golf ball to save my life and see no point in it either. Steve knows the guy who works behind the bar and I felt a bit embarrassed, wondering if the barman assumed we were having an affair. But Steve reassured me he's never taken Olivia to that particular golf club so as far as the barman needs to know, I was his other half. Actually, it did make me feel pretty good when he said that. I'm definitely falling for him. This thought scares me a bit as I've never felt this way about a married man before. I'm starting to take our relationship a bit more seriously as I know someone could get hurt here. Hopefully not me.

Monday 15th April

I'm not really enjoying the weekends at the moment. Monday mornings don't come round quick enough and I thought I'd never say that. But I'm missing Steve when I don't see him. Is this something I need to worry about I wonder. I could be getting a bit infatuated but seeing him this morning was an amazing feeling. I was almost turned on, especially when he blew me a kiss.

We met up at lunch time and walked to the chip van on the Industrial Estate, then sat on a dry patch of grass and ate our chips. Olivia makes Steve sandwiches every day and he shared them with me. At one point, Brenda drove past us in her Renault Clio and nearly crashed it into a lamp post when she saw us sat together. She's such a nosey old bag. But still, she's my boss and I don't want her prying. She's known Steve and Olivia for a long time. He says I shouldn't worry about her as he can wrap her round his little finger which I do actually believe. In fact, if I didn't know better, I'd say Brenda has the hots for Steve and she's probably jealous that we're so close.

****

Kelly rang me last night to say her and Greasy Graham are back together. I can't believe she's taken him back after he slept with that slag Joanne. But I guess she loves him, and love is blind as they say. I hope for her sake he keeps it in his trousers this time round.

Tuesday 7th May

I haven't updated my diary for ages. There's nothing much happened and I couldn't think of anything interesting to write. I've seen Steve twice in the last two weeks, which was a couple of hours at the Plough and Horses and an hour at the driving range. He hasn't been round to the flat as Olivia is off work with a bad back and she said she wants him home. Starting to think Steve could be henpecked.

He came into reception at lunch time and asked if I wanted chips from the van but I said no. I've decided to play hard to get for a while. Just because I'm young, free and single doesn't mean I'm always available and there at his beck and call. He needs to learn that I'm a woman first, not just his bit on the side. That sounds so awful when I say it out loud, but I guess that's exactly what I am. Still, I'm not letting him take advantage of me.

Thursday 9th May

It's his eyes that get me I think; I couldn't resist them as he leaned over my desk and asked if he could pop round last night. And I gave in. I was so determined to tell him it wasn't convenient.

He turned up at 7.30 with a bottle of Blue Nun. Before I got chance to open it he grabbed me and started ripping my clothes off. He's an amazing lover. It was a bit chilly in the flat so we got in the bed and just lay there, panting like two over-excited dogs. I pretended I was Meggie in The Thorn Birds in the scene where she and the priest are having a post-sex chat, as I turned over and put my hands on his chest, leaning my head against him and running my fingers through his coarse, silver hairs. He stroked my bare shoulders and grinned at me like the cat that had just got the cream. Eventually I got up, went to get two glasses and opened the wine. Then we sat up in my bed, clinked glasses and acted like two people who were on their honeymoon.

Writing that has made me go all tingly.

Friday 10th May

It's going to be another weekend of not seeing Steve. I'm going to my mum's for tea on Sunday so that'll take my mind off him, plus I'm going to buy some new underwear tomorrow afternoon as it seems Steve quite likes lacy lingerie.

Saturday 11th May

I'm pretty cut up as I saw Steve in town with his wife. I noticed them on the other side of the street looking in a shop window. He turned round and saw me staring but turned back to Olivia quick. Felt such an idiot as I stood there gobsmacked holding the Bessie's Lingerie bag. The first thought I had was that the surprise of him seeing me in my new black lacy knickers and bra would be ruined as I assumed he'd seen the pink Bessie's carrier bag.

Then I woke up to the reality of it. I'd seen my lover with his wife. I've never felt so gutted in my life, ever. I couldn't concentrate on doing anymore shopping so hurried back to the car and drove home in a daze. God knows how I reached the house in one piece because I don't remember any of the twenty minute drive back to my flat. After seeing Steve and Olivia together, I'm not sure I can carry on doing this. I don't want my heart breaking by anyone but this has hit me like a bolt of lightning. It's a serious situation and up until now Olivia has just been another person in Steve's life, and the woman on the end of the phone. Now I know she's not just another person but the woman he married and the woman he's been sleeping with for at least eighteen years. I need to ask him about his daughter, Susan. He did say once that he doesn't want to talk about her to me as he feels it's a part of his life that needs to be kept separate from our relationship, but I need to know more about him. It's either that or I'm calling it a day. The worst thing is that Olivia is really attractive with mousey-blond hair in a shoulder length curly bob, and a lovely slim waist. She doesn't look anywhere near mid 40's, more like mid 20's if I was guessing. I'm starting to get a little worried that Steve's been lying to me.

Monday 13th May

Steve walked into reception this morning looking a bit sheepish. He asked me if I wanted a brew and I said yes. By the time he came back with the cups, bloody fat cow Brenda was hovering near the filing cabinet. I reckon she's got her eye on us. He left the cup of coffee on my desk and scarpered. I didn't see him again till home time. He was stood by his car so I went over to him. He told me that Brenda's mentioned he spends too much time in reception and it's putting me off my work, so he decided to avoid me for the rest of the day. I noticed

Brenda exit the building and I made a point of turning round to face her. It's none of her damn business who I see in my personal life. Just because she's a fat old cow with no life doesn't mean no one else can have a life either. Though any man who went near her would probably need therapy.

Anyway, Steve apologised for being in town with Olivia on Saturday, but I assured him it wasn't his fault I saw them together. I've asked him how old she is and he says she's 44. I told him she's very attractive and he agreed, which made me feel like shit. But then he kissed me, in the frigging work's car park of all places. I was a bit taken aback to say the least, but I admit it felt good. I've invited him over one night this week, told him I have a surprise for him. He's trying to get away on Wednesday night so long as Olivia is on a late shift at the old people's home where she's worked for ten years. He said that will enable him to get home before she does and have a shower before he goes to bed. I thought about that afterwards. Not sure if his expectations for us to have sex are a bit high, or whether he feels he needs to wash away my scent. Either way, once again I felt a bit shit. Still, I'm looking forward to some quality time with him again. If we have sex, I won't complain.

Thursday 16ᵗʰ May

The sex was brilliant last night and Steve was on fire. He absolutely loves my seductive underwear and couldn't stop touching the bra, even when I'd taken it off. Olivia is one lucky lady to sleep with this man every night.

Friday 17th May

I have just read that last sentence back from yesterday's diary entry. I don't want to imagine Steve having sex with Olivia, that's too much to bear. He did tell me that they don't do it much these days and when they do it's usually after a drunken night out. I'm not really sure if he said that to make me feel better, but to think he's having sex with his wife actually makes me feel a bit sick. I'm starting to get really protective over this relationship and have to keep reminding myself that I'm 'the other woman' which I don't like, but I know it's either that or going back to being on my own. Right now, I'm enjoying the thrill of it all even though I'm not enjoying the thoughts that keep cropping into my head.

When I see him at work and he smiles at me with those piercing blue eyes and gorgeous white teeth, I melt, every bloody time. But whenever Olivia rings to speak to him my stomach turns over. She's the main person in his life, not me. I'm just a holiday, whereas she's all year round. I'll have another chat with Kelly this weekend. Think I need to talk to someone about all this. I keep wondering if Steve has told anyone about us.

Sunday 19th May

Kelly and I went to the pub on Saturday night and had a really good girlie chat. Greasy Graham was on a stag do so she needed something to do. I knew she'd end up living her life around him again, he's so manipulative. I explained how I felt about Steve, about the fact I think I'm falling for him and she surprised me by saying I need to be careful. I asked her how she felt about her best mate seeing a married man and she scowled at me before telling me she doesn't really approve of the fact he's married but she's glad I'm enjoying my life and that's more important right now. She seems to have changed her tune a bit recently and I wonder if it's because she and Greasy Graham are back to being very much together.

I'm now hoping I haven't offended Kelly and her being happy for me when I first announced my relationship with Steve, hasn't turned sour. We've been best friends for years and without her to talk to my life will consist of the bottle bank and walks up and down the aisles in Tesco.

I feel shit again now and half wished I'd never told Kelly about Steve. Lying in bed last night, Kelly's words going round in my head together with the six glasses of wine and three Curacao's, I started thinking about Steve and Olivia probably cuddling on their marital sofa watching their marital telly, before hopping into their marital bed. I so need to get these thoughts out of my head. I need to learn to separate Steve and Olivia's life to his relationship with me. He seems to have no problem doing it, so why can't I? And I still haven't asked him about his daughter.

(Note to self: don't let Steve shag you again until you've asked him about Susan.)

Thursday 23rd May

Steve came round last night, it seems like he's able to get away on Wednesday's though he's a bit worried as he keeps missing practice sessions at the driving range. Still, I think the sight of my unbuttoned blouse compensated. I did pluck up courage to ask him about his daughter but he wasn't in the mood to talk about her so I decided to leave it. As I'm trying to separate his home life with our relationship I suppose I shouldn't push it. Think I'm feeling a bit confused.

He stayed until after half past ten last night, which is quite late for him. Said he'd told Olivia he was at the golf club and would probably stay for a drink with the guys. I took advantage of his extended stay and we had a shower together which meant he didn't stink of my perfume when he got home. Two birds, one stone, and all that jazz.

Monday 10th June

Again, nothing interesting to add so I haven't bothered updating the diary recently. It's coming up to three months since I started seeing Steve and up to now it's been a case of a trip to the golf range or a couple of hours at my flat. I definitely prefer time at the flat of course but would really love to do something different, like go out for a nice meal somewhere and look like we're a proper couple.

Only we aren't, are we. It's just sex between two people, one who's married and the other who's a saddo.

Some nights I stand at my bedroom window hoping he'll surprise me and just turn up; that I'll see his car coming round the corner into my cul-de-sac and he'll have an overnight bag with him. It's turning into a fantasy now, maybe even an obsession. I'd love him to stay over one night but I know it's not going to happen and that makes me feel a bit sad really. The only time we can get together is when Olivia is working or when he's got an excuse to go out, like a trip to the driving range because he has a match coming up and needs to practice on his swing. I'm not a fan of the golf club; it's full of toffs with posh cars, not to mention the wives who look at me like I'm shit off their Jimmy Choos. They all sit in the club house drinking Pimms looking bored out of their tree. I know I would be if the highlight of my social life was waiting around for my husband to get to the nineteenth hole.

****

Mum asked me if I want to go away with her this summer. She's looking at going to a nice little hotel in Wales where my dad used to take her, except she wants me to go with her so she won't be on her own. I really, really don't want to go. For several reasons; 1, because it's a hotel that's about as exciting as a pile of ironing; 2, because it's full of pensioners; 3, because she'll be reminiscing about dad before he buggered off to New Zealand, and 4, because I'll miss Steve. No, a week in a pensioner's hotel in South Wales really doesn't appeal to me. I'll have to decline her offer and tell her to ask Auntie Maud instead. She's not my real auntie, just one of those close family friends that mum has known for donkey's years and insists I call her auntie. I don't think she'll mind me not going, plus Auntie Maud's a hoot so the two of them will have a much better time without my sour face maudlin about.

Thursday 20th June

I'm pleased to report that Steve did come last night. He turned up at the flat at his usual time, half past seven, bottle of wine in one hand and a bunch of flowers in the other. He apologised when he handed me the flowers and said he'd picked them up from the local petrol station. I told him it's the thought that

24

counts, before a carnation drooped before my eyes. This time I opened the wine first and we sat on the sofa. I was just going to reach for the remote control when he put his hands either side of my face and turned me round to look at him. He had a really serious expression that I didn't like very much. And then he dropped the bombshell.

Olivia's booked a holiday for them as a surprise. She reckons they don't spend enough time together. They're going to Majorca for a fortnight in the middle of July and staying in a luxury five star hotel, just the two of them. She said it'll be like a second honeymoon.

I'm gutted. Seriously gutted. I'm so gutted in fact that I drank a full glass of wine in one fell swoop then refilled the glass and downed that one, too. I think Steve was a bit shocked at that but I didn't care. How could he do this to me? What am I supposed to do while he's away playing Mr Faithful in Majorca? Damn him. Damn this relationship. Damn me for falling for a married man.

I made sure he knew I was upset about it. The binge drinking probably gave it away, but I asked him to leave. I couldn't look at him because I just wanted to cry. Or throw something.

After he'd gone I looked at the petrol station flowers and realised why he'd bought them for me.

Saturday 22ⁿᵈ June

I wouldn't speak to Steve at work yesterday, even when he came into reception. I acted like a complete twat and picked up the phone to have a pretend conversation with Mr. Nobody. He must

25

have thought I was being really childish, which of course I was. It was inevitable that this was going to happen sooner or later. But when Olivia rang late in the afternoon, I snapped at her and told her Steve wasn't available. She was a bit cross with me I could tell. I imagine he was asked about the rude receptionist at work again.

Sunday 23rd June

It's nearly midnight and I'm wide awake, I'm going to be so knackered at work tomorrow. Brenda will probably fire me and then I'll never see Steve again. But I can't sleep. I can't stop thinking about him and Olivia sunning themselves on a beach in Majorca before they go back to their hotel room. It hurts so damn much. Three months ago I was young, free and single with a crush on a married man called Steve Harris. Now I'm young and single and not really free anymore because I've turned into this uncharacteristic person in my life known as 'the other woman'. Does that make me free, I wonder? I have no idea. But I know one thing, if Steve still wants to see me I'm going to carry on seeing him. I've decided I can't live without him. No matter how much his marriage to Olivia hurts, I enjoy his company and love the attention he gives me. Until someone single comes along I'm going to carry on seeing Steve and try to get used to being 'the other woman'.

****

Shit, it's two am and I'm still wide awake. My eyes are hurting because I've been crying. I need to get a grip.

(Note to self: tell Steve you insist he comes round tomorrow night so you can talk about how you feel. And don't take no for an answer.)

Tuesday 25th June

Fortunately, Steve was able to get away last night so we met at the Plough and Horses which is easier for him to get home from, rather than coming along country lanes to get to my flat. I told him I didn't want him to go away to Majorca but accepted that he was going anyway and I won't go on about it. He nodded at me as though he was telling me I was being a good girl. If I hadn't been driving I'd have ordered a pint at the bar to give me a bit of Dutch courage in order to tell him to fuck off. As it happened, he suggested going for a drive in his Golf so we could park up somewhere and be completely alone. I mentioned the woods located at the back of the pub so we went there and found a lovely little spot in the trees. It was pretty dark and he switched the light on in the car before leaning over to kiss me. I responded, a little more passionately than I expected I would, but he gets me every time. We ended up getting into the back seat and stripping off. I have to admit it wasn't the easiest of sexual positions but it was good all the same. I think he might have been a bit cold.

He took me back to my car an hour later and as I kissed him goodnight, I realised we hadn't talked at all but had just spent the last hour having sex in the back of his Volkswagen Golf. Why does he do this to me? I need to stop making myself so available all the time. I wanted to talk about why I don't want him to go away on holiday, not with his wife at any rate, but perhaps with me. I also wanted to tell him that I love him. But that's something that can wait. Maybe he isn't ready to hear that yet. Maybe he never will be. I'm still not absolutely sure how he feels about me. I know he cares about me and I know he likes me but I can't help thinking this is just about having good sex to him, like he's copped off with a younger woman and feels he's still 'got it'. Maybe he's going through a mid-life crisis and I'm at the centre of it.

Friday 12ᵗʰ July

I'm a bit upset so decided not to update the diary. Not been in a great mood recently due to Steve going away tomorrow on his 'second honeymoon'. Brenda really pissed me off when she wobbled into reception and gave me a pile of filing to do. We have a filing clerk but apparently she's off sick so Brenda has kindly decided I have to do it in her absence. Claire manned the phones for an hour and took great pleasure in having a chin wag with Olivia when she phoned to tell Steve she'd just been to collect their pesetas. I definitely get the impression that Claire knows about me and Steve because when she finished her cosy chat with Olivia, she turned to me and made a point of saying how romantic it was that they were going on a second honeymoon. I bit my lip, thinking it was a better option than throwing the Cotton and Associates file at her. Starting to wonder why I work here when I can't stand most of the staff. Then again, if I didn't work here I wouldn't see Steve would I. Best to put that thought to the back of my mind for now.

Anyway, Steve left at five and stood by his car waiting for me to exit the building. I let Brenda drive away, watched Claire and Yvonne link arms and skip off like they were in a primary school playground, then I walked over to him and smiled pathetically. He kissed me in the car park again. I hope someone saw us this time because I've been so down lately that I'm not sure how much longer I can continue this charade. We got into his car and he gave me a little box. It's a pair of gold heart-shaped earrings. I can't believe it. They're absolutely gorgeous. I kissed him hard on the lips and told him how much I love them, and then he handed me a note which he told me to read once I got home.   It reads:

Rachel, while I'm away I will be thinking of you all the time. Please know that I don't want to go on this holiday but couldn't refuse otherwise Olivia would be really suspicious. I want you to know that when I get back I'm going to spend more time with you and put my foot down with Olivia. I'm going to start going to the driving range at least three times a week and will stay for a drink afterwards. I realise my swing won't improve but at least we'll be able to spend more time together.

Missing you already.

Yours, Steve x

Yours? What the hell does that mean? Is he telling me he's mine? Am I reading too much into this? Not sure I want to answer that. I reckon I'll have to wait until he gets home to see where this relationship is going. And I'm not sure I believe he doesn't want to go to Majorca for a fortnight. I mean, I'd love to go to Majorca for a fortnight. After declining mum's offer of a week in Wales I've realised that I'm going nowhere this year. Even Kelly and Greasy Graham are going away; having a week in Greece, how appropriate. She's always wanted to visit Athens and Greasy Graham agreed it would be good for them to get away. So that's me then, Billy-No-Mates, as per.

Saturday 20th July

Steve has been away for a week now and he hasn't sent me a postcard. I really thought he would. Maybe he's forgotten my address. I'll ask him when he gets back. Kelly went to Athens on Wednesday and on Thursday mum went to Wales with Auntie Maud. They're doing a few nights at the pensioner's hotel in South Wales then a week in a hotel in Cardiff. If I'd have known they were going to bloody Cardiff I might have gone. I hear the nightlife's awesome.

I rang Denise this morning to see if she wanted to go out tonight but she's going to a wedding reception. As I'm totally depressed about my lack of a social life, not to mention my lack of a sex life, I've decided to buy a few bottles of cider and drown my sorrows whilst watching The Thorn Birds.

****

The phone rang at 6pm but when I picked it up there was a click and then the line went dead. I reckon it was Steve and he couldn't get through. Damn bloody stupid British Telecom and their crap service. Mind you, it could have been at his end I suppose.

Sunday 21st July

Another phone call at 11am and the same thing happened. I shouted really loud down the phone 'Steeeeeve!' but it just went dead again. Fucking brilliant, I muttered to myself, cursing British Telecom again. I hope it wasn't mum. If she heard me say Steve, she'll insist on knowing who he is and I have no intention of telling her I'm seeing a married man. She'll flip. Especially after dad did a moonlight flit to Auckland with Auntie Anna (another friend of mum's whom I had to call auntie, though once mum found out about their fling, as she called it, she was no longer to be known as Auntie Anna but 'that bitch who stole your father').

Monday 22nd July

Last week without Steve at work was bad enough. This week I have to endure a temp in the office who's been hired in to sort out the filing cabinet after Gaynor, the filing clerk, decided not to bother coming back and resigned. Can't say I blame her really, filing is so boring. And she's got no ambition so I imagine she's quite content sat at home all day waiting for her weasel of a husband to come home so she can make his tea. We used to have many a conversation about her husband, as I think he's a chauvinist pig and she's thinks he's just old-fashioned. But we all know he's just a lazy tosser who takes full advantage of his wife's low self-esteem and ability to make herself look like a desperate housewife. Anyway, she's gone now and I have to put up with some dozy temp from Julia's Temping Agency in town. We've had temps from there before and they've all been useless.

Tuesday 23rd July

Adele walked into the office at nine this morning. She's gorgeous. No, I mean seriously gorgeous. She has long, brunette hair with a little curly kink at the bottom, soft brown eyes and a complexion to die for. And her figure, oh my, I wouldn't be surprised if she thinks I bat for the other side after she caught me eyeing up her chest umpteen times today. She had just a bit of cleavage on show, though enough to tease, which I know for a fact sent Brian into a frenzy in the canteen. I reckon the poor man's not getting any at home. He was sitting at the table with his tongue hanging out, not even looking at the Daily Star in front of him, when I took her in there to get a bacon butty. She sat at the table next to him and I swear I noticed a bulge in his pants, the dirty get. Though I imagine Adele knows how gorgeous she is and wears such clothing because she can get away with it. If I wore a blouse like that I'd be really conscious of showing too much boob. And I'm quite in awe of my own boobs for what it's worth. They're nice and round and firm. Steve says more than a handful is wasted anyway. Maybe that's his way of telling me they're small.

Wednesday 24th July

I didn't sleep much last night as kept thinking about Steve. Still haven't had a postcard and the phone hasn't rung since Sunday morning. Even my mum hasn't phoned. Still, at least that must mean she's enjoying herself. She went through a lot when dad left. It was ten years ago now, but she was left with me on her own and I was at that awkward age of 16. I guess it can't have been easy for her. Dad has offered for me to go and stay with him anytime I want but every time I've mentioned it in front of mum she's always pulled her face and made a point of telling me 'that bitch who stole your father will never make you welcome. They moved over there to start a new life, and that doesn't involve us.' Bit harsh I know, but I can see where she's coming from. I get the odd postcard from him and of course he sends birthday and Christmas cards with money. He also sent me a cheque for three thousand pounds when I bought my flat. But, as time has gone by I've just never bothered about going over to visit him. He'll never come back here so I guess there's a chance I'll never him again.

Anyway, where was I? Oh yes, Steve. I keep thinking of him with Olivia and it's driving me mad. If he hasn't got a tan when he returns I'm going to be really upset because that can only mean one thing, especially on a second honeymoon. But now I'm worried about Adele. Not her personally, but I'm worried that when Steve clasps his eyes on her he'll want a bit of her as well. Shit, he might even dump me in favour of *her*. I know I'm acting like a complete idiot. I obviously don't trust him.

Saturday 27th July

Steve is due back today. I've been watching arrivals all day on the television for his flight details. He said the plane would arrive in Manchester at 15.15. The arrivals page tells me it's on time. That means in ten minutes my lover will be back on British soil. This makes me happy. I can't wait till Monday morning. Just hope Adele doesn't wear that bloody blouse again.

Monday 29th July

OMG! Steve has the most amazing tan. He looks sensational. I couldn't speak when I saw him, no words would come out. I must have looked like a guppy fish when he first looked at me. I just stared into his eyes and smiled like a gorp. He mouthed to me 'see you later' when he saw someone in reception, not realising it was Adele and she wouldn't have been bothered because she had her head stuck in the filing cabinet. Much to my relief she was wearing a polo neck but she still looked incredible and I'm sure Steve will be asking who she is.

****

I met Steve at his car at 5pm. We let everyone drive away then we got in the car and kissed each other like we'd been prised apart for two weeks. Two very long weeks, that is. I didn't realise just how much I've missed him. It was really intense. He said he's had a lovely holiday and the hotel was really fabulous, but he wishes it had been me he'd gone with. I wasn't sure I believed him but I kissed him again for saying it, just as Adele walked past.

Shit, bollocks and shit. I can't believe she looked in the car just as I was pulling away from him. She smiled at us and waved a silly little wave where she didn't move her hand just her fingers. I'm going to have to ask her to keep quiet. I'm going to have to bribe her. Maybe I could ask her round for a meal one night this week and we could chat about it. Oh God, I can't do that, she already thinks I fancy her, now she'll think I'm batting for *both* sides. Steve suggests I just tell her the truth and ask her not to say anything. She's a temp after all and won't be working with us for long. Hopefully.

Thursday 1st August

I was hoping Steve would have come round last night but he said he needed to go to the golf club and pay his fees for the following year. I couldn't go

34

with him because he's been to many functions there with Olivia so I pretended I was okay with it and we arranged for him to come round tomorrow night instead. He said he'd show me his white bits.

Adele hasn't said anything about Steve all day. Think I'm going to forget about her seeing us in his car last night and hope to God she doesn't mention it to anyone. She's acted quite normal so I have a feeling she's going to be discreet.

Saturday 3rd August

Steve doesn't have many white bits, but he looks amazing with a tan. I'd have loved to have seen him in his trunks and he's promised to show me photos next week once Olivia's picked them up from Max Spielmann. I felt a bit weird when he said I could see the photos because I imagine there'll be loads with Olivia on as well. Might need a drink before he comes over with them.

****

It was a pretty magical night, one that I'm going to remember for a very long time. We didn't just have sex last night, we made love. Steve told me he's in love with me. I thought I heard him say 'I love you' while we were at it, but I was in no fit state at the time to ask him to repeat it. Anyway, he rolled off me, reached for the glass of wine by his side of the bed then turned to face me and said 'I'm in love with you.' I was gobsmacked at first and thought he was just meaning he's in 'lust' with me, enjoys the sex and all that, but then he scooped me up under his right arm and pulled me towards him. He kissed my forehead and said it again. He also told me he's been thinking such a lot about me while he's been away that he had to keep going off for walks on his own. He also confirmed it was him that tried to ring me but every time I picked up, the line at his end went dead. After the second attempt on Sunday morning he gave up.

I don't know where he got his energy from last night, but we made love again after that brief conversation, and it was incredible. He left at half past ten but said he might be able to get away for a few hours on Sunday afternoon if I was at home. I reassured him I would be. I can go and see mum on Monday, find out all about the holiday with Auntie Maud.

Sunday 4th August

It's 9pm and I'm pissed as a fart. I haven't a clue how I managed to turn the laptop on but I did. Steve didn't come over, nor did he ring to say he couldn't come. I'm really disappointed in him and will make sure he knows tomorrow when I see him at work. He could have at least rung me. Oh, bollocks to men. I'm going to bed.

Monday 5th August

I arrived in work today to find out that Adele won't be coming in again. She told the agency that the filing job is boring and she needs more stimulation (I bet she does). The agency clerk asked me to pass the message onto Brenda who was on the phone at the time. The clerk also told me that Adele wanted to pass on her best wishes to me for the future and said she hoped it all turned out okay. I cringed at that bit, knowing full well what she meant. I feel a bit lonely in reception on my own now and even though Brenda didn't ask me to do the filing, I have a feeling she might tomorrow when she sees how much crap Brian has dumped in the filing room. If she asks me I'm going to be brave and say I think we should get another temp in as I'm always so busy on the switchboard and typing up Mr. Winterson's letters. He doesn't give me that many admittedly, but I'll be damned if I'm going to be Brenda's filing clerk. Being the receptionist is boring enough.

****

Steve has promised me he owes me an explanation but doesn't want to discuss it at work so he's coming round tomorrow night. He says he couldn't get away yesterday because of a personal family issue and that's why he feels it wouldn't be right to tell me while we're at work. I forgave him, mouthed 'I love you' and turned back to the switchboard before old bag Brenda caught me with my trousers down, so to speak.

Wednesday 7th August

Steve's explanation about his absence on Sunday afternoon was quite lengthy but I do understand now. His daughter Susan, went round to his house on Sunday after lunch. Apparently, she lives with her boyfriend Keith, but he's a bit of an arsehole. They had a big row and she decided to move back home but Steve isn't happy about that, simply because it could scupper his plans to see me so often, especially when Olivia's at work. So he told her to sort her relationship out. But then Olivia decided that Steve was being the arsehole and told Susan that she was always welcome to move back home. Steve had no choice but to go along with it otherwise Olivia would start asking questions about why he was so against her moving in with them, so he had to go round to her flat and collect the rest of her belongings. As it happens, Keith was there and he was really cut up, crying that he wanted Susan back and hadn't meant to call her a selfish bitch. Steve felt he should stay and calm Keith down which gave Susan and her mum time to have a chat as well. Steve and Keith ended up in the local.

Two hours later, they both went back to Steve's house to see if they could make Susan see sense, which fortunately she did, and so all's well that ends well. The thing is Steve told me Susan isn't actually his real daughter. Olivia was in a relationship a couple of years before they got married and Susan was the result. Susan's biological father never bothered with her so Steve offered to raise the child as his own and a year after she was born they got married. No one knows that he isn't Susan's real father except immediate family. I told him it's none of my business anyway but he can always talk to me about anything and it won't go any further. I want us to be completely honest with each other.

Mind you, I still think we should keep our relationship separate to the one he has with Olivia; not sure I want to be bothered with all his complications.

Friday 9th August

Fortunately, Brenda has hired another filing temp. This one is called Sandra and she's in her fifties. She's very nice if not a bit set in her ways and just wants to get on with the job which is good, means she won't be asking me too many personal questions. She's also only working three days a week which means I'll have reception to myself on Monday's and Friday's. The only drawback with that is I'll probably have Claire and Yvonne keep popping their heads round to see if I'm okay, their code word for 'any gossip?'

Kelly rang me at work today and asked if I'd go on a hen party with her tonight. I'd already invited Steve round so I was reluctant to accept, but they're going to Jerry's, my favourite nightclub in town. I told Steve and he said he didn't mind.

Sunday 11th August

Think I might be passed going to nightclubs. Spent all day yesterday in bed feeling rough as a dog's arse. The phone rang mid-afternoon and it was mum wondering where I was because I haven't seen or spoken to her since last week. She was full of the Welsh holiday, telling me how amazing the hotel was and how much I would have loved the spa. I just nodded and thought about Steve. No spa masseuse could ever give me a massage like he can.

****

Poor mum, feel a bit awful now. I'll go and see her tomorrow night.

Monday 12th August

Just been to mum's. She's not happy with me because she says, in her words, 'you're not interested in anything I'm doing.' I'm concerned that my relationship with Steve is starting to interfere with my relationship with mum. We've always been so close, especially after dad left, and I really hate upsetting her. I wanted to tell her about Steve but didn't. I'm pretty sure she'll never understand in a month of Sunday's. But I have promised to take her out for lunch this Saturday. We're going to her favourite garden centre because she loves their beef stroganoff.

Wednesday 14th August

Steve and I went to the chip van for lunch today. It's been a really hot day so we sat on the grass up the road where no one could see us. Except Claire that is, when she jogged past in her lycra. She looked the part, I'll give her that, but she's such a show off. She smiled and panted what sounded like 'Hi' on her way past. We smiled back and carried on eating our chips as though we had every right to be sat on the grass together. I'll await her interrogation as it's bound to come at some point.

Thought she might have nipped into reception this afternoon but she didn't. She's probably been filling Yvonne in on the cosy scene set by Steve and Rachel on the grass at Priestfield Industrial Estate.

Thursday 15^h August

As predicted, Claire came to see me today, cup of coffee in one hand and a file in the other. She sang 'hello' to me as she strolled in and sat down at the other desk. I watched her put the file down and take a noisy slurp of coffee before she looked at me with a suspicious smirk.

'Anything to tell me?' she asked.

'No,' I replied.

'Sure?' she asked again.

'Positive.' I replied.

'Oh, come on, Rach, you're not telling me there's nothing going on between you and Steve Harris, it's obvious, for god sake. I won't tell anyone, honest.' She made a cross symbol against her chest then pressed her hands together as though she was going to start praying.

I told her nothing was going on and that we're just close friends and even if there was something going on it would be none of her business and I wouldn't tell her anyway.

'I don't believe you,' she smirked.

'I'm not bothered whether you believe me or not, it's the truth. Sorry I can't make your day and fill you with gossip but there's absolutely nothing to tell,' I said, smirking back.

She stood up then, slurped her coffee again, picked up the file then wandered to the door.

'You're right,' she said, 'none of my beeswax, I won't ask again.' I turned back to the switchboard, willing it to light up. Then she did something that really touched me, really made me see another side to her, a side that I honestly never knew existed. She said, 'Rachel, be careful, you're a lovely person and I don't want to see you get hurt.'

I sat there gobsmacked for a moment, wondering if I'd heard her right, but yes, she seemed genuinely concerned about me. I reckon she's alright really, and maybe it's Yvonne that's the bad influence. Maybe when they're together they're thick as two thieves, but Claire has definitely gone up in my estimations. She didn't hang around for a response so once I'd got over the shock of her being nice to me, I picked up line one that was flashing red for an outside call.

It was Olivia, needing to speak to her husband.

Friday 16th August

Steve came to the flat last night. I wasn't sure if he could definitely come but he turned up at 8pm. We had a coffee as I've been on a tee-total mission this week, then we made love on the sofa after getting bored whilst watching Honey, I Shrunk the Kids. I told him about the awkward conversation with Claire and he just smiled. Said he's always thought Claire is a nice girl and if I were to tell anyone at work it should be her. But I said I'm not telling anyone so he doesn't need to worry. He reckons loads of people know anyway, which kind of shocked me I have to say. He said Brian's always joking with him about us going out for lunch together and he has a feeling Brenda knows something as well. When I asked him how, he said he has no idea but every time Brian's poking fun at him for fancying me she always seems to be in the vicinity giving him dirty looks. As I wouldn't put it past Brenda to ring Olivia, I told Steve we need to be careful from now on as I really need this job to help me pay the mortgage amongst other things. I'm not sure whether he agreed or not because he was too busy fondling my boobs and not really concentrating anymore.

Saturday 17th August

Took mum to Paradise Garden Centre for lunch and we had a great time. She was really chatty and very grateful that I treated her. Think she's over being pissed off with me now. At least I don't need to feel guilty anymore for not visiting her as often. I just wish I could tell her I've got a man in my life but I'm not going to. I'm enjoying my relationship with Steve and I know if she finds out she'll do everything she can to stop me seeing him on the principle that he's married. The fact that he's a nice guy won't come into it. Still, I can understand. She said I look radiantly happy but didn't ask why that was, so I changed the subject and pointed out how lovely the pansies looked this year.

Monday 19ᵗʰ August

Claire's being really nice to me and I have to admit that I'm finding it a bit weird. She's asked if I want to go for a drink with her on Wednesday night but I've declined. It's obvious what she's up to and I'm not being made to look a fool. I might like her now but we'll never be best friends. I have this notion that she and Yvonne are plotting something and she's going to be wired up in the pub and I'll end up spilling the beans after she's got me pissed. I'm not falling for that one.

Steve laughed when I told him and said it could've been worse; it could've been Brenda wanting to take me out for a drink. He's got a point. Still, I'm not going out with Claire and that's final.

Friday 23ʳᵈ August

Met Steve at the Plough and Horses last night and we went back to the woods to make love. It was so romantic and he was so horny. I think it's the danger of someone finding us in the woods, stark-bollock naked in the back of his Golf, with the windows steamed up and Michael Bolton playing softly in the background. It's a bit squashed in there but it really is a lovely place. Fortunately, there's never anyone about so even on these light nights we can get away with it. We talked about meeting here one weekend and having a walk through the woods. I think that will be perfect. He's playing golf all of this weekend so I'll see if he wants to do it next weekend. Fingers crossed.

Tuesday 27th August

Brenda came in the office today and said I need to take some annual holiday as I still have two weeks left for this year and if I don't take it soon she won't let me carry it over. Apparently, according to her, it's a new policy for employees that joined the firm within the last two years. I'm going to query it with Brian because I think she's just made it up to get rid of me for a couple of weeks. Though I could manage a week off as I need to paint my bedroom.

Wednesday 28th August

I've told Brenda I'll book next week off if she's able to find a temp and as I suspected, she said she'd already found one. I think she's got something up her sleeve for when I'm not here, like finding the perfect receptionist and finding a few excuses to get me off the premises. She'll have a fight on her hands if that's her game because I'm going nowhere.

****

Steve's face dropped when I told him I'll be off next week. He says he's going to miss me which made me fall in love with him all over again. He also says he's going to take a day off as well so that we can go for that walk in the woods. I'm so excited right now I need a stiff drink to calm me down. I can't wait to see Brenda's face when she realises that both me *and* Steve are off on the same day. I imagine Claire and Yvonne will have a field day, too.

Friday 30th August

Had a lovely, romantic evening last night with Steve when he turned up unexpectedly at 8pm. He said he'd been to the driving range and wanted to see me so we could make arrangements for our day out next week. We've planned to meet up in the little lay-by where it seems quietest, in the woods, at half past ten next Wednesday. If I manage to get any sleep between now and then, it'll be a miracle.

****

Mum rang earlier to ask if I wanted to go to a spa hotel for a few days next week as I'm off work. Shit. I really would've said yes in any other circumstances, but I've told her I'm going to paint my bedroom and give the flat a good deep clean. Think she blacked out for a while as she didn't speak for about a minute. Then she cleared her throat and croaked, 'on your own?' She must know I'm seeing someone, she can read me like a book. I might have to tell her that I've got a boyfriend but we're not serious so I won't be introducing him to her just yet. I'll pop round for Sunday dinner and tell her then.

Sunday 1st September

It's my favourite season, autumn. Mum made a delicious roast beef dinner with Yorkshires and all the trimmings. As she'd invited Auntie Maud as well I couldn't fill her in on my mystery boyfriend. She did try to collar me when I was loading the dishwasher but Auntie Maud walked in and asked for some Gaviscon. I'm always telling mum that her Yorkshires are a bit stodgy but she never listens.

****

Steve has just rang and it's nine o'clock at night! He's never rung me at this time; in fact, he hardly ever rings me at all. He said he was going to the off licence as Olivia fancied a bottle of wine so he stopped off at the phone box and thought he'd just say hello. Says he's missing me already and is dreading this week at work without seeing my smiling face in reception. He says the loveliest things to me. I don't know what I'd do if he wasn't in my life, and that scares me. I keep thinking what will happen if Olivia finds out about us and he decides to ditch me and stay with her. It's a thought that's been kicking around for nearly a month or so now, ever since he said he'd fallen in love with me. Part of me has this awful feeling that this will go tits up. But, when we're together on our own, I think one day it's just going to be him and me, no Olivia and no Susan either. Although, I imagine Susan will always be a part of his life. It's not something we've talked about but I know that if he left Olivia tomorrow I'd let him move in here with me and I'd be determined to make a go of it.

I told Kelly how I feel and she still says be careful, even though I know she's glad that I'm happy. She and Greasy Graham seem really content these days and I don't see as much of her as I used to. But that's okay as I understand she's moved on with her life so I'm not going to get in her way. She did say she'd be there for me though, when it all went wrong. I wasn't too sure if I appreciated her saying that but I know she meant well. I pointed out that it was a case of 'if' it went wrong, which I'm absolutely certain it won't. She's a good friend and I'm lucky to have her, especially now.

Monday 2nd September

I got up at half past nine this morning and watched a bit of telly before going to B&Q for paint supplies. Didn't realise how bloody expensive it all is. Anyway, I've started sanding down the walls and skirting boards so I can start painting tomorrow. The paint is a gorgeous light green colour with gloss white for the wood work. And I've bought a really posh-looking stick on border, too. Cost a small fortune but it's better than paying someone else to do it.

Tuesday 3rd September

I'm really nervous about tomorrow. No idea why. I haven't eaten all day because I'm excited, but now I just feel sick. What if someone sees us, someone who knows us from work? I can't stop thinking about how Steve must be feeling as I bet he's just as nervous if not more so. He's the one who has to tell all the lies, making the excuses for going out of the house. I haven't asked him where he's told Olivia he's going for the day but I assume it's the golf club. I only hope she doesn't take the day off and suggest going with him as she seems to be trying to attach herself to his hip right now. Oh bugger, I need to get to sleep but the paint's given me a bad head and my mind is like a whirlwind of thoughts. It wasn't long ago that I would have just walked away from this relationship but now, I feel I'm in too deep. I'm a different person, in love with a married man, wanting to spend every waking moment with him.

I keep asking myself why I love him so much. I mean for God's sake, he sleeps with another woman every night and for all I know he could be lying to me about his non-existent sex life; they could be at it like rabbits. No, scrap that thought, I don't want to know if they are. Or do I? Do I have a right to know more about his personal life with Olivia? Am I entitled as 'the other woman' to know what goes on behind closed doors in his marital home? Maybe I should mention it, tell him that it's on my mind and I want him to be honest with me. What if he tells me the truth? But what is the truth? And why am I sat up in bed at nearly midnight with my laptop writing all this crap? Get a grip, Rachel, get a grip.

Wednesday 4th September

I've just had one of the best days of my life. Steve was already parked up in the lay-by when I arrived at twenty past ten, said he'd been there half an hour as Olivia left for work at nine and he didn't want to hang around the house. I could tell he was nervous when I first saw him because he didn't give me that gorgeous, broad smile where he flashes his teeth at me and makes me feel like a million dollars. He got out of his car slowly and waited for me to turn my engine off before he came to open the door for me. I stayed in the seat and he knelt down and kissed me. Then I got out, locked the car door and we went for a stroll under the trees, hand in hand. It's been a long time since I've held a bloke's hand and it felt a bit odd at first, but his grip was so strong that he eventually made me feel really secure, as though it was meant to be. We walked for about half a mile before he stopped, put his arms around me and kissed me really affectionately. There was absolutely no one about so we sat down in a little clearing where I got a wet backside and he had a fumble. There was a bird singing in the tree nearby and it sounded beautiful. Steve reckoned it was a nightingale, but I'm useless with birds so I just took his word for it. It set the scene though, made the atmosphere really romantic and momentous.

Then we walked back to the cars, got in his and drove to the Plough and Horses for a lovely pub lunch. It was quite busy but we managed to get a table in the corner so hopefully weren't seen by anyone we knew. I really fancied the hot chocolate fudge cake but decided not to bother as I didn't want to end up with it all down my top. Though, Steve pointed out that he wouldn't mind licking it off me.

(Note to self: melt some chocolate next time he comes round.)

It was about two o'clock when we got back to the cars again and this time we sat in mine. He told me he can't stop thinking about me and it's definitely having an effect on his marriage because Olivia says he's in a world of his own half the time. He tells her it's the golf tournament coming up in November and he's got loads on at work, and luckily she believes him. When he mentioned her I decided it was the right time to ask about his marriage. Not sure he appreciated me asking because he said he'd rather not talk about it, but when I turned away and looked through the window, he put his hand on my face and turned my head gently. I remember exactly what he said because it was exactly what I wanted to hear.

'Olivia and I don't have sex anymore, we haven't done for a few years now. She slipped a disc in '93 and we couldn't do anything for a long time, but she's lost her sex drive. I think she's going through the change.'

I have to admit that a part of me was a bit shocked when he told me something so personal, but I did ask him to be honest with me so I thanked him for telling me the truth. But then I wondered if he's just with me because Olivia won't satisfy him anymore. I soon put that thought to the back of my mind though when he kissed me and asked if we could come back here to make love. He makes me laugh and he listens to me and he's great in bed. If only he wasn't married.

We parted company at four so he could be home before Olivia got back at tea time. I just chilled out on the sofa when I got in and thought about what an incredible day I'd just had and how much I love Steve Harris.

Friday 6th September

I finished painting the bedroom this afternoon and it's looking great. I'm really pleased with the border, too. Mum came late afternoon to inspect and even *she* was impressed. She wouldn't dream of doing a job like this herself; she just gets 'a man' in to do all her DIY. But she can afford it. I can't.

I made us both some tea and was dying to tell her about Steve, but I chickened out. I'm worried that she'll just start asking awkward questions about him, like how old is he, where does he work, where does he live, that sort of thing. It'll probably just lead to more lies and I'm not happy about lying to mum, so it's probably best that I don't mention him at all. If she asks why I haven't got a boyfriend I'll just say I'm happy on my own. She won't be bothered, though I imagine she wonders sometimes about whether she'll ever have a grandchild. Heaven forbid that would ever happen. Think I'd shoot myself.

Monday 9th September

My first day back at work after a week off went quite well considering a temp's been covering reception for me and she's just about made a complete cock up of my filing system. It'll take me a few days to sort it out but it gives me something to do when Brenda's on the prowl. She caught me reading Take A Break magazine once and told me to put it away. Mind you, I've seen Claire and Yvonne sat at their desks a few times with magazines and I know Brenda makes personal calls because her 'friend' Carol is always ringing to return her call. She must think I'm stupid.

Steve came into reception and said how much he enjoyed last Wednesday and asked if I would meet him again this coming Saturday. My tummy did a little cartwheel and I agreed to meet him at one o'clock in our usual spot.

Just as he was leaving, Brian walked in with an odd look on his face. Think it could be his piles playing up again; poor guy is always moaning about them, much to my embarrassment.

Wednesday 11th September

Steve came round last night and we had a really nice cuddle on the sofa. He only stayed an hour or so but asked me what I wanted for my birthday. It's on 23rd September and I'll be the grand old age of 27. I'm not sure what I want him to get me though I did say it would be nice to spend the night in a hotel somewhere. I could tell he wasn't sure about that idea when he laughed as though I was a child who'd just suggested moving to Disney Land. Guess I could suggest some jewellery to him, something he can buy me without it being noticed too much. I'll write a few things down this week.

Friday 13th September

I'm always a bit anxious on a Friday the thirteenth. Being a bit superstitious I tend to avoid walking under ladders and putting my umbrella up inside a building, and if I see a single magpie I spend ages frantically looking round for another. Was going to ring in sick this morning as my head's banging with the cider I drank last night, but decided to go in as I still haven't sorted out the mess that the temp left last week. Feel like strangling Brenda for taking her on when she could have just asked Claire or Yvonne to man reception for the week. They might be a pain in the arse but at least they know what they're doing and wouldn't have left me so much work.

It was raining at lunch time so we didn't bother walking to the chip van. Instead, Steve asked me if I wanted to go for a drive with him. I was a bit shocked that he'd asked as it must look obvious now to the other members of staff. He says he's sick of hiding it and is getting irritated by Brenda making snide remarks about him always being in reception, and Brian winking at him every time he walks past his desk. There are a few others who work on the shop floor who are also starting to talk about us. Apparently, Pinky and Perky in packing asked Steve outright earlier this week, 'are you shaggin' t'receptionist, ya dirty get?' He smiled and said he might be which I'm not sure was a good idea because now it's all over the building that there's a rumour of Steve Harris 'havin' it away with 'er who works on't'switchboard.' And of course everyone knows that Steve is married, and that I'm not. This is bound to get back to Olivia at some point.

However, when I got home tonight and poured myself a glass of Southern Comfort to wind down, I couldn't help feeling rather proud that I'm the one who's supposedly shagging Steve Harris, because he's probably the best looking bloke at Winterson's and is also very popular with the ladies. Being proud isn't something I know I should be, but my feelings for Steve have gone way beyond a crush now. If anybody asks me where I see myself in five year's time I think I'd answer, 'in a nice three-bed semi with my husband, Steve, and perhaps a dog.'

Saturday 14th September

I met Steve at the woods this afternoon. He was late today and I started to doubt that he would turn up, but he arrived at 1.45, saying he half expected me to have gone. I assured him I wouldn't have done that and I do understand that sometimes he won't be able to get away for one reason or another. Not sure if I'm being too soft with him but I do think that if I started giving ultimatums like 'it's Olivia or me', then he'd probably bugger off and I wouldn't see him for dust. Yes, I am insecure. In fact, I'm jealous of his wife. In actual fact, it's turning me into a drinker I think, as I'm getting through far too much alcohol in a week. I seem to be spending a lot of time at the bottle bank on Tesco's car park and I'm now on first name terms with the trolley man. He's called Derek, and he's really sweet.

Anyway, we had a walk in the woods and held hands again. There were a few people milling about and I felt quite proud to be with Steve, like we were a proper couple. We probably looked a bit odd as we'd both arrived in our own cars, a sure sign of an affair, but I wasn't bothered. I've gone past the point of caring what other people think. It's none of their business. Steve is my lover and I want to be with him. End of.

He couldn't come back to the flat because he didn't have time so we had a good snog in his car and a fumble when no one was about. Though I think in future we'll keep our personal moments to when we're in the flat as I'm sure I saw someone loitering in the bushes. I mentioned it to Steve but he was too busy at the time to acknowledge me. Think he feels the same to be honest; gone past the point of caring.

Monday 23rd September

Nothing much happened last week apart from the usual Wednesday night in with Steve, a bottle of wine and my nice cosy bed. I didn't see him much at work as he's hoping to get promoted in the next six months and has to attend meetings about what his new job could entail. Much to Brenda's amusement, she made sure I was inundated with minutes to type up after each meeting, with Claire and Yvonne being delegated to check them over. Yvonne being the petty bitch that she is made a point of telling me I needed to take my time more as there were quite a few typos in one of the documents and she insisted I did it again. I felt like saying, 'shove it up your arse' but thought better of it. She's like *that* with Brenda and I have a feeling her mum is a personal friend of Brenda's, too. Probably best not to rock the boat.

It's my birthday today, I'm twenty-seven. Steve left a card in my desk drawer with a note inside saying, *'meet me at my car at lunch time,'* which I did. He was sat behind the wheel, keys in the ignition, big grin on his face. He said, 'Fancy a pub lunch?' I wasn't going to refuse so we went to The Red Lion on Charley Road, a few miles from the industrial estate, and I spent half the time wishing someone from work would walk in and the other half scared that they would. It wasn't the most relaxing pub lunch I've ever had, though Steve seemed to enjoy himself. He's getting very blasé about the situation now and it wouldn't surprise me if he's told people, like Brian for one. We've been seeing each other six months now; it must be obvious that we're an item.

As we sat down at a table he gave me a little square box. It was dark blue and my first thought was that there was a ring inside. There wasn't. He's bought me some gorgeous gold earrings in the shape of love hearts and I absolutely love them. I must admit my stomach turned over when I saw the box because for about five seconds I wondered if it *was* a ring. But I'm not disappointed because we're nowhere near that stage yet and I love the earrings. Besides, he's still married.

I asked him to come round tonight but he couldn't. I was a bit disappointed when he said he couldn't come as I honestly thought he might have surprised me and taken me out for a meal, or at least just come to see me for an hour or so to give me another birthday present. But not to worry, he said he's going to make up for it this weekend and meet me at the woods again on Saturday, only this time we're meeting earlier so that we can have lunch out then come back here.

(Note to self: pop down town and get that lingerie from Debenhams with the birthday money from mum.)

Speaking of mum, she's given me £500 for my birthday which is really generous of her. I went for tea after work and she made me a lovely chicken curry, her speciality. She was going to invite Auntie Maud but I asked if it could be just the two of us as we don't get to see each other much these days. It turned out to be a really lovely evening. Mum told me one of her insurance policies has matured and she'd like to buy me a new car. I suggested she treat herself first then see if there's anything left but she's insisted. I think it must be a large sum if she wants to buy me a car but I didn't like asking how much. Anyway, we're going to a Vauxhall garage on Sunday as I've had my eye on the new Astra's for a while; they're much more sophisticated than my old one now. She also asked me what dad had sent for my birthday. I'm not too bothered that I haven't had anything. I guess I'm a grown woman and should just live with the fact that he probably doesn't think about me anymore.

Kelly has sent me a gorgeous card with 'Special Friend' on the front, and a Next voucher. I think it's the first year she hasn't bought me an actual item for my birthday since we were teenagers but I'll let her off because she knows how much I love Next clothes. And a £30 voucher isn't to be sniffed at. She must be *really* happy to be forking out that much.

****

Woke up at two am wondering why I haven't even had a card off dad. Cried myself back to sleep.

Tuesday 24th September

I went in work today with eyes like piss holes in the snow. Even Brenda commented that I looked shit and offered to send Claire in to look after reception if I wanted to go home. I told her I was fine and thanked her for being so considerate. She probably just wants another excuse to get rid of me, the old bag.

When Steve walked in the office and said more or less the same thing I told him that I'd been crying in the night as I hadn't had a card off my dad. He said I shouldn't worry because New Zealand's a long way away and it's probably on its way. His smile and kind words made me feel much better, as did the carton of chips he bought me at lunch time.

Thursday 26th September

I decided to go to the driving range last night as Steve was going anyway and stopping here on his way home. I surprised him as he was in full swing. He got me a basket of balls to have a practice and said if I wanted, he'd take me on the golf course one weekend and we could do nine holes. I pointed out that nine holes would probably take me a week to get round and he laughed. Think I'll just stick to the driving range, even though I still find it really boring. But just being with Steve is worth the sacrifice of me making an idiot of myself.

He followed me back to the flat and I put the kettle on hoping a hot drink might warm us up. He did that lovely thing again where he puts his arms around my waist from behind, turns me round and kisses me tenderly. Then the kettle gets forgotten about in favour of my bed.

Saturday 28th September

I met Steve at the woods again this afternoon and it was much quieter. Probably had something to do with the fact it was chucking it down, but it meant we could get passionate in the back of his Golf. Some nutter jogged passed us at one point, just as Steve was unhooking my bra, and I'm sure he got an eye-full as he had to dodge the nearest tree. We sat in the car after making love and drank the coffee I'd made for us in a flask. By then it had stopped raining so we went for a little stroll to our favourite clearing. We couldn't sit down as it was obviously too wet so we stood and held each other. He hugged me like I've never been hugged before. And then we heard the bird again. I'm sure it was the same one as it had the same pitch and seemed to be singing the same tune. Steve's pretty convinced it's a nightingale and said he's going to find out properly. We've decided to call our special place 'Nightingale Woods'.

Sunday 29th September

My lovely and generous mum has bought me the most gorgeous car! The insurance policy that matured was one she and dad took out when I was nearly 7 and it's brought in thirty thousand pounds. She's supposed to send dad half of it but she's not doing; said he doesn't deserve it because he stopped paying into it when he left her. I'm so proud of her determination to stay independent but I'm thrilled at the fact she's just written a cheque for six grand to pay for my new car. She's bloody amazing is my mum.

If you ever read this diary, mum, which I do hope you never will, but if you do, just want to say I love you and you're the best mum in the world.

Wednesday 2nd October

I have just got home from the Vauxhall garage with my new Astra. It's a 1.6i GLS and is bloody gorgeous. It's bright red with a cream interior and far too many dials that I'm going to have to learn how to use, but I'm sure Steve will help me. I can't wait to take him for a spin in it later.

Thursday 3rd October

Steve didn't turn up last night. I was more disappointed because I wanted to show off my new car but then I got a bit annoyed because he never bothered to ring me and explain why he couldn't make it. As it happens, Susan's pregnant.

There are all sorts of thoughts going through my head now. As soon as he claps eyes on his grandchild he's probably not going to want to know me. He's pretty shocked about it as is Olivia but they had a good chat about it all last night and have decided to support Susan and Keith. Not sure where this leaves me but I imagine it'll get talked about eventually. I'm not seeing him this weekend as they're all going out for a family meal to celebrate the good news. I'm going to get seriously pissed.

Sunday 6th October

Another hangover to add to my collection. I'm too upset to update the diary so I'll not bother.

Tuesday 8th October

Steve wants to come round tomorrow night but I'm not sure it's a good idea. I can't stop thinking about him being a granddad in seven months time. It's really upset me and he doesn't seem to realise just how much. He isn't looking at the big picture and what this could mean for our relationship. It's alright for him; if Olivia never finds out about our affair he can just go back to living a normal life with another family member to love, but me, well, I'll be back to being Billy-No-Mates again, lonely and bored with my life. And I'll probably have to leave Winterson's because I won't be able to face him every day. Olivia's rang three fucking times today and the third time I picked up I almost told her to piss off. Steve's been in reception a few times, grinning like a Cheshire cat and if he thinks I'm going to pretend I'm happy for him he's got another think coming. I suppose I'm happy in an odd kind of way, like if we were still-just-friends-and-we-weren't-having-an-affair-and-he-wasn't-the-man-I-want-to-spend-the-rest-of-my-life-with kind of way. But how can I be happy knowing that this could be the thing that splits us up? This baby will most probably take him away from me and make him realise his family responsibilities, not just as a husband and father, but as a proud granddad as well. Oh shit, what a mess.

Wednesday 9th October

I gave in. Steve's just gone home after we spent two hours in bed, shagging for England. I think he feels he needs to prove a point to me, that the news about Susan's pregnancy isn't going to affect our relationship. He was really tender tonight and very sensitive, more than I've ever known him to be.

We didn't talk about the baby or how it would affect us but I think we both know we're going to have to at some point.

Talking about babies, I've just realised I'm late.

Tuesday 15th October

I rang Kelly to tell her I still haven't come on. Could tell she doesn't know what to say as it's not like her to be speechless. I've been on the pill for two years after my periods started getting a bit irregular and my doctor thought it might be best, but if it hasn't worked and I'm up the duff, I shall kill that doctor.

Plus, occasionally we use condoms, just as an extra precaution. I used to think this was because of STI's and Steve still having sex with Olivia, but after he reassured me he doesn't have sex with her anymore, I suggested ditching the condoms and going bare-back.

Wednesday 16th October

I found a back-bone and told Steve tonight that my period's late and he went a funny shade of grey. Thought he was going to pass out for a moment so I got him a glass of water. I was half hoping he might have flung his arms around me before telling me he'll leave Olivia and we could live happily ever after. But instead he gulped down the water and went to the bathroom. When he came out he asked if he could make a brew, which he's never asked before as he usually just helps himself. I told him to sit down then I made it instead. We sat in silence drinking our tea and staring at the telly. He left at nine which was quite early so I was a bit pissed off with him. I'm wondering now whether Steve and I being parents together is such a good idea.

Thursday 17ᵗʰ October

Still no period. I'm starting to brick it now.

Steve came in the office first thing and asked me the inevitable question of 'have you come on yet?' When I said no he turned away from me and said 'shit.' I've told him that if I don't get my period by Monday that I'll go to the doctors and ask for a pregnancy test. He offered to come with me which I thought was really sweet of him, but this is something I'd rather do on my own so I declined. I love him more for asking though. At least it means he cares.

He has a golf tournament this weekend which is probably for the best as I don't think we'd have much to say to each other right now. But I'll stay off the booze, just in case.

Monday 21ˢᵗ October

I literally couldn't wait to get in work this morning and tell Steve the good news; I came on last night. Phew. That was a close one. Might pop to the doctors anyway and make sure these pills are safe enough, or at least I'll ask for some free condoms. I don't see why I should feel insecure with a contraceptive pill and have to buy condoms as well, that's just taking the piss.

****

Steve wants to celebrate the fact that we're not pregnant. Not sure how I feel about that but I guess he has a point. Looking at it logically, it could have been really awkward. And there was always the chance that he wouldn't leave Olivia for me and I'd end up having to bring up the child myself. My mum would have gone spare, though I imagine once she'd have stopped lecturing me on the responsibilities of having unprotected sex she would have been happy. She's mentioned more than a few times that she'd like to be a grandma. And then she'd definitely have wanted to know about the man I've been seeing, mainly because she would have wanted to kill him.

Friday 25th October

I haven't seen Steve outside work all week as I've been knackered due to having a really heavy period. He took me to the pub on Wednesday lunch time which was lovely but apart from that we haven't spent any time together. He's still really busy at work and determined to get this promotion so I've just kept my head down and tried not to annoy Brenda.

Saturday 26th October

God, I love that man. He rang me early this morning and asked if we could meet at Nightingale Woods. Said he's really missed me this week and feels he needs to make it up to me for acting like a bastard when I told him the possible pregnancy news.

We met in our usual place at half past one and he got straight out of his car when he saw me turn the corner. He got into my front passenger seat and kissed me really tenderly before admiring the dashboard of my new Astra. He told me he was really sorry for his reaction last week but hoped I understood why it wouldn't have been a good idea for us to have a baby. He also said he wasn't sure if he wanted any more kids but he realises that I'm in my prime and appreciates that I might want a family at some point. I told him it was fine, that I forgave him and no, I didn't want kids. Snotty noses and dirty nappies have never appealed to me anyway.

Though there was a little part of me that felt like it had died this afternoon.

We strolled through the trees, leaves crunching under foot. I love autumn, it's such a romantic season with the change in colours, and Nightingale Woods is no exception. It's absolutely beautiful at this time of year.

Monday 28th October

Steve has told Brian about us. I had a feeling he might have done as I've noticed Brian grinning inanely recently, every time he walks into reception. He said he told him because he asked, and he's known Brian a long time and doesn't want to lie to him. I reckon this means we don't need to hide as much because now that Brian knows for definite, it'll be round the building like wild fire. Though Steve has asked him not to tell anyone, but I'm not sure Brian is the sort of person that can keep a secret as big as this to himself.

Olivia rang the office this afternoon while Steve was with me and I just passed the phone to him. He was laughing and joking with her and talking to her like she was his best mate. I felt sick when he hung up. I was dying to ask him what it was about but his pager went off so he had to go.

Tuesday 29th October

Just before I left work today Brian came up to me. I think he'd been standing outside the door to collar me.

'I won't tell anyone about you and Steve but I'm not going to lie for you either so if anyone asks me if you're having an affair I'll have to tell the truth,' he said. Then added, 'I hope you understand my dilemma?'

'I understand,' I said, obviously putting his mind at rest as his shoulders seemed to droop at bit out of relief.

'Are you happy?' he asked, much to my surprise.

'Yes, though I wish Steve wasn't married of course,' I replied.

'Be careful won't you, I don't want to see you get hurt, Rachel. I've known Olivia a long time and I like her. She and Steve have always had a good marriage from what I've seen but he obviously thinks the world of you.'

I nodded. My inability to speak probably made me look like I hadn't listened to him but his little speech about Steve and Olivia's marriage has made me feel pretty bad. In fact, I've just been sick.

Thursday 31st October

I know my relationship with Steve is really complicated and definitely not ideal with him being married, but after what Brian said on Tuesday, I can't help feeling like a complete slag. What I'm doing is wrong, I know that. But I can't stop myself. I love Steve and he loves me. We're good together and I know we can make this work. I'm trying to stop thinking about how nice Olivia apparently is, and think more about what *I* need, what *I* want from life. I know I'm being a selfish bitch but this is how I feel right now.

It's Halloween and I've already had three trick or treaters. I always buy a few big bags of mini chocolate bars and hurl them at the annoying kids. But I've run out now so if anyone else comes to the door I'm either going to tell them to bugger off or just not answer it. Maybe I'll just tell them to bugger off.

Saturday 2nd November

Steve came round last night, unexpectedly. He said Brian rang him to have a chat with him about me. It looks like Brian is trying to make Steve end our affair. Luckily for me, Steve said he isn't going to do that and has told Brian that he loves me. I keep thinking any day now Steve will leave Olivia. It could just be wishful thinking but if he's even told Brian that he loves me, then this must be serious for him as well.

We made love on the sofa and afterwards he said, 'I don't want to live my life without you in it.' That's the most romantic thing any man has ever said to me. Not that I've had many boyfriends over the years, Steve being my most serious, but I've never been this close to anyone and it's the most amazing feeling in the world.

Monday 4ᵗʰ November

Yvonne has been asked to organise the Christmas do this year. She wants to have it at the local Labour club as it's big enough to get all employees in, plus their other halves. She wants me to be there especially because I didn't go last year due to having a shitty cold. Obviously, Steve and I weren't together last Christmas so I wouldn't have bothered about him taking Olivia, but when I mentioned this year's do to him and asked if he'd be taking Olivia, he said he wouldn't be going. That's made my mind up then. I'll tell Yvonne tomorrow that I'll help her organise it if she needs a hand, but I won't be going. The last Christmas do I went on was three years ago when I used to work for Craving Canvas and I got completely hammered and ended up snogging my boss, George. I was the talk of the firm for months after that and George kept winking at me. When he asked me to join him and his wife for a night out at the local swinger's club, I realised what a muppet I'd been. I handed in my notice shortly after and did some temp work for a while before landing the job at Winterson's.

Wednesday 6ᵗʰ November

I've just got back from the driving range with Steve. He didn't come back here as he was feeling tired, but I'm not feeling great myself. Think I'm coming down with a cold.

Thursday 7th November

I woke up this morning with a stinking cold so rang in sick. I won't be going in tomorrow either. Steve rang me at lunch time and asked if I wanted anything which I thought was lovely of him, but I don't want him to catch this cold so I thanked him and said no. He said he'd ring me on Saturday morning and if I'm feeling better he'll pop round for an hour.

I'm lying on the sofa feeling sorry for myself, stinking of Vicks. There's a bottle of Benylin and a packet of Lemsips on the table and I'm praying I'll be better by Saturday.

Saturday 9th November

I'm still not feeling great but had a hot bath this morning and waited for Steve to ring me. He eventually did at 11 o'clock and I said it was okay for him to come round but I'm still not back to normal. He arrived at 2pm with a box of chocolates and a bottle of Hock. I don't think drinking the wine is a good idea as I'm rattling on Paracetamol, but I opened the chocolates and we almost got through the first layer.

I wouldn't let him kiss me on my lips as I really don't want him being off work next week with man-flu. So I let him have a fumble instead, though he moaned a bit when he pulled his hand from under my jumper and realised it stunk of Vicks.

Monday 11th November

I went back to work today as I'm feeling much better. Told Yvonne that I'm not going to the

Christmas do but will help her organise it, and she's given me a list of things to do ranging from phoning the caterers to phoning the Labour Club, to collating a list of all employees and finding out how many vegetarians there are. I doubt they'll be many though; reckon the only thing that lot will be interested in is getting pissed.

Anyway, I've booked the Labour Club for Friday 13th December as they'd had a cancellation, and the only other date they could have given me was midweek which Yvonne said was no good as everyone would come in work the next morning with a raging hangover. Except Brenda of course; I doubt a drop of alcohol has ever passed *her* lips. She'll probably not even be going.

I managed to book the caterers too, though will need to finalise details with them nearer the time. It's going to be a finger buffet to make it easier, and that way they'll put vegetarian food at the end of the table separate from all the meat. Mr. Winterson is being really generous as he's told Yvonne that he's willing to pay up to £5 per head. I imagine it'll be more or less a full turn-out if he's paying for it all so I hope he realises how many people work there. He also said it'll be a free bar. I really do think Mr. Winterson needs to retire before he gets the bill for this Christmas do. Poor old man seems to think his employees will have a glass of sherry and a mince pie. He's in for a shock, I fear.

Tuesday 12th November

Brenda asked me if I was going to the Christmas do today. When I told her I wasn't she scowled at me and said, 'neither is Steve Harris, funny that.'

69

I think Brenda knows about us. And I couldn't give a shit anymore. Brenda-no-life-Appleton can go and play on the M6. That woman is a bitter and jealous old hag. It's nothing to do with her.

Thursday 14ᵗʰ November

When Steve came round last night he told me that Brenda has asked him if we're having an affair. He said he ignored her and walked away but she shouted after him, 'Everyone knows, so there's no point in hiding it.' Of course she's wrong; Olivia doesn't know.

Saturday 16ᵗʰ November

I met Steve at Nightingale Woods today. It's been a glorious autumn day and we had a lovely romantic walk through the trees. There wasn't a soul about and it was so peaceful. We lay in our clearing and made love with only the sound of the nightingale and our methodical panting to be heard. Walking back to our cars hand in hand felt so right and I honestly can't imagine my life now without Steve in it. We've even got our own song that we listen to in the car; it's by Michael Bolton and it's called 'Said I Loved You...But I Lied'. It's the most beautiful song I've ever heard.

When we sat in my car afterwards, Steve asked me if there is anything I want for Christmas. I looked into his eyes and just said, really quietly, 'you.' He smiled and kissed me then pulled away and said he needed to get back as Olivia wanted to go out for a meal tonight with Susan and Keith. That kind of spoiled the mood somewhat but we did have a truly magical afternoon. I keep wondering if he realised I was being serious about my answer to his question about a Christmas present. I do hope so.

Tuesday 19*th* November

Steve's just gone. He came for a couple of hours which was nice and we just relaxed on the sofa watching telly like an old married couple. We're so comfortable with each other. Even though we've only been together just under nine months, it feels like we've known each other forever. I can't imagine what it must be like for him having to go home to Olivia after he's been with me. He said he's used to it now but does feel guilty sometimes. But he's trying not to let his marriage interfere with our relationship, at least until Susan's baby is born which won't be till next May. I'm not sure I want to be his mistress till next May as I really hoped we'd be a proper couple well before then. But if it means having to wait or lose him altogether, then I'm prepared to wait. What we have is too special to throw away because of me being impatient.

Friday 22*nd* November

Brenda's bringing in a new temp next week to cover for Gail in packing who finishes for maternity leave today. Poor Gail looks like a beached whale and has put me off having kids for life. I'm going to miss her. She comes into reception every day with packages in one hand and a bottle of Gaviscon in the other, and we always have a bit of a chin wag. She has never once enquired about Steve even though I'm sure she's heard the rumours, like everyone else seems to have done now. I do hope Brenda's new temp will be a good substitute. I'm meeting Steve at Nightingale Woods tomorrow so I'll ask him if he knows anything.

Saturday 23rd November

Steve doesn't know anything about the temp as he says he doesn't talk to Brenda much anymore after she quizzed him about having an affair. I'm glad really, because at least she'll never know for definite and won't be able to make a sneaky phone call to Olivia.

But what Steve did ask me was if I was doing anything on the night of the work's Christmas 'do. I haven't come down from cloud nine yet after he told me he wants us to spend the night together and he'll tell Olivia he's going to the do then staying over afterwards so he can have a few drinks. He said she'll believe him so I'm going to leave him to deal with that one. He's asked me to choose somewhere for us to stay and get it booked, and better still, he's paying.

Sunday 24th November

I couldn't wait to book a hotel room for me and Steve at The Round Table Hotel in Greenley. It's a small hotel with individually styled bedrooms and a really good reputation for food. I'm so excited about it. I'll start making a list of things I need to take, like lacy underwear for starters.

Monday 25th November

I told Steve I've booked the hotel and he's thrilled as he's never been there before and always wanted to try it. Plus he said no one will know us so we can pretend we're properly together and no one will suspect. I booked it in my name and he quite likes the thought of being incognito which made me laugh.

We walked to the chip van at lunch time but it was too cold to sit outside on the grass so we walked back to the car park and sat in my car, which unfortunately now stinks of chips. Oh well, worth it for an hour with the love of my life.

Wednesday 27ᵗʰ November

I told Kelly that Steve and I are spending the night in a hotel and she was a bit worried. She says I need to make sure *I* keep all the receipts and don't let Steve go home with them in his wallet. She always thought that Greasy Graham had spent the night with Joanne but he swore blind he never did. I think she believed him in the end though I have my doubts. But I can't say anything because she's been so kind about it after everything she went through. It could have been very different and I could have completely lost my best friend.

Thursday 28ᵗʰ November

The cheek of Yvonne; she's asked me to print out all the invitations for the Christmas do, write out the envelopes and make sure everyone gets one. I have a feeling she's taking the piss now because I can't for the life of me work out what she's actually doing as the official organiser apart from barking orders at me. I feel like telling her to stick the invitations up her arse but she's too friendly with Brenda and I know that'll just give Brenda ammunition to fire me. Mind you, on the grounds of telling someone to shove Christmas-do invitations up their arse, I'm not sure Brenda would get away with it, though she'd probably have a damn good try.

****

Steve came round last night and brought me a Michael Bolton video. We watched it together, snuggled up on the sofa, and when he started singing 'Said I Loved You...But I Lied', Steve kissed me really passionately and we ended up making love on the sheepskin rug. That song will always be very poignant to us now, and if we get married, I'm going to make sure it's played when we do our first dance as a married couple.

Sunday 1st December

I love Christmas, more so this year for obvious reasons. Mum came round today and helped me put my tree up. It looks gorgeous and Christmassy and all twinkly and sparkly. Christmas is such a romantic time for lovers I always think and this year I'm going to make sure it's the best year of my life so far.

I've promised mum I'd go to her house next weekend and help put her tree up plus all the decorations. She has loads that she places all around the house and makes it look like Santa's grotto. Dad used to love Christmas too, though not as much as mum. He used to leave all the decorations to us and would just say, 'Oh, they look nice,' after all our hard work. The only thing he did at Christmas was carve the turkey because mum bought him an electric carver one year and he was dead chuffed. Looking back on it, my dad was a lazy sod really and pretty miserable with it. Over the years we've realised we're better off without him, especially mum who seems to be really happy these days. I think a part of her will always be bitter but she's a strong woman and done a good job bringing me up. Well, I think she has anyway.

I haven't seen Steve this weekend. He just said he wouldn't be able to see me as Olivia wants to go Christmas shopping. Apparently, she likes to go the first weekend in December every year so he couldn't say no. As I wanted to put my decorations up and mum had offered to come and help, I decided not to sulk and just have a nice weekend to myself, with mum of course.

Tuesday 3rd December

I forgot to mention Brenda's new temp last week after all the excitement of booking a hotel for me and Steve. Anyway, she's really nice, about 25 with long blonde hair. She's quite rounded and she's married with a little boy. She gets temp jobs from October to Christmas to help pay for presents for him which I think is really cute. Her husband is an air steward. I didn't tell her I always thought male air stewards were gay as I wasn't sure how she'd take it, though she does seem to have a sense of humour. She's staying with us till 20th December when her little boy breaks up for Christmas. And she said she might come back next year and carry on covering Gail's maternity leave as she really likes it here. Plus, it's only a five minute drive from where she lives so it's ideal. I think Brenda did good there, for once.

But the best thing about Tina the temp is that she's on the ball and has already sussed about me and Steve. I asked her on Friday if it embarrassed her and she laughed and said, 'God no, we only live once, make the most of it, flower.' Yes, I like Tina.

Thursday 5th December

I've told Steve that I'd like a CD and a book for Christmas so he's giving me a Woolworth's voucher then I can get them myself. I asked him if he would come shopping with me this weekend and he said he might, but he's all shopped out after being dragged round Manchester with Olivia last weekend. I said I'd meet him at Nightingale Woods at 1pm and if he felt like shopping we'd go in my car and leave his there, but if he didn't then we'd just stay put. I think I already know that I'll be going shopping on my own.

Friday 6th December

Mum rang to ask if I'd go and help her tomorrow but I've told her I've already arranged to go shopping with Tina from work and would she mind if I went on Sunday instead. She agreed and hung up. Can't believe I've just lied through my teeth to my lovely mum. I'm going to have to buy her an extra nice present this year because I feel really, really guilty now. She's never once asked me outright if I have a boyfriend so I've never needed to lie to her. Until now.

Saturday 7th December

As I thought, Steve didn't want to go shopping so we sat in his car for a while then got into mine. We made ourselves comfy on the back seat and had a cuddle to warm each other up. It's quite spacious in the back considering it's only an Astra. But I need to have it valeted again now as Steve wasn't quite as careful as he usually is.

Sunday 8th December

We put mum's tree and decorations up and the house looks gorgeous. I hope I'll have a lovely big house like hers one day. She went to the garden centre yesterday and spent a fortune on new ornaments and decorations for the tree. Auntie Maud called round at 3pm and was in awe at the beauty of it all. Mum's asked her to have Christmas dinner with us which doesn't bother me but up until today I hadn't really thought about what would happen over Christmas when I won't see Steve. It's not going to be great knowing he's at home with his wife and family, being the loyal family man that I guess is expected of him.

But I have this Friday to look forward to and I'm so excited I might burst.

Monday 9th December

Claire and Yvonne came in the office today with two boxes of Christmas decorations and a large artificial tree and told me I could put them where I wanted so long as it looked really classy. A few thoughts went through my head when they said that but I kept quiet. I'm getting really sick of them bossing me about as they are only secretaries and not my actual boss. Yvonne asked me if I've finalised everything with the caterers and I took great pleasure in telling her it was all done and dusted last week and she has nothing to worry about. Claire smiled a bit too sweetly for my liking before walking out of reception and back to her office. They're up to something and it had better not include me and Steve.

Tuesday 10th December

Steve has just gone and I'm knackered. We made love in my bed and I nearly fell asleep on his chest. I reckon this is what it'll be like on Friday when we spend the night together. But right now I need to get some sleep as I have a lot to do tomorrow at work after Brenda asked me to write a hundred Christmas cards for suppliers and customers and get them in the post first class. The stupid woman forgot to do it last week and as she hasn't got time this week, she's decided I can do them instead. Foreplay with Steve might be out of the question tomorrow night if he comes round as my wrist will no doubt be aching.

Wednesday 11th December

Got the Christmas cards done and in the post by lunch time, much to Brenda's disappointment. I think she was expecting me not to finish them and then she could have had a go at me. She's got a face like a slapped arse at the moment and I suspect it's because she's a bitter, dried up old sow with no man and no life.

Steve didn't manage to come round tonight and even though I was a bit disappointed I managed to get my overnight bag packed ready for Friday and iron my outfit. I've drunk half a bottle of wine and feel a bit tipsy but it could be excitement as well. I wonder if he's as excited as me.

Friday 13th December

It's here, our big night. I'll fill you in on the details tomorrow when I get home. I'm going to the hotel in half an hour to meet Steve for seven pm. We've booked the table for half past so we can get back to the room and make the most of our 'night in'.

Saturday 14th December

I had to sit and think about this diary entry for a while as I'm not sure what to write. Apart from the fact it was an awesome night, it wasn't all good so I'll start with the bad news first, that way it might not seem so bad by the time I get to the end.

Olivia has asked Steve if he's having an affair. Last weekend when they went shopping, she was getting the bags out of the car and found an earring in the foot-well. It's a little gold stud shaped like a dolphin and is definitely mine because I'd noticed it was missing but hadn't put two and two together. Bollocks. He swore blind that he had no idea whose it was and assumed it was one of the girls from work when he'd transported them to town the other day. That was a lie of course, but fortunately he reckons Olivia believed him. Though she has asked where exactly the Christmas do is and why wasn't she invited. He got round that by saying the other guys he works with aren't taking their wives either so he didn't think it would be her cup of tea. He's not entirely convinced that she believed him but he says if she's still suspicious she'll probably ask him again when he gets back on Saturday. It kind of put a downer on the night a bit and neither of us felt like eating much so we ordered a prawn salad with side order of chips then went back to the room. I felt a bit sick really; not sure whether it was because the prawn sauce was quite vinegary or whether I was panicking that Olivia would come knocking on the bedroom door. But she didn't and once we got back to the room, we turned the telly on and sat half naked on the bed watching Michael Parkinson interview Roger Moore.

Steve loved my new black lacy lingerie and kept running his fingers over the bra cups. Eventually, Michael Parkinson wrapped up his show and Steve tenderly lifted my face towards his then kissed me fervently and so full of lust that I think I had an orgasm just thinking about what was going to happen next.

He unhooked my bra, slowly removed my thong then slid inside me. I can honestly say I've never had sex like it ever. It was the best shag in my life. The bed was really comfortable and even though it creaked a bit every time Steve penetrated, it made it all the more exciting. I imagine the people in the bedroom next door heard us because we did make a racket with all the yes, yes, yes's and give it to me's.

We rang for room service at half past ten and ordered some ice cream and a bottle of wine. Steve answered the door to a sinewy young lad with acne who hung around a bit too long waiting for a tip. Steve gave him a couple of quid and thanked him. I think the clientele of this hotel are a bit more upmarket than us because the lad seemed a bit pissed off by the two pound coins he stared at in the palm of his hand. He was probably expecting a note at least.

Then we really got down and dirty. I'm not going to reveal everything that we did in this diary just in case someone reads it one day, like my mum, but in a nutshell, I didn't think ice cream could taste as good on the human body, in places I never thought it would reach.

We decided to try and sleep when it got to one am because apart from the fact we were completely knackered, we had also drunk far too much. As we had to drive home in the morning it seemed only the sensible thing to do. To be honest, I'd sobered up but I think Steve was a bit drunk. He fell asleep shortly after but I lay awake, staring at the ceiling wondering if this was the beginning of the rest of my life.

I also wondered if Steve would mind us having separate bedrooms once we're married, because he snores like a bleedin' pig.

****

We got up at seven am, knackered, eyes like piss holes and still feeling a bit light headed. I jumped in the shower first as I was desperate to wash off the remnants of last night's ice cream, and Steve watched the news on telly. We decided against going down for breakfast and ordered a continental to our room. All I wanted was a strong coffee but Steve ate four pieces of toast, a bowl of cornflakes, two cups of strong coffee and the complimentary shortbread biscuits. He says he's always hungry after a night on the booze.

I was quite upset when we had to go our separate ways. It didn't feel right. I hope no one saw us from the hotel because I'm sure they'd guess what was going on. He kissed me as I was getting in my car then closed the door gently. I wound my window down and he leaned in and kissed me again before saying, 'I love you. See you on Monday.'

I wish we could have spent the day together and gone to Nightingale Woods, but he'd promised Olivia he'd be home by mid-morning. Still, putting aside the fact that she quizzed him about having an affair, it was a wonderful night and I can't wait till we can do it every single night, for the rest of our lives.

Monday 16th December

Seems the Christmas do at the Labour Club went well. The food went down a treat as did the free bar, no surprise there. Everyone was completely shit-faced and had a fantastic time. Claire was quite sweet really when she said it would have been nice if I'd been there, too. She also pointed out that Steve didn't go to the Christmas do and that was the first time for years.

I said, 'Oh, right, did he go last year then?'

'Yes, he did go last year and took his wife, Olivia. She's great fun.' Then she smiled at me, an irritating sickly smile as if she knows something and is just waiting for me to confirm it.

She said, 'You don't need to hide it anymore, Rachel. Everyone knows you and Steve are having an affair.'

I didn't know what to say so I just sat there and looked away, not sure whether I should laugh, cry or go over and slap her. I decided against slapping her as that would definitely have been grounds for my P45, so instead I said quietly, 'I'm not bothered what you all think, Claire, and neither is Steve. We're in love.'

She didn't laugh, which I was surprised about. I half expected her to fall over in hysterics but she came over to me, put her hand on my arm and said, 'it's okay, it's no one else's business what you and Steve do in your spare time. Steve's a good bloke and I'm sure he'll do the right thing.'

I'm not too sure what she meant by that because she walked out then, but I'd like to think she was being kind. You never can tell with Claire.

Tuesday 17th December

Steve rang me last night from a phone box. He said he just wanted to hear my voice, which I thought was particularly sweet of him. I think he'd been rowing with Olivia because when I asked if he was okay, he said, 'I've been better, just needed to get out of the house.' I told him what Claire had said and he replied with, 'who gives a shit what they say or think; they can't get to us now.'

I've got a funny feeling something's going on in Steve's mind, but I can't quite put my finger on it.

(Note to self: empty a few drawers just in case Steve lands on the doorstep with a bin bag.)

Thursday 19th December

I met up with Steve last night at the Plough and Horses. He'd been to the driving range again and was 'out for a drink with the guys from the golf club'. He gave me the Woolworth's vouchers and I gave him a blow job when we got to Nightingale Woods.

****

Kelly came round tonight for a pre-Christmas drink. We usually go out on the lash the week before Christmas but this year she says she's skint as her and Greasy Graham are saving up for their own place. She's currently bunking up with him at his tiny flat but it's far from ideal. Plus, she reckons they'll get married either next year or the year after and she's hoping to have a baby as well. Fortunately, she's got a well-paid job but I'm not sure their salaries will stretch to her dream apartment on the docks.

I told her all about our night in the hotel last Friday and how amazing it was. I left out the bit about the ice cream because she loves Walls Vanilla and I thought it might put her off for life.

I also told her what Olivia had said to Steve about finding my earring and him having an affair. Kelly tutted at me and said I should be more careful otherwise it'll all end in tears. It's bound to do that anyway, though I'm hoping they won't be mine.

Saturday 21ˢᵗ December

Steve came round to the flat this afternoon to tell me his plans over Christmas. Once we've finished on Tuesday, which will be Christmas Eve, he won't be back at work until the 30ᵗʰ December and then we'll obviously all be off again on the 1ˢᵗ January, though many people have taken the full week in between Christmas and New Year to be with their families. I'd thought about doing the same if Steve told me he was off too, but waited to see what he was doing first.

I've invited him round on Monday night as it'll probably be the last opportunity for us to be alone until after the New Year.

Monday 23ʳᵈ December

Once again, I don't know what to write in the diary as I can't think of the right words. Excited doesn't cut it, nor does fucking-hell-I-can't-believe-it's-really-happening. Okay, so this is what happened tonight:-

Steve arrived at seven pm with a bottle of Liebfraumilch. His eyes were bloodshot. I didn't say anything straight away but took the bottle off him, opened it and poured out two glasses then handed him one. Then I sat next to him on the sofa. He put his glass of wine on the coffee table and turned to look at me with tears in his eyes. My first thought was 'shit, he's breaking up with me,' then he put his arms around me, pulled me into him and cried. He was literally sobbing, resting his chin on the top of my head. I didn't know what to do or say so I just lifted my head up and looked at him. He said really quietly, 'Olivia knows about us.'

I sat up quickly and stared at him. 'How?' I asked.

He stroked my face and managed a really weak smile. 'She asked me about the earring again and I just couldn't carry on lying to her so I told her the truth. She's devastated.'

My initial reaction to this news was probably a bit insensitive as I smiled like the Joker out of Batman then kissed him. I told him it was okay and if he wanted to stay here for the night he could. I wasn't sure what else to say.

He said, 'I can't stay. I need to get back and tell Olivia that I'm leaving her.' Then he held me really tightly and added, 'Do you definitely want this, because there's no going back once I've told Olivia I'm leaving?'

I confirmed to him that I did want it and I would support him every step of the way. He pointed out to me that I'd most likely be cited as a third party in the divorce and at some point Olivia, and probably Susan, would want to meet me and probably string me up. That concerned me a little but I assured him that I would be prepared for the backlash and understood that I was just as much to blame as him, so I would therefore take what was coming to me.

After much kissing and cuddling on the sofa and me mithering him with plans for our future together, he left at nine o'clock in order to break the bad news to his wife.

I finished off the bottle of wine when he'd gone and stared into space, thinking about needing more wardrobe space and perhaps making a trip to MFI in the January sales. The flat is a bit small for us both but it'll have to do for now. I doubt we'll be able to afford a bigger place for a while, at least while the divorce is going through. And besides, we've no idea what Olivia will demand as financial settlement. I keep thinking it's all happened so quickly, so out of the blue, but really, it's what I've been hoping for and so I shouldn't be too surprised at the enormity of it all.

I'm sure we'll cope though. One way or another we'll get through all the shit that will no doubt come our way. Maybe I should change my phone number and get a few extra locks for the front door. Just to be safe.

Tuesday 24th December

I didn't get much sleep last night and I'm very tired, grumpy and completely devastated. I can't believe what's happened.

Steve didn't come in work today. Brian came into the office and asked what was wrong with him as he'd rang in sick before I'd got in myself. I told Brian I didn't know and then went on to tell him what had happened last night. Both Brian and I put two and two together and decided he needed to spend the day packing and discussing things with Olivia. The phone has only rung twice all day and one of the calls was Steve asking if he could come round tonight to talk to me, of which I naturally agreed. I was particularly disappointed when he turned up without a suitcase, or at least a few bin bags.

Instead, he came into the flat, sat on the sofa and cried again. I don't think I've ever seen a grown man cry as much. And then he dealt me the blow. The biggest bollocking blow I've ever had in my life.

He's decided not to leave Olivia after all. He says he can't do it because she's so upset and he feels sorry for her. 'I had no intention of letting our affair get this serious,' he said, and added 'I don't think you did either,' though I think he said that just to make himself feel better. He's going to spend the next few days with his family, have as normal a Christmas as is possible under the circumstances as they haven't told Susan, and will see what happens in the New Year.

Before he left he said, 'You should know that I love you. I always will and if this hadn't hurt Olivia as much as it has, I'd be here now, living with you.'

I'm really angry. Like, really fucking angry. Did he honestly think this wouldn't hurt Olivia? Did he assume he could just walk away from her and she wouldn't feel anything? I told him he's a selfish prick, but I said it whilst crying on his shoulder, just before he walked out the door.

This has to be the worst Christmas on record, even worse than the one in 1986 when my dad left.

I can't believe Steve has done this me; he loves me; he said it to me only tonight. Last night we were planning our future together and tonight he's planning his future with Olivia. I know I'm gullible sometimes, and perhaps a bit naive, and I've always been a selfish cow, but this just takes the biscuit. How dare he hurt me like this; one day tell me he's leaving his wife for me and the next day tell me he's leaving me for his wife. What's the man on? He's obviously confused. He has to be. How can he do this to me?

****

It's two am on Christmas Day and I'm sat on my sofa watching shit on the telly. There are two empty bottles of wine on the coffee table and three bottles of Budweiser. I hope Steve is lying awake in bed thinking about what he's done. Right now, I hope Olivia chucks him out anyway. At least then he'll have nowhere else to go and will come back here with his tail between his legs. And yes, I will take him back. I love him. And right now, I reckon I always will.

Boxing Day

It was, as I expected, an awful Christmas Day. My mum made a splendid turkey dinner like she always does but I hardly touched it. Told her I think I'm coming down with something and asked if I could go and lie on the bed for a bit. Her and Auntie Maud were waiting for The Queen's speech on the television anyway and had already got through half a bottle of Harvey's Bristol Cream, so I buggered off upstairs and lay on my old bed, crying into my pillow and wondering if my life could get any worse.

I could hear mum and Auntie Maud laughing downstairs as they washed the pans and filled the dishwasher. Mum's bought me a beautiful set of bedding, just what I wanted. I chose it with Steve in mind after he told me he loves chintzy fabric. It's got pink, yellow and blue flowers on it and green foliage woven in between. She also gave me the usual smellies like talc and bubble bath, plus a voucher for a weekend spa break, pointing out that I could do with a weekend away because I was looking worn out. Auntie Maud has knitted me a cardigan and I must admit it's really nice, not at all like the usual monstrosities she tends to knit. I thanked her and gave her a little kiss on her cheek, noticing how old she's looking close up. I bought her some posh bubble bath from Marks and Spencer, and a box of Milk Tray; she was very grateful. I got mum a new handbag. She pointed it out when we went to the garden centre and said how much she'd love one like it, so I went back and bought it as a surprise.

My bed at mums always feels so cosy. I took an overnight bag as I knew I'd end up getting hammered. Auntie Maud never fails to put half a bottle of sherry in her trifles, plus mum likes to make sure we've always got a full glass on Christmas Day. But I didn't feel pissed when I lay on the bed, just utterly pissed off. It was like a truck had run me over and I couldn't breathe. My head was pounding and my eyes hurt. I wanted to speak to Steve so badly but I knew I wouldn't be able to. Then I started thinking I should get back to the flat in case he tried to ring me. But I decided against it because apart from the fact I'd probably get done for drunk driving, I wasn't sure it was the best thing to speak to him just then as I was so upset.

****

I have to wait until Monday now before I can see Steve, though I doubt he'll be in work anyway. He's probably phoned Brian and told him what's happened and Brian's encouraged him to take some time off. Maybe it's for the best if I don't see him for a while. Mum wanted me to stay for a few nights as she does get lonely by herself, especially over Christmas, but her friends, Jean and Gordon arrive today and are staying over until next Wednesday so I declined. I said I'd go round tonight for tea just to be sociable. I don't want to go but I do love Jean and Gordon, they're like family to us. Plus, I don't have to call them auntie and uncle.

Monday 30th December

It was a very long weekend. But there's been a breakthrough. First, I had a lovely time at mum's house and decided to stay on Boxing Day night when Jean and Gordon were there, because as usual, mum kept filling my glass up and I ended up being unfit to drive home. But we had a great time playing Trivial Pursuits and eating crap.

On Friday the 27th, I got home and checked my messages on my new answering machine. There were two from Steve. The first one told me he was really sorry for everything and hoped I'd had a nice Christmas with my mum and that his Christmas had been really miserable; and the second just said, 'We need to talk. I love you, Rachel.'

I arrived in work at nine o'clock, usual time. Thankfully, Brenda has booked all this week off which means I won't have her wandering in and out of reception pissing me off when I'm not in the mood. I could have seriously been in danger of losing my job with the mood I've been in lately. But after today's developments, well, she can sack me if she wants because Steve and I are back together!

Yes, you read that right. He came in at 9.30 and walked straight up to my desk in reception. He was smiling at me in that lovely way, the way he smiles at me after we've just made love at Nightingale Woods. It was as if he couldn't care less who was about when he bent down towards my face and kissed me full on the lips. I pulled away after a few seconds because I wasn't sure what he was playing at, but then he asked if I could go with him for a walk as he needed to talk to me urgently.

I checked with Brian that it was okay and as Brian already seemed to know what was going on, he agreed and said he'd man the phones. I doubt they'd ring, but still, it was good of him to be understanding. So, Steve and I went for a walk around the industrial estate; not the most romantic walk we've ever had but at least we were on our own.

'I've had a really shit Christmas, love,' he said. 'It's been impossible to enjoy even a minute of it because I've missed you so much.'

I told him I'd missed him too but he told me to shut up and listen.

'Olivia has told Susan about our affair and Susan has naturally hit the roof.' He bowed his head as though he was ashamed about upsetting his daughter more than his wife. He continued. 'They've been having a right go at me for the past four days, love, and have just about driven me out of the house. I can't take it anymore and I've decided to pack my bags and leave.'

I turned my head in the opposite direction, not sure whether to believe him or not.

'Would you mind if I came to live with you until we can get a bigger place?' he asked.

At first, I questioned that he meant what he said and he wasn't just annoyed with himself and the fact that Olivia now knows. But he assured me that he loves me, wants to spend the rest of his life with me and will be going home at lunch time to pack up and leave.

'Olivia has asked so many questions about you; what you look like, how old you are, who are you, what's your name, where do you work.' Blimey, I thought, nosy cow. 'She also says she wants to meet you and tell you what she thinks of you and until she's done that she'll not let it rest.'

But Steve's told her nothing about me (which I'm quite relieved about to be honest) and he says he has no intention of telling her anything either. He said once the divorce starts to happen only then will she know who I am.

I'm grateful to him for keeping my identity secret. I'm going to have to leave Winterson's now of course, because once she does find out who I am she'll probably come to work and make a scene in front of Brenda and, heaven forbid, Mr. Winterson which would be so embarrassing. But I'll get some temp work again, it always pays well.

****

It's now Monday night and I'm just sat waiting for the phone call from Steve to tell me he's on his way here with his stuff. I've cleared three drawers and moved loads of things out of my wardrobe to fit his suits in. Plus, I've given the bathroom a really good clean in case he wants to have a bath later. I feel quite nervous about it in a way, but an excited kind of nervous. He should be ringing any minute now so I'll close this entry for tonight.

****

Once again, I'm awake at two in the morning, but for all the wrong reasons. Steve didn't ring; neither did he turn up at my place. I haven't a clue what's going on and I'm really worried. I know where he lives even though I've never been inside his house, and part of me is itching to get into the car and drive there. I do hope he's okay and Olivia hasn't murdered him or something.

Tuesday 31st January

It's lunch time and I'm at home.

The reason for that is because Steve didn't come into work this morning but instead rang me and asked me to meet him here.

I'm so angry I can't see straight. In a nutshell, Olivia has begged him to give their marriage another chance and he's agreed. She suggested they give it three months and see how it goes. She says she loves him too much to just let him go and he says he feels he owes her at least three months to see what happens. He also said he's not sure it'll work and thinks she'll just drive him away after a week or so but he has to try, for hers and Susan's sake. He's even told Brian about what Olivia has suggested and Brian rang me a few minutes ago to say how sorry he was that it's all turned out like this and if I needed some company he would come round. I declined his offer though did thank him when he suggested I take some time off and come back when I feel ready. I'll stay at home this week and see how I feel at the weekend and if I'm still this angry and upset I'm going to hand my notice in at Winterson's, then register again with the temping agency.

I think I can hear Brenda cackling from here; she'll be revelling in this once she finds out.

****

It's now seven pm and I'm once again shit-faced. Mum rang at tea time asking if I'd like to go and see Jean and Gordon before they leave in the morning but I told her I've had a drink and can't drive so to wish them a safe journey and we'll catch up soon. I feel pretty bad for not seeing them; in fact, I had hoped I'd be introducing them to Steve but that's gone tits up now hasn't it.

I can't believe I've let him do this to me. Again.

I've been 'the other woman' for nearly ten months and for the past five months at least we've been deeply in love with each other. I feel like he's used me, made a fool out of me.

But I love him. God, I love him.

The thought of sitting in the house on my own for the next six days doesn't bear thinking about. Right now, all I want to do is curl up and die.

New Year's Day

This isn't how I wanted to start the New Year. Mum has phoned twice this morning already asking what time I'll be there and if I'll pick up some Elmlea from the Spar shop. I'm going to need to put on a brave face for a couple of hours then make my excuses and leave. I hope Steve feels as miserable as I do. And right now, I hate Olivia.

Thursday 2nd January

I managed to last three hours at mum's yesterday before coming home. She said I was really pale and tried to insist I stay the night but I just had to get home so I could cry. The tears were killing my eyes all day and it was a real struggle trying to pretend to mum that I just had a cold and it was nothing to worry about. She said she'd ring me today to make sure I'm okay but I've taken the phone off the hook. I just want to be by myself and I don't want to talk to anyone, ever again.

Friday 3rd January

I woke up at three am and put the phone back on the hook after having an awful thought that Steve could have been trying to contact me.

****

It's nine am and I can't eat anything because I feel sick but I've just had a long hot bath and do feel a bit better now. I'm going to ring Kelly later and tell her what's happened. I'm sure she'll be a little bit relieved but I'm sure she'll be upset on my behalf.

****

Brian rang me. He wanted to check I was okay. Said he spoke to Steve this morning and things are very strained in their house. Olivia is in pieces and Susan says she's never going to speak to her dad again. She's also told him he won't be able to see his grandchild. But my stomach did a little cartwheel when Brian told me Steve said he still loves me and always will. It's given me a bit of hope and I'm now wondering if he and Olivia giving their marriage another chance is really what he wants. I don't think it is, but Brian says he at least owes her that much as they've been together for years. Brian's also offered to come round this weekend to cheer me up. I'm not in the mood to be cheered up, I told him. He was really sweet and said. 'No worries, I'm here if you need me.'

Saturday 4ᵗʰ January

I went to Nightingale Woods today and sat in the lay-by for an hour and a half listening to my Michael Bolton cassette. Thought there could be a chance that Steve would turn up but I was kidding myself. Now I'm at home, on my own again, with an almost empty bottle of Liebfraumilch. I just want him to ring me, just to see if there's hope or if I should leave Winterson's and get on with my life elsewhere.

I feel like a sad and lonely idiot and if anyone tells me that they could see this coming I'm in serious danger of strangling them. I know that a lot of affairs end in tears with 'the other woman' coming off the worst, but I honestly thought me and Steve were for good. He's let me believe that and I did. A big part of me still believes there's a chance for us and he'll leave Olivia and come to live with me. And then there's a small part of me that just wants to run away and hide, or perhaps move to a different country and start a new life. Going back to work on Monday is going to be a nightmare. I imagine Claire and Yvonne will have a field day taking the piss, and Brian will be all over me with 'I told you so.' I like my job and the money's good so I'm going to give it a chance, see if we can just get on with each other and work something out maybe, but if it's hopeless then I'll give the temping agency a ring and ask Joanne to find me something.

I just wish Steve would ring me.

****

Saw two magpies before, sat on the grass outside my lounge window. That's got to be a sign.

Monday 6th January

I went into work today and it wasn't as bad as I expected. Brian was really lovely and didn't say I told you so once, and Brenda even stayed out of my way, too, which tells me she definitely knows about us and thinks she should give me some space. Plus, Claire came in and said if I needed to talk she was always here and she's given me her home phone number. I think she likes me underneath. I'll stay clear of Yvonne for this week because if she does say something to me about Steve I think my reaction will be a swift slap across her face.

Steve came into reception at lunch time and asked if I could spare half an hour in the canteen to talk. I really wanted to say yes but I didn't. He seems really down in the dumps and I've decided I don't want to bring up the subject of 'us' just yet, not until he's had time to think about how much he's hurt me. I honestly don't think he realises.

I didn't see him for the rest of the day and when I went to my car, he'd already gone.

Tuesday 7th January

The atmosphere in reception is really crap, though Tina came back today as she's agreed to cover Gail's maternity leave, so that did cheer me up a bit. I told her what's happened with me and Steve and she was really shocked. I thought she was putting it on at first when she did a really melodramatic gasp and threw her hands to her mouth, but then she said 'Oh my God, I honestly thought you and Steve were made for each other, you look so good together.' That made me cry, and I sat at my desk blubbing like a muppet. She had to answer the phone twice whilst I was blowing my nose. I thanked her and she gave me a gentle hug then said she'd be around if I wanted to chat. I think I'm starting to realise that I've got more friends at work than I used to think; Claire is being really lovely as is Tina, though Brenda's been in to see me today and told me I'd have more work as from next week because they've taken on a new contract.

According to her, the contract is going to bring in millions of pounds to the company over the next five years and they'll be recruiting loads of new staff, plus they're going to have the offices revamped which will mean reception will be in a different part of the building for a while. I asked her whereabouts I'd be and she said, 'probably in with Brian, but it's not been decided yet.' I'm okay with that, after all, Brian is a nice guy and has been very kind to me since the split with Steve. I just hope he's good to work with in the same office all day because I do quite enjoy working on my own.

****

Steve has just rung me. I was sat on the sofa finishing off a Hawaiian pizza when he rang. I thought it was going to be either mum or Kelly so I was completely surprised when I heard his voice and nearly dropped the phone. He says he needs to talk to me and explain what's happening because he feels we haven't discussed it properly. I told him that I didn't want to get hurt again and he didn't need to explain anything to me if his plan was to stay with Olivia.

'I don't know what my plans are yet, love. That's why I need to see you. Will you meet me at Nightingale Woods tomorrow night?'

'Why don't you come round here?' I suggested, but he says he doesn't feel comfortable coming here at the moment. I didn't ask why but I have a feeling he thinks Olivia or even Susan might follow him and if he leads them here they'll know where I live and will hound me. He's a thoughtful man, even if he has ripped my heart out.

Wednesday 8th January

I met Steve at Nightingale Woods; he was already there when I arrived. He got into my car and we just sat there for about five minutes not knowing what to say to each other. Then he leaned over and kissed me. I responded and it felt so bloody good. He says he still loves me and isn't sure what's going to happen with him and Olivia.

Apparently, Olivia keeps asking him really personal questions about our affair, like did we use condoms, how many times did we have sex, where did we do it. He's also told her that we stayed in the hotel that night and he didn't go on the Christmas do, and she threw a pan at him that was full of frozen peas. That actually broke the ice (not to mention the kitchen door) and we both started laughing. He says she's turned into a different person and keeps hissing insults at him, telling him he needs to lose weight and she's surprised he managed to pull anyone with the way he looks. She's also asked again about the earring she found in his car and he told her it was mine. Plus she mentioned the Woolworth's voucher that she found in his wallet when she was rummaging around for a tenner for a Chinese. He didn't know she'd found the voucher and as she assumed they were for her, she didn't say anything because she hadn't wanted to spoil what she thought was a surprise present.

I told him I was sorry that he was going through all this but he says he's fine and it'll most likely stop eventually. He's upset that Susan still won't speak to him though and I think he's a bit worried that she's going to stop him seeing his grandchild. Part of me wonders if the reason he's told Olivia he'll give their marriage a go is because of Susan and her baby, which is ridiculous I think, because even if he does leave Olivia, I'm sure Susan will come round once the baby's born. I haven't said this to him but I might do at some point.

We sat in my car for an hour listening to Michael Bolton and chatting about Olivia and her moods then he kissed me again and touched the top of my leg. I thought he was going to ask if we could get in the back but he pulled away and said 'goodnight, see you tomorrow at work.' Looking back on it now, I'm not sure getting in the back would have been a good idea, but I probably would have done it at the time.

Friday 10th January

I've got a problem. I'm not sure whether Steve still thinks we're having a relationship or whether he just wants us to be friends. He wants us to meet up at Nightingale Woods tomorrow afternoon and I have no idea what to do. I know I shouldn't go and should just let him get on with making a go of his farcical marriage, but I want to see him so much. I really love him and I'm terribly confused. I'll sleep on it and see how I feel tomorrow. He said he'd be there at one pm and would wait for half an hour, and if I didn't turn up he wouldn't hate me for it.

Shit, I hate having a dilemma before I'm going to bed. I'll never get a wink's sleep tonight.

Saturday 11th January

I gave in. When I woke up I had a massive urge to see Steve, so I got myself dolled up, put on some sexy underwear then set off. I got there at five past one and true to his word, he was already parked up. As it was a nice day we had a walk to our clearing. The ground was too damp to sit down but he pushed me up against a tree and took my breath away when he planted his lips heavily on mine. Someone jogged past just as he was putting his hand up my top but I couldn't have cared less if it was Olivia herself; I was enjoying being with him too much.

When we got back to the cars, we got into mine. I asked him what was going on between us and why he wanted to keep seeing me. He says he isn't going to leave Olivia, not yet anyway, but loves me and doesn't want us to end. I told him he's having his cake and eating it but he laughed and said, 'What do you want?' He got me with that question because he knows full well that I want to carry on seeing him. He said we won't be able to see each other much, maybe just once a fortnight for now, but we'll obviously see each other at work so it's better than nothing. Maybe it is, for now.

****

I can't friggin' sleep. I shouldn't have had that last glass of Southern Comfort because now I've drunk myself sober. I hate it when that happens. I'm lying on my bed typing this as if I stay horizontal it might fool my body into thinking it's not time to get up yet.

I can't stop thinking about what Steve said to me today, well, yesterday now as it's Sunday. He's not going to leave Olivia but still wants to see me. Part of me feels he's just taking the piss, but because I love him I don't know what to do. I can't ask Kelly because she'll just tell me I need to leave Winterson's and get on with my life. I might have a chat with Tina at work, or even Claire. She's been really nice to me recently and I think I can trust her. She did give me her phone number so perhaps she wants us to be friends.

Right, I've made a decision; I'll ask Claire round for a drink this week and we can have a good girlie chat.

Thursday 16th January

I haven't seen much of Steve at work; think he's getting his shit together for this promotion he's going after. Probably thinks I'll be a distraction. Anyway, Claire came round last night and I'm pleased to say we had a great time. She's actually a lovely person and I take back all the bitchy comments I made about her. She's also very down to earth and a good laugh. She turned up with an expensive bottle of red wine which got opened and poured before she'd even had chance to take her coat off. She's promised me that nothing I tell her will be repeated anywhere and she also told me something really interesting, probably the reason why she's suddenly decided she wants to be my friend.

Six years ago, she had an affair with a married man and it went on for eighteen months until his wife found out. I can't believe I gasped in horror when she told me; how lame am I?! So she thought this affair was the bee's knees as far and was convinced they would one day settle down and get married, have kids and live happily ever after, amen. But he left his wife for a week, moved in with her then went back to the wife leaving Claire absolutely devastated. She had tears in her eyes when she was telling me so I know she was telling the truth. She said she'll never trust a man again and they're all arseholes, but I told her that Steve was an exception. She looked at me with one eyebrow raised when I said that.

She lives with her girlfriend now. She and Melanie have been an item for three years. Now that did shock me and she laughed when she saw my face. She said, 'Don't worry, I'm not going to come on to you.' Then went on to tell me she's always had lesbian tendencies and her affair with Paul was to try and prove, especially to her very old-fashioned parents, that she wasn't gay. It didn't work though and now she's shacked up with a lovely girl from Stoke-on-Trent.

We've agreed to be friends and make a regular thing of getting together. I've told her to bring Melanie round for a drink sometime as I'd love to meet her. Claire made me laugh when she told me she couldn't stop staring at Adele's tits, you know, the temp from last year. I smiled but didn't bother telling her that I couldn't stop staring either.

Wednesday 22ⁿᵈ January

I think Yvonne's a bit jealous of mine and Claire's new friendship. She keeps coming in to reception when Claire and I are chatting. I know for a fact that Yvonne's happily married so I'm pretty sure there's no romantic attraction there, but I do wish she'd fuck off and let me enjoy my new found friend. Claire said Yvonne can be a bit bitchy sometimes but she's harmless really. And the best thing is that Claire reckons Yvonne will leave Winterson's in the next few months as her husband's being relocated to the South. All we need now is for Brenda to leave and this will be my dream job.

Wednesday 29ᵗʰ January

Steve came round tonight to help me assemble a HiFi cabinet that I've bought from MFI. I could've done it myself really but it was nice to have him help me. He brought me some chocolates as well, even better.

We didn't do anything other than have a little cuddle on the sofa after the cabinet was finished, but I think if he'd have stayed longer we'd have ended up in my bed. He was very turned on, I could tell.

Monday 3ʳᵈ February

Brenda brought me some boxes today and told me to start packing up my files and move them into Brian's office as the building work starts on Wednesday. Brian's made room in his office for my clutter and he helped me move everything in. Jake from accounts, came and wired up the switchboard for me as I didn't know what went where. It's quite cosy in Brian's office as it's much smaller than the bland reception and he's got a huge radiator along one wall that he has on all day. He seems quite excited that I've moved in with him and has made me three cups of coffee and offered me his chocolate biscuits that apparently no one is allowed to touch.

Steve popped his head around the door and said with a grin, 'you'll need to watch him.' We all laughed though I have a feeling Brian was a bit embarrassed.

Friday 7ᵗʰ February

I met Steve at the driving range tonight. I didn't hit any balls, not that I can anyway, but I just sat on the chair and watched him. It was really cold and he lent me his bomber jacket. Not sure I want to go to the driving range again as it's so bloody boring, not to mention freezing.

We sat in my car for a bit after he followed me to a lay-by a mile away from golf club. It's very deserted round there so there's no danger of us being seen, but I still felt a bit uncomfortable. Steve didn't seem to though, and was very amorous. He asked if we could get in the back but I was shivering and couldn't be arsed to strip off. So we've arranged to meet at Nightingale Woods next weekend.

He says Olivia is a bit better now and seems to be getting over what's happened. She questions him whenever he's going anywhere which is why he doesn't want to go out too often, but it seems she's accepted that our affair is over. I'm not sure where this leaves us now, because if they're getting their marriage back on track then it's pretty obvious he's just using me for sex. But he still tells me he loves me. Like, really loves me. And he's even said tonight that he's not sure his marriage will work or not. Do I carry on seeing him the way we are, or do I give him an ultimatum? I'll have a chat with Claire next week and see what she thinks.

Wednesday 12 February

I'm really enjoying working in the same office as Brian, he's such a hoot. He's about ten years older than me and lives with a flat mate in Appleworth. He split up with his girlfriend a few months ago and hasn't been out with a girl since though he says he used to fancy Claire until she told him she was a lesbian. Then he said he *really* fancied her. We have such a great laugh.

The building work in reception is coming along nicely and there are lots of hunky guys strolling about outside with saws and drills and flasks. Still, I love Steve. I'm not going to let another man tempt me while there's still a chance with him.

Thursday 13th February

I asked Steve if he wanted to come round tonight and he said he might do, but it depends on whether Olivia's working. She's been doing a lot of day shifts recently and he assumes she's changed shifts with someone so she can be home in the evenings and keep an eye on him. I can understand her not trusting him but it must be awful having to live like that. He only needs to say the word and he can come and live here.

****

Steve's just gone home. I couldn't believe it when he turned up at eight pm. Said he'd been to the driving range for an hour and is supposed to be having a drink with the lads. He hugged me really tightly when he walked through the door and it felt amazing. I've really missed his hugs. Then he kissed me and asked if we could go to the bedroom, but I said no.

I don't know what's come over me lately as I've become really assertive. It's like I feel in charge of the situation all of a sudden and I can see that Steve doesn't know what to make of it. I actually think my new found confidence is making him love me more because judging from the bulge in his pants that I felt as he pressed himself against me, he was certainly turned on tonight.

Friday 14th February

Steve came into the office with a Valentine's card for me. He's asked me to meet him at Nightingale Woods tomorrow afternoon. I have to admit I'm a bit confused about it all as he seems really happy at the moment and it doesn't seem that long since he was completely depressed about everything. Wish I could read his mind.

Tina reckons he's still madly in love with me and is just towing the line as far as Olivia is concerned, but I know him and I think there's more to it. I'll ask him tomorrow how he really feels about me. If it's bad news then I think I might need to seriously consider leaving Winterson's because this not knowing what's going to happen between us is driving me nuts.

Sunday 16ᵗʰ February

Stayed at mums last night as she'd invited Auntie Maud over and wanted me to go, too. Auntie Maud has got herself a fella. Think mum's really embarrassed about it actually because every time Auntie Maud mentioned the wondrous William, she looked at me and rolled her eyes. We get to meet William in a couple of weeks as mum's invited them both round for dinner. I got a bit tipsy on the Harvey's Bristol Cream that Auntie Maud brought with her which is why I stayed over at mum's.

But the real excitement happened when I met Steve at the woods this afternoon. He was stood leaning against his car when I arrived and had a huge grin on his face. As I parked up I saw him reach into his car for something and it turned out to be a gorgeous Figaro design, gold bracelet, my favourite. He says it's for Valentine's day. I flung my arms around his neck and kissed him then we went for a walk to our clearing where the lovely nightingale was singing away. It was incredibly romantic. I asked him how he was managing to get away and wasn't Olivia suspicious anymore. He said he didn't want to talk about her and then pushed me against the nearest tree. I'm still confused though as I didn't get chance to ask him what's going on.

Tuesday 18ᵗʰ February

Brian asked me how it's going with Steve today. He said he's glad that things seem to be getting back to normal and it's good to see Steve looking happy again. Then he put his head down and carried on writing up his report for Mr. Winterson. I'm finding Brian a little odd recently; it's as though he knows something I don't and he's dying to tell me. I wish he'd get on with it because he's starting to really bloody irritate me.

Friday 21st February

I answered the phone to Olivia today, for the first time since she found out about me and Steve. She obviously has no idea who I am because she just asked to speak to Steve in her usual cheerful voice. I so wanted to tell her that it's me who her husband is in love with and that I want her to end their marriage so he can be mine. But of course I didn't and just put her straight through to her husband.

I asked him this afternoon what she'd wanted and apparently they're going away for the weekend once he gets home from work, to a little hotel in Scotland. They've been several times to the same place and she thinks they need some time away. I was hoping he would have come round to the flat tomorrow as I think I'm ready for us to make love again, but I'll pop to the garden centre with mum instead.

Monday 24th February

I asked Steve if he's had a nice weekend in Scotland and he said it was very pleasant and they did a bit of shopping in Perth on Saturday. A part of me felt jealous that they were spending time together, away, in a hotel, but a bigger part of me was just glad he was waiting by his car to talk to me at home time. He's asked me to meet him at Nightingale Woods on Friday night as Olivia is going on a night out and he can get away for a few hours. It'll be a bit cold no doubt, but I've agreed.

Wednesday 26th February

The building work should be finished by Friday so I'll be moving into the new reception area on Monday morning. It's looking really swish and Brenda has even asked me if I want to take some money from petty cash and get some yucca plants. I'm amazed she's asked me as it's usually Claire or Yvonne who get to do errands during working hours. Anyway, I popped to Turnstall Farm and bought three yucca plants and a few miniature roses to add a bit of colour. I almost bought a fish tank and some fish as well but thought better of it. I'm quite looking forward to being in a smart reception area for a change, instead of the scruffy old bland one with a skanky switchboard and stained carpet.

Saturday 1st March

I met Steve at Nightingale Woods last night and it was bloody freezing. I had to turn the engine half on and keep the heater blowing as even Steve's cuddles couldn't warm me up. In future, I'm not going there in the evening; he'll have to come to the flat instead and we'll meet at the woods at weekends.

I plucked up the courage to ask him what was going on with him and Olivia though I really wish I hadn't. Their weekend away in Scotland proved to be a dirty weekend from the sounds of it. I must admit, Steve didn't really want to tell me but I begged him to as I've asked a few times now for him not to keep things from me. She'd bought a new outfit and some sexy underwear and told him she was feeling 'fruity'. He said he was totally taken by surprise. He also said it reminded him of how they used to be years ago. When he noticed my thunderous expression, he thankfully added, 'I'd rather not talk about my marriage to you, it's not fair, and I don't want to see you upset.' Unfortunately, that doesn't make me feel any better because now I know he's having sex with his wife again. Apart from the fact I now feel like a second rate whore, I'm not happy about the fact that he's dipping his wick with Olivia and dipping it with me; and we don't use condoms.

****

Sat on the sofa with a half empty bottle of wine thinking about Steve and Olivia in their marital bed. I'm really not happy about this set up. I honestly don't know whether I ought to just give him an ultimatum now.

Monday 17th March

It's been a couple of weeks since I added an entry to my diary and the simple reason for that is because it's been the most boring two weeks of my life. I moved in to the swish new reception area and managed to work out the new switchboard after Jake from accounts talked me through it. Why he's not assigned to technical stuff I've no idea, because he's a complete whizz with computers and anything technical. He's actually a bit of a geek really, but very nice with it. Brian keeps coming into reception to make sure I'm okay. I think he's missing me, bless him.

Steve seems to be walking round with a permanent grin on his face lately and every time he walks through reception he winks at me. I smile back to be polite but I'm half thinking the smile is more aimed at the fact him and Olivia are at it like rabbits. He hasn't mentioned us meeting up at all and it does make me feel sad. I'm really hoping I'm wrong, but I can't help thinking this 'giving it a go' that Olivia insisted they try, has gone right against me. She mentioned three months when it all came out and it's almost passed now. Still, I live in hope. I think if after the three months is up and we're still just ticking along as we are now, I really need to think about leaving Winterson's. I'm 28 this year and being on the shelf with only a married man to keep me company whenever he can get away from his wife, isn't much fun anymore. Plus, I'm sick of being pissed every night and having a headache every morning. I've no sodding willpower.

****

I've been reading back through my diary and just realised I missed our official twelve-month anniversary. I went on my first date with Steve on 13th March and it would have been really nice to have met up again and done something romantic. But I forgot and he didn't even mention it, so I assume he's forgot, too. I'm just sat listening to Michael Bolton belting out 'Said I Loved You...But I Lied' and it's made me cry. Can't help thinking that this could have turned out so much better than it has.

Friday 21st March

Steve noticed that I'm wearing the bracelet he gave me for Valentine's day. He says it makes him happy to see it on me and could he come round to the flat tomorrow afternoon. I said he could though I get the impression it's just to talk.

Saturday 22nd March

Steve turned up at two pm with a huge bouquet of flowers. They're absolutely gorgeous and must have cost him a fortune as they have a tag attached to the wrapper that says, 'Callender's Flowers' and that's one of the most expensive florists for miles. It also means that he's made a special trip into town to buy them. I couldn't resist him when I felt the rod in his trousers and we ended up making love in my bed. It felt like the first time again. His touch sent shivers down my spine and we almost lifted the roof as we both reached orgasm at the same time. God, just thinking about it is making me weak at the knees.

We didn't talk about Olivia once. Neither of us mentioned her name even though I nearly did when he was leaving because I was dying to ask him to stay the night. But of course I didn't and he left at five pm. I've just ordered a pizza and I'm going to settle in front of the telly for the night and stare at my beautiful flowers.

Sunday 23rd March

Auntie Maud's new fella, William, is such a hoot. He must be at least seventy but he has a fabulous sense of humour. Mum did a lovely roast beef dinner with her Gaviscon-inducing Yorkshire puddings and Auntie Maud made an extra strong sherry trifle. William and I sat in the lounge while mum and Auntie Maud did the washing up.

'You should find yourself a nice young man, Rachel and settle down,' he said, 'because you're a lovely looking lassie and could get any man you wanted.'

I think he was just being kind and I didn't tell him about Steve, even though I probably could have done. I think he'd be the type that would just say something like 'go for it if it makes you happy.' If Auntie Maud carries on seeing him, I might tell him sometime. On the other hand, if he were to tell Auntie Maud she might feel obliged to tell mum, so maybe that wouldn't be such a great idea. Oh well, I'll see what happens. But mum commented that I look radiant and seem to have put a bit of weight on which isn't surprising with all the chocolate biscuits Brian keeps offering me.

(Note to self: no McDonald's this week.)

Tuesday 25ᵗʰ March

I'm really pleased for Steve; he's got his promotion. He showed me the letter at lunch time and says he's over the moon. It means he'll move into his own office just down the corridor from me and he'll now be in charge of the shop floor. Plus it means an extra ten thousand pounds a year which is pretty amazing. I asked him if he'd be celebrating and he said he'd like to come to the flat this weekend and we can celebrate together. What I actually meant was would he be celebrating with his family, but I didn't like to ask. I'll get some new lingerie for Saturday and make sure he realises how pleased for him I am.

Saturday 29ᵗʰ March

It's Easter Saturday and Steve has just rang me to say he won't be coming round after all as Olivia wants to take Susan and Keith out for a meal to celebrate his promotion. I feel quite angry actually because I went to Debenhams to do some late night shopping on Thursday night, and spent thirty quid on a black bra and knickers. Plus, I've spent ages in the bath titivating myself and sorting out my bikini line.

I'll make sure he knows how pissed off I am when we're at work next week.

I've always known that I come second, but it seems lately he's making it obvious to me that I'll never be his first thought. And it really hurts. *Really* hurts.

Tuesday 1st April

Steve didn't come in till ten am this morning as he had to go to a meeting at head office in Burnside. He looked very smart in a new suit and tie and I think he's had his hair cut. I smiled at him when he walked through the main entrance and he gave me a gorgeous smile back. But I'm still angry with him about Saturday. It was really out of order what he did. The fact that he's smiled so sweetly at me does tell me that he hasn't a clue how much he's upset me, again. So I've decided to ignore him for the rest of the week, or at least until he apologises and offers to take me out somewhere nice.

Thursday 3rd April

Brian keeps coming into reception and asking if I'm okay. I'm actually getting on really well with him at the moment. I think it's since we shared an office and he's realised that I'm not as bad as everyone has been making out.

Friday 4th April

Steve had the cheek to ask me if I fancy Brian. What a stupid thing to ask, mind you, it could mean he's jealous of our friendship. Maybe this will finally make him sit up and realise it's me he wants and then he'll leave Olivia and move in with me. Could be a result waiting to happen.

Wednesday 9th April

I'm in a real quandary. I've been head-hunted by another company that is a customer of Winterson's. They're called Campbell & Co., and they're based in Burnside, just down the road from Winterson's head office. The money is much better than what I'm getting on reception and it means I'll have a lot of spare cash left over when I've paid the mortgage and bills. But I'm not sure I want to leave the job I'm currently doing.

I'm not sure I'm ready to say goodbye to Steve.

Thursday 10th April

I've confided in Brian about the job offer and he thinks I should go for it. He says the job prospects for a receptionist at Winterson's aren't that great and he doubts I'll ever be promoted, and even if I do get offered another job at Winterson's, it'll most likely be working with Yvonne or Brenda, both of whom I can't stand. I mentioned my worries re Steve and was a bit saddened by his answer, though I know he's probably right.

'Don't you think it's about time you realised that Steve isn't going to leave Olivia?' he said. 'You really should think about getting on with your own life.' He also said something else that's really made me think; 'Steve told me that his marriage to Olivia is better than it's ever been and the affair you had seems to have brought her out of her shell. He says they're on fire in the bedroom.'

I stared at him with my mouth open doing my best guppy fish impression. After a minute or so I just smiled and said 'oh, that's nice,' whilst inside thinking what a shit-stirrer Brian is. I knew they were getting on okay and I also knew, or at least suspected, that they were sleeping together, but I honestly believed that there was still a chance for us.

****

I'm sat on the sofa, pissed again, crying into my laptop. It feels like Steve's left me all over again. I've been a stupid gullible idiot. I need to do something to make him see that he can't get to me anymore and I'm not bothered if he and Olivia are shagging the pants off each other every night. Revenge is sweet.

Monday 14th April

It's been a few weeks now since I've been alone with Steve. We've had lunch together a few times and walked to the chip van, but he hasn't asked to meet me at the woods, nor has he asked if he can come round to the flat.

So, I've decided to ring Mrs. Brewer at Campbell & Co. and tell her I'll accept her job offer. I'll have to give Brenda a month's notice but I can't see her objecting. I've told Tina and Claire and they're really pleased for me. Tina said she's going to ask Brenda if she can take over as receptionist as she doesn't want to leave once Gail comes back, and Claire was crying. I hugged her and said I'd like us to keep in touch and that I'm not going for another month. Brian asked if I'd keep in touch with him also, and I agreed.

Tuesday 15ᵗʰ April

Steve came into reception today and asked me why I hadn't told him about leaving Winterson's. I said I didn't think he would be bothered as we didn't seem to be as close anymore, but he came over to me and hugged me, in full view of the reception area. I wasn't sure how to react so I just hugged him back then sat down in my chair, probably looking quite flustered. He said he's going to miss me but this is a great opportunity and one I shouldn't let pass by. He also said he will ring me all the time so we can still arrange to meet up at Nightingale Woods and perhaps he can come to the flat.

Then Brian came to me at lunch time and gave me his home phone number and asked for mine. I wrote it down on a post-it note and passed it to him. He said he'll ring me at the weekend if I didn't mind.

Wednesday 16ᵗʰ April

Mrs. Brewer rang me today and asked if there'd be any chance of me starting work for them next week as they're really short staffed. I said I'd speak to Brenda and let her know tomorrow. I could have done with more time to prepare myself really. Mrs. Brewer seems really nice and I think she'll be a better boss than Brenda's ever been, plus I really do think now is the time for me to move on and try to get Steve out of my system.

He really upset me when he said I should take the job at Campbell & Co., it kind of gave me the impression that he feels it would be best for me to leave anyway. He also said if I'm only holding back because of him then I shouldn't because he doubted very much he'd be leaving Olivia now. After today, I think I've finally realised what an arsehole Steve Harris is. And this weekend I'm going to invite Brian round for a drink when he phones me.

****

I'm actually gutted about what Steve said today. I *do* still love him. I think I always will. And I believe that deep down he still loves me. Maybe once I've left Winterson's, I'll get my life back on track and will be able to make some new friends. I just feel so sad about everything; Steve, leaving Winterson's, not being able to have a laugh with Claire and Tina. God, I'm even going to miss Brenda and not spending half my day moaning about her. Oh shit, have I done the right thing?

Friday 18th April

I've finished at Winterson's now. I can't actually believe I don't work there anymore. I've been there for three years and on the whole it's been a really great job. I got a huge card, signed by everyone, even Brenda, and a Marks & Spencer voucher for £100 that I think is really generous. Everyone gave me a hug, except Brenda, not that I'm bothered about that, but she did have a stupid grin on her fat face, obviously delighted that I've finally left. Claire was crying and Tina was a bit emotional as well, and Yvonne shook my hand and wished me luck. Brian gave me a great big bear hug that felt really lovely. His aftershave is still lingering on my blouse.

Steve waited for me after work and was stood by his car when I walked out of the main entrance. He called me over and obligingly I went. We sat in his car and he handed me a leaving card that reads inside, *'I'll miss you. Please keep in touch. All my love, Steve xxx'* I'm not sure he means the 'All my love' bit, but it was a nice gesture. How he expects me to keep in touch with him I don't know because I obviously can't ring him at home and if I phone him at the office it's going to raise suspicion again. I'll just have to hope he phones me sometime.

Claire and Tina came round tonight and we had a great time. They brought two bottles of red wine and Claire treated us all to a Chinese takeaway. Tina says she's looking forward to starting her new job as receptionist on Monday and I warned her about not getting involved with married men. Then we all pissed ourselves laughing and scoffed the Chinese.

Claire told me she doesn't speak to Yvonne much these days because she got fed up of her gossiping about me and Steve. That made me feel good actually, because I now know that Claire is a true friend. I'm sorry that she isn't close friends with Yvonne of course, but it's good to know I've got a friend who has defended me.

I told them about Steve. Virtually everything. We'd drank both bottles of red and had started on the Southern Comfort by the time we got round to the gory details, but it felt good to get it all out, and especially to them as they know Steve. Claire said she honestly thought at one point that he was going to leave Olivia and would have been really chuffed for me if that had happened. Tina said she wasn't sure because she's worked with someone who had an affair with a married man before, and it all turned sour. In fact, so she says, the wife threatened to kill the mistress and it ended up going to court and everything. She hadn't wanted to tell me before because she could always see how much I loved Steve. How thoughtful of her!

They think he's a bastard for breaking my heart twice in a matter of days though, and especially over Christmas, but they said I'm probably better off now and should find myself a nice bloke and have some fun for a while.

Which is exactly what I plan on doing, as soon as Brian rings me tomorrow.

Saturday 19th April

The phone rang at midday and it was Brian. He sounded really gentle. I told him if he wanted to come over for a coffee sometime he was very welcome. So he's coming one night next week but will ring me nearer the time. He said he's missing me already at work and he doesn't know how he'll go on without seeing my smiling face behind reception every day. I laughed and said, 'Don't be daft,' making a camp hand movement that he obviously wouldn't have seen, but there were butterflies in my tummy and I'm not sure whether that's a good thing or a bad thing.

When I hung up, I couldn't help wishing it had been Steve who'd rang me, rather than Brian.

Monday 21st April

My first day at Campbell & Co went really well, better than expected actually. Mrs. Brewer, who insists I call her Margaret, is my immediate supervisor and my duties include typing her correspondence and trying to decipher what she's saying on the Dictaphone. I've never used a Dictaphone before and was a bit wary when she introduced me to the cassette player and the foot pedal, but I soon got the hang of it. I'm a bit worried about losing the cassettes though, as they're so small. She has a very quiet voice so I have to keep turning the volume up. There's another girl who works in the same office as me; she's called Julie and she's really nice. She's married with two kids and is probably in her thirties, but I think we're going to get on really well. Then there's Kevin and Tony, two clerks who more or less run the firm. Mr. Campbell is a supposedly high profile solicitor but he doesn't come into the office much these days as he has another office in Stretdale where he spends most of his time. The other managers, Christopher and Hugh, have their own offices with plush leather furniture and floor to ceiling bookshelves, though Julie reckons they do very little apart from have a meeting to arrange another meeting. Margaret says it's a really friendly environment and everyone will make sure I'm okay. She's right. I think I'm going to like it at Campbell & Co.

Thursday 24th April

Brian came round to the flat last night. He rang during the day and left a message on my answer phone, saying he didn't like ringing me at work as I'd only just started there, but would I ring him on his home number and say if it was okay for him to call round. I rang him straight away and within the hour he was on the doorstep. I think he's quite keen.

Anyway, he brought a bottle of Chianti with him and we sat on the sofa, quite close up. We chatted for two hours. He told me all about his ex-girlfriend, Chantelle, and said he still has feelings for her but there's no chance of them getting back together because she's now shacked up with a new bloke. I admit to feeling a bit disappointed when he said he still has feelings for her because I was under the impression he'd got over her and was perhaps on the loose. He asked me if I'm still seeing Steve and I told him the truth, that I wish I was but it looks like he isn't interested in me anymore.

But then Brian told me that Steve's been walking around the offices with a face like a slapped arse ever since I left and he has a feeling he'll be in touch. I have a few mixed thoughts about that because if Steve does get in touch and we carry on seeing each other, which is obviously what I'd like to happen, then it could mean that Brian *won't* want to keep in touch. I'm not sure whether I should be so choosy with my friends just on the off-chance that Steve may one day decide he doesn't want Olivia but wants me instead. I mean, how long will it be before he makes that decision? And is it right that I let him keep me waiting like this? I told Brian I'd like Steve to still be in my life and if he contacts me I won't turn him away. I noticed a bit of disappointment in Brian's expression when I said that.

And then when it was time for Brian to leave, I opened the front door for him and he gave me a long, lingering and particularly romantic kiss on the lips. I haven't been kissed like that since Steve and although it felt different, it felt really nice. I was confused before. Now I'm losing the will to think in case my friggin' brain explodes.

Friday 25th April

I've discovered that Margaret is quite nosy. She asked me today if I have a boyfriend and when I replied with a cagey 'I'm not sure,' she insisted on knowing all about me so she could fathom out for herself whether or not I did indeed have a fella. I cut my love-life story very short as I don't want her to know about Steve just yet, and she said I shouldn't have a problem finding someone as I'm really attractive. I thanked her for the compliment then turned the tape player on. I really don't want to start explaining all the shenanigans to everyone at Campbell & Co. as I don't know them well enough. And besides, this is supposed to be a fresh start.

Saturday 26th April

Brian phoned me this morning to see if I'd like to go out for a meal with him tonight. I told him I'm already going out but I'll ring him next week and we can arrange something for another time. We had a chat for half an hour and he said he really enjoyed spending time with me last Wednesday night and can't wait to see me again. I hope he doesn't think we're an item now, because I'm not ready for another relationship. I'm still hoping things will work out with Steve.

Tuesday 29th April

I couldn't believe it when Steve knocked on my front door tonight. Stood there, bold as brass, jangling his car keys and smiling like a loony. I wasn't sure whether to ask him in or not at first but I caved and offered to make him a brew. We sat on the sofa, snogging and having a fumble, but then he suddenly asked me if I minded the fact that he hadn't left Olivia and probably wouldn't be doing. I pulled away from him and said I was disappointed that it hadn't worked out how I'd wanted, but I didn't want us to lose touch and I was quite happy for him to come round and see me. We've agreed to meet up at Nightingale Woods this weekend. He said he'll ring me on Saturday to confirm if he can definitely make it.

Saturday 3rd May

Steve did ring and we met at the woods in the little lay-by. It was like old times. We sat in my car for a while before going for a walk to our clearing. There was something different about him though, something I can't put my finger on. We sat on the ground and listened to the nightingale for a while before he pulled me against his chest and kissed my forehead. He said, 'I love you, Rachel, and I want you to know that I always will.' Then he stood up, reached for my hand and we walked back to the cars. He kissed me before I got into mine and even though a young couple with three kids walked past, he didn't pull away.

I'm not naive enough not to realise that Steve was saying goodbye today. He does love me and that makes this so much harder. He must know how much I love him but it obviously isn't enough. His marriage naturally means more to him than I do and I can partly understand that, though it hurts like hell. Susan's baby is due any day now and he did say he'd ring me once it's been born. Hopefully we'll keep in touch, maybe not how I'd like, but if I can just hear his voice occasionally, that'll have to be enough.

****

I'm sat at home on my own as usual, wondering if I'll ever be happy. My life has been so exciting these past twelve months since Steve came into it, and even though it's been a dangerous kind of excitement, it's still given me something to focus on. I've enjoyed being Steve's girlfriend. Not so much 'the other woman', but having the opportunity to be in love with a man like Steve has changed me. It's made me grow up, mature, find a pair of balls to face the world with, so to speak. It's given me confidence in myself and made me realise that even though I'm gullible, I'm also attractive to men and *can* be choosy if I want to be. My relationship with Steve might not have gone to plan, but it's been a memorable experience.

I'm listening to Michael Bolton and his dulcet tones as he sings 'A Love So Beautiful', one of the nicest songs I've ever heard with incredibly fitting words to how I feel right now. Maybe *our* love so beautiful could have been even *more* beautiful if Steve hadn't been married. But to me, it's been a beautiful relationship and I know that I'll love Steve for the rest of my life, even if I do meet someone else one day.

Wednesday 7th May

Brian came round last night again. This time we had a long snog on the sofa and I let him have a fumble up above. I wouldn't let him go any further as I don't want to just jump into bed with the next guy that comes along, plus I haven't got over Steve yet, but it was very lustful, and we were extremely horny. Whether it'll ever materialise into a proper relationship I don't know at this stage but I'm not counting it out.

He told me that Steve's daughter had a baby girl and they've called her Sonia. He was off work today as the baby was born yesterday and they wanted to help Susan get home and settled in. I was a bit disappointed as I did hope Steve would ring to tell me about it himself, but I guess I shouldn't have expected him to. Brian also said that he's told Steve he's been to see me just to make sure I'm doing well after leaving Winterson's. Not sure how I feel about that because I wanted to tell Steve myself that Brian's been here. Now it'll look like I've been playing away behind his back. Which of course I haven't, but as I've told Steve I want to carry on seeing him, he'll probably assume that I was lying and I'm just some cheap tart. Brilliant. Thanks, Brian.

Friday 9ᵗʰ May

The phone was ringing when I walked through the door from work. It was Steve. The first thing he said was about him now being a granddad and I congratulated him, asking the usual naff questions like how much does Sonia weigh, are mother and baby doing well. Then he asked, 'How do you know she's called Sonia?'

I had to come clean and tell him that Brian told me. Bollocks. I really didn't want it to happen like this but Steve got a bit frustrated with me and said he knows Brian and I are seeing each other and he can't believe I haven't told him after everything we've been through. I explained that it isn't serious between me and Brian and we're just friends, but he said by the look on Brian's face in the office he can tell we're a lot more than just friends. Shit, shit, shit. Steve went on to say he wished me all the best and even though he's upset I haven't told him myself about Brian, he hopes I'll be very happy in my new life. Then he hung up.

I've just been to the off licence and the kebab shop and I'm now going to get pissed and stink of chilli sauce. Life as I know it has officially come to an end.

Part Two

Present Day

CHAPTER ONE

I found a diary from seventeen years ago, buried underneath a pile of what I now refer to as 'junk'. It was fun to read through it. Though it brought back some very painful memories of which I thought I'd got over. Now I know that I've just put them to the back of my mind whilst getting on with my life. There are tons of cassettes too, many of which I can't play anymore because I don't have a tape recorder. And videos, again obsolete. It's a shame really because some are ones that I'd love to watch or listen to again. I'll have a proper look through them all this week and might order some of them on CD and DVD. One cassette in particular that I thought I'd lost is Michael Bolton so I'm definitely buying that on CD. My taste in music has changed over the years and I'm more into classical now. But I can still hear those beautiful, dulcet tones, filling the atmosphere in my old Astra and giving my cosy, little flat a romantic ambience. So many wonderful memories to cling onto.

Life's been relatively kind to me over the years as I think back, though losing Christopher was quite a painful time. Especially when Mrs. Richards from next door kept bringing me casseroles with far too much salt in them and I ended up with dreadful heartburn. I didn't have the heart to tell her because she was only being kind. I expect she felt a lot of empathy as she'd been through the same thing many years previously, losing her husband I mean, not the heartburn, though I imagine she lives on remedies if she puts that much salt in her food. The only difference was that she'd loved her husband throughout their marriage.

Moving to Cornfield was the best thing I could ever have done. I don't miss my old life with Campbell & Co. and pretending I was happily married to a man who only wanted me because he needed a decoration for his arm. Christopher hated being on his own; when we got together, it was only three months into our courtship that he asked me to marry him. I wasn't sure at first but then I discovered how wealthy he was, apart from the fact he was extremely good looking. Trisha in accounts kept telling me how lucky I was and how much she wished he'd asked *her* to marry him. I felt like saying often that she was welcome to him, but then I'd think about the lifestyle and the money and all the long haul, expensive holidays we would go on together. 'No, hands off, Trisha,' I said, 'he's all mine.' Then I'd grin inanely and pretend I was so in love. My friend Claire was really happy for me of course and was my chief bridesmaid.

My relationship with Brian from Winterson's lasted nearly ten months. We were, or so I thought, really happy and saw each other every weekend. I didn't see him during the week as that was when he was seeing Chantelle, his 'ex'. What a bastard *he* turned out to be. I can't believe I went from one arsehole to another in the space of two years. I really was gullible back then. But I guess I lived and learned, as the saying goes, and now I'm quite happy living on my own in this beautiful and very picturesque Scottish village. I have money in the bank and do a couple of day's volunteer work in the Cancer Research shop in Tewsford. I guess if someone had asked me in my twenties where I saw myself in seventeen years time, I wouldn't have said a little village in the Scottish Highlands working in a charity shop. No, I most likely would have answered, 'Happily married to the love of my life,' with a pretentiously smug smile and an assertive tone in my voice. As it happens, the love of my life couldn't bear to leave his wife. I sometimes wonder if I'd have had kids with the love of my life, would our togetherness have been more certain. But I don't regret not having children because I'm not maternal anyway, though there are times when I've thought about my affair with Steve and maybe regretted it a little.

I have no idea where he lives now or what he's doing, and even though I do think about him from time to time, like today when I found the Michael Bolton tape, I haven't missed being with him. He hurt me terribly and I've moved on. I had no choice really, as it was obvious in the end that he had no intention of leaving Olivia, even though he might have led me to believe otherwise. Still, he's a notch on my bedpost and a memory that I can now think briefly about before shrugging it off as one of life's experiences.

I suppose the sad thing has been losing touch with Kelly after her and Greasy Graham got married and moved to Spain. We stayed in contact for about two years, just texts and the odd email, but then she had a baby and I think we decided we didn't have much in common anymore. Every conversation seemed to focus around nappies and the price of formula and to be honest, I didn't know how to respond. I was married to Christopher at the time and even though he'd mentioned having a baby, I was dead against it. Kelly kept telling me I didn't know what I was missing but I just couldn't have had a baby with Christopher. I've been brought up with the morals of loving someone before you start a family with them. Kelly did keep asking why I married Christopher, which she was perfectly qualified to ask being my best friend at the time, but I didn't want to tell her it was because I was lonely and liked the thought of having a six figure bank account. I doubt she'd have approved of my reasons for marriage. I'll give her credit though, she was, and I imagine still is, completely in love with Greasy Graham. But it's been seven years now since we've been in touch and I think too much water has passed under the bridge. I wrote to tell her I'd moved to Scotland but she never wrote back. Sad really, when you consider we were friends for such a long time.

I haven't been back to Manchester since mum died. She had a heart attack seven years ago, just a year after Christopher died so it wasn't the best twelve months of my life. I'd only been up here six months when Auntie Maud rang me to say she'd been admitted to hospital and it looked serious. Naturally I bombed down to Manchester, collecting a speeding ticket and three points on my way after doing 65 in a 50 zone. Bloody road works on the M62 are a nightmare. But by the time I got there she'd already passed away. We only spoke on the phone the previous day and the last words we said to each other were, 'I love you,' so even though I was devastated, at least she knew I loved her. I spent about eight months living like a hermit after her death until Claire and Melanie came to stay and lifted me out of it. They've both been very good friends to me and I'll be forever grateful to them for supporting me in my hours of need.

Mum left quite a lot of money when she died, money that she'd been saving up over the years; money that dad had been sending her. She'd never told me about it but he'd been paying a thousand pounds a month into an account for her and me, maintenance he'd said it was. Even though dad and I lost touch years ago, I was ecstatic when I realised there was over a hundred thousand pounds due to me as mum's benefactor. And that didn't include the other money she had from her pension and savings bonds. I still wish I had her with me of course, but the money has definitely been useful. Christopher left me with a massive inheritance also, and I've not needed to work since living up here. But I find things to do like volunteering at church events and helping keep the village in bloom. I'm not very churchy, but there are some lovely people in the village and as they welcomed me with open arms I've always felt I want to do something in return.

Poor Auntie Maud lives in a home now. She and William did a world cruise four years ago but it was too much for William and he dropped down dead on their return, still holding a bag of duty free sherry. She was naturally beside herself and never really recovered from his death, though she did manage to save a couple of bottles of Harvey's Bristol Cream. Her niece, and only living relative, took care of her for a while at their house in Dorset, but after six months it was obvious that she needed constant care so they found her a nice care home near where they live. She's been there ever since and still writes to me occasionally, telling me how much she misses mum and William and how she'd love to see me again. I've just never had the inclination to go all the way to Dorset as I'd probably have to stay with her niece and I really don't want to. So we just write letters to each other, though I haven't heard from her for about eight months now so I do hope she's okay.

Mrs. McCraikie from the village popped by yesterday to ask if I'd help with the church flowers this weekend as there's a wedding and the bride has been very specific about what she wants. She sounds like a complete fusspot to me, as she's insisting on ivory roses and green foliage to be interwoven around the pews and it's going to take absolutely ages. She chose our church in particular as it won 'Best Kept Graveyard Competition' last year and is completely landscaped with rockery and begonias because relatives keep it looking tip top. There's also a marquee being erected in the vicarage garden which looks pretty impressive. I've agreed to help purely because I want a peek inside it.

The village is currently buzzing with excitement at it all, it's as though nothing ever happens in Cornfield, which I guess it never does, and Andy, the local taxi driver, has been recruited as chauffeur. He's picking the bride up from her hotel in Tewsford, ferrying her to the church, then him and some of his taxi-mates will be doing journeys back to Tewsford after the reception to take guests back to the hotel. I think Reverend Holdsworthy is quite excited about the whole thing too, because when I saw him in the village shop the other day, he gave me a little kiss on my cheek and said how well I looked. I didn't get too overwhelmed as he's probably pushing 80.

Since moving to Cornfield I haven't had a proper boyfriend. I've been on a few dates over the last eight years but none have been particularly flamboyant. There was Angus who was a bit younger than me and very quiet, not really much conversation, just hands that kept slipping on to parts of my anatomy that I'd rather he didn't know about. When he asked me to marry him after our third date, I realised that he wasn't for me. He got married to a lovely young girl in the end and they had a baby within their first year of marriage. It turns out all he wanted was to be a dad and fortunately his new wife was quite content at being a mum, so they have a marriage made in heaven. I see her occasionally, walking their three children to the village school, though I think one of them might not be his because she has brown hair and looks like she's been to Spain for a month whereas both Angus and his wife are vibrant red heads. Still, he's very happy now and I'm happy for him. I rarely see him as he travels quite a distance to Edinburgh and I believe he stays there during the week sometimes. I've thought about befriending Janice, his wife, but she always seems so preoccupied with her brood of kids and really, I'm not sure we have a lot in common, what with me being a single woman living on my own with no family, and her being the busy mum, involved with the PTA and chief organiser of school sport's day.

There was also Phil who I have to admit I did quite like. We got on really well for a while and spent quite a lot of time together back in 2006. He was really tall and dark and extremely handsome, but he was also very ambitious and had no intention of staying in Tewsford, where he lived. He wanted to move to London and work on Fleet Street. The Tewsford Echo wasn't ruthless enough for him and it was obvious when we were together that his heart would never have been in Scotland. Local news about someone's cat being stuck up a tree and a grandmother having her knitting needles nicked just didn't enthral him. He stayed over at my cottage sometimes and I stayed at his, and Mrs. McCraikie kept asking me when she should buy a hat, but then one day he came to see me and said he'd been offered a job with The Guardian and would be leaving next Tuesday to start his new life. I was more annoyed than upset because I did think he would have told me he'd even been for the interview, but keeping it from me just seemed a bit sneaky. He asked if we could keep in touch and I told him to get stuffed though I was on my fourth Southern Comfort at that point. He couldn't give a shit about me, I realised that when he moved away and his cousin Terry rang me to say he was shacked up with some bird from the newspaper office. He'd only been living in London for a month.

Stewart was a nice chap, probably more my type if I'm honest with myself, but we became more like brother and sister after a while and having sex with him just felt wrong. He didn't turn me on like Phil did and I was sick of comparing them when we were in bed. So I finished with him after a few months and have never seen him since. Looking back and thinking about Stewart, I reckon we could have made a go of it if I hadn't been so judgemental of him. But maybe it was for the best as I really am happy being on my own.

CHAPTER TWO

The wedding was beautiful. Mrs. McCraikie, Helen from the village shop and Joan, the vicar's wife all helped to interweave the flowers and I must say they looked absolutely gorgeous. The church was awash with colour, down to the bride's exquisite taste I assumed. When we'd finished decorating the church I popped to the vicarage gardens and had a look inside the marquee which again was very tastefully done. It wasn't a huge space, probably about six round tables with a long top table for the wedding party. Ivory fabric covered the high-backed chairs and ivory roses were placed in the centre of each table. The marquee company really went to town and I suspect it cost a pretty fortune. There was even a wooden stage area at one end and a DJ setting up his equipment. Reverend Holdsworthy and Joan stayed all night apparently, bopping away to old 60's music. I wasn't invited of course as I'm not known to the bride and groom but they didn't mind me watching the wedding in the church. The Reverend conducted a very intimate service and everyone clapped when he said, 'You can now kiss your bride.'

Helen went to watch the service too, and sat next to me whispering that she hoped the bride wouldn't flop out of her wedding dress. It *was* a bit low with rather a substantial amount of cleavage showing, but it was very beautiful all the same; the dress, not the cleavage, though the cleavage *was* pretty impressive.

Helen's husband left her a few years ago as they kept arguing about the shop; he wanted to sell up and buy a bigger franchise but she's always been very content in Cornfield, plus the shop belonged to her parents and they'd passed it on to Helen and her husband. I feel a bit sorry for her really as the only friends she has are me and Mrs. McCraikie, and as Mrs. McCraikie is in her late 60's she isn't really an ideal BFF. Helen and I have become quite close since her husband left, though she doesn't do herself any favours when she won't go anywhere or do anything if there's something on telly that she wants to watch (she won't upgrade to Sky Plus, says it's too technical for her). Though I know I've changed since my younger days as I'm quite unsociable now, too. But on a Sunday night we walk to the local pub together for the pub quiz and have a few glasses of wine then get George, the landlord, to walk us home. There are no street lights in the village and it's pitch dark in the autumn and winter months. I nearly got run over one night by some knob head in a zooped up Astra. Bloody Astra drivers, they shouldn't be allowed on the roads.

George is married to Hazel and they run the pub together but he came onto me on one of the nights he walked me home. I think he'd been having sneaky pints in the back as he stunk of beer. But when we reached my front door and I started fumbling about in my bag for the keys, he put one hand against the wall and the other against my shoulder. Then before I knew what was happening he started stroking my cheek with his chubby fingers and said he found me attractive. I laughed, probably a little too loudly, and I think it offended him because he pulled away quick and said, 'be like that then.' Anyway, the following week, Helen and I went to the pub for our usual night on the tiles, and he came over to apologise for his behaviour. He didn't say he'd been drinking but he did say he'd had a row with Hazel and just needed some light relief. Helen stared at me as he walked away and I had to fill her in on the gory details, making sure she realised that he most certainly *didn't* get his light relief. She was pissed off that I hadn't told her before but I pointed out that I was tipsy myself and also a little embarrassed about the whole episode. Fortunately, he's never tried it on since and we still let him walk us home. Men.

But getting back to the wedding that took Cornfield by storm, you would have thought Royalty were descending upon us with Hello magazine, as our little village was lined with newly planted pansies to add even more colour to an already rainbow-effect country lane. George and Hazel gave the bride and groom a discount on barrels of ale, bottles of champagne and wine, as the couple thought the catering company they'd hired were charging too much on the booze. Hazel said she'd have done the food as well and was a bit peeved that they hadn't been asked, but the pub food is more like pub-grub, chunky chips and battered cod, chicken in a basket, that sort of thing, so I'm not sure it would have suited this couple. Judging by the expensive marquee and the cost of the church flowers I reckon they would have had caviar canapés and plenty of oysters on the menu.

I could hear the music from my cottage and by midnight I was getting a bit sick of it. I sat up in bed reading a book but couldn't concentrate as they'd started playing 80's music at about quarter to twelve and I suspect everyone was pissed as I could hear people singing to 'Don't Leave Me This Way'. I read the same paragraph four times until I gave up and went downstairs to make a cuppa. I imagine the locals in the houses right near the vicarage would have been fuming at the noise. And then at one am I heard about six car horns beeping in unison, most probably started by Andy who's always good for a laugh. I wasn't laughing though. It finally went quiet about half an hour later.

I don't go to the Sunday services at church, much to Joan Holdsworthy's disgust. She's always saying I should make an effort, but I imagine the Reverend's head was banging somewhat after all the excitement of the wedding. Helen tells me he read out a message to the congregation written by the bride that said, *Thomas and I would like to send our heartfelt thanks to the ladies of the village who did such a beautiful job with the church flowers,*' and she's left a donation of £100 to put towards next month's flowers which I'm sure Mrs. McCraikie will have no trouble in spending.

Helen came round for lunch today as she closes the shop on a Sunday. She was still banging on about the bride's cleavage and said the dress looked ridiculous because she was bursting out of it. I think Helen was a bit jealous really because she's finding it hard to get a man and I know she misses the sex because she told me after we got shit-faced at Andy's 50th. I think she misses her husband but she won't admit it. Whenever we go out for a drink she always manages to bring him into the conversation, telling me about something amazing he once did. It's a shame he left really because I reckon they got on like a house on fire.

Claire and Melanie are coming up next weekend for a week and I've invited Helen to come over for dinner when they're here. I spoke to Claire on the phone quite early this morning; she has an annoying habit of ringing at eight am after she's been for her morning run, and even though I was still in bed trying to catch up on last night's missed sleep, it was lovely to hear her voice. She and Melanie have something to tell me and they want to tell me face to face. God, I hope they're not pregnant. I think Melanie would make a great mum but I'm not sure about Claire. She's a bit too prim and proper and I couldn't imagine her being all mumsy and adapting their gorgeous dockside apartment to fit in with a baby. In fact, they'd have to move. They could move up here, to Cornfield. There's a lovely little cottage for sale in the village, needs a bit of work but it'd be superb for those two. Maybe that's what she wants to tell me, that they're moving up here and starting a family. Oh wow, that would be awesome. Mind you, I'm not sure Melanie would want to leave her job. She's a solicitor and works with a big firm in Manchester city centre. As the main wage earner it would have to be Claire who'd give up her job and as she's just been promoted to Director of Accounts at Patterson Dale, I doubt moving to Scotland is on the cards.

She left Winterson's shortly after I did and got a typing job at a small firm in Salford Quays that make and sell kitchen units. She kept in touch with Yvonne for a while but it soon fizzled out as she realised what a bitch Yvonne really was. I have no idea what the others are doing because Claire lost touch with them all when she left but she did tell me that old Mr. Winterson died last year. His obituary in the local paper said he was 93.You have to commend him for he still popped into the offices occasionally. I nearly went to his funeral but I wasn't sure whether Steve would have been there so I decided against it. Claire didn't go either so I've no idea who went. Maybe if I ever go back to Manchester again I'll pop to his grave and lay some flowers on it. He really was a lovely man, very generous and playful and not at all like you'd expect your millionaire boss to behave.

I wasn't sad about losing touch with the guys at Winterson's, especially after Brian and I split up. I felt that that part of my life had ended and I was ready to start a new phase. The fact I earned lots more money at Campbell & Co., plus got together with Christopher did help of course. But there was always that little niggle at the back of my mind when I would think about Steve and what he'd be doing. I even drove past his house once. I've no idea why I did that because if he'd have been outside I probably would have just carried on driving. But his car was parked in the drive, the same Golf we'd made love in so many times at Nightingale Woods. I was surprised he still had it and Olivia hadn't insisted he get rid of it, though she probably never realised what went on in the back seat.

CHAPTER THREE

I've had a fabulous week with Claire and Melanie. I went to pick them up at Tewsford Station on Saturday afternoon and brought them straight back to the cottage so they could unpack before walking down to the Cornfield Arms for supper and lots of wine. I asked Helen to join us but she considerately said she'd leave me to catch up with them on their first night and would join us another time. I was dying to hear their news but they wouldn't tell me till we'd had a drink.

Anyway, the big news is that they're getting married. It's a civil ceremony obviously but they're so happy. I'm absolutely thrilled for them. There was no baby news and they both nearly fell over when I told them I thought they were pregnant, and they've assured me that's something they don't want as they're very happy being on their own. It's lovely to see Claire looking so at ease with life, such a change from how she was at Winterson's all those years ago. When I first met her I used to think someone had rammed a rod up her arse as she'd often look at me with steely eyes and a thunderous expression. But I've since realised she just didn't enjoy working with Brenda either, and she was fed up with Yvonne's bitching. It just shows that you never really know a person until you..., well, until you get to know them properly.

Anyway, they want me to be a witness at the ceremony and they've asked Melanie's cousin, too. The wedding will be held at the Register Office in Manchester city centre in November which is only a few months away. I'm really excited. It means this will be my first trip to the North West since I said goodbye to mum at her funeral. It's going to be quite sentimental I don't doubt but I intend to have a drive around and remind myself of my old haunts.

I've already introduced George and Hazel to Claire and Melanie on one of their previous visits, so they know what to expect. Having two lesbians in a little country pub isn't something I thought the locals would adapt to, but I was pleasantly surprised. I noticed George kept looking over whenever Melanie touched Claire's leg. I don't imagine Hazel would have got away from him last Saturday night, unless his hand is his best friend these days. I told them Claire and Melanie are getting married and Hazel brought over a complimentary bottle of champagne. The other locals kept looking over at us, probably wondering what the special occasion was as I doubt the ones I don't know that well would even think Claire and Melanie are an item. It might be a lovely place to live but Cornfield is a village with a lot of pensioners whose biggest excitement of the day is being able to clip their own toe nails.

We were all a bit in shocked when Reverend Holdsworthy and Joan walked in and saw us celebrating. He asked what the special occasion was and when I told him he smiled really broadly and said he'd love to marry Claire and Melanie in the village church if he could. We all thought that was a lovely gesture, though I get the impression Joan didn't when she went bright red and grabbed her husband's arm. She cleared her throat and said, 'come on Bert, we should leave these youngsters to it. They don't want us old fogies spoiling their fun.' I wouldn't have minded the Reverend joining us actually; he's quite a rum bugger.

On Sunday we just chilled in the cottage. Typical British summer brought rain and a rather cold wind so we opted for a day in with Trivial Pursuits and a few bottles of wine for company. Claire asked if I'd be comfortable going down to Manchester for the wedding and I asked her why she thought I wouldn't be.

'You haven't been down for years and I wouldn't want you to bump into anyone you don't want to see.' She's so thoughtful, but I put her mind at rest and told her I wasn't bothered.

'I'll probably stay a few days,' I said. 'I haven't kept in touch with anyone down there so it's not like I have anyone to visit. But I will do a bit of shopping in Manchester and have a snoop around Salford Quays.'

'And have a drive past Steve's house knowing you...' Claire said, with a cocked smile.

'Well, I might,' I replied. And we all burst out laughing then Melanie shook the dice.

By six pm we were out of wine and I volunteered to walk to the pub and get some more. It was busy in the Cornfield Arms and I noticed most of the locals huddled together near the bar. They shouted me over and said they were having a meeting about a property developer who'd applied for planning permission to build six executive style homes just opposite the pub, meaning most of the village would be smothered in road works for months, and we'd end up with modern properties amidst the tranquil and particularly picturesque scenery that we currently enjoy. I explained that I couldn't stay and had just popped in for a few bottles of wine. Helen was there, sat next to George and Hazel, and they said there'd be another meeting next weekend, and if I cared about it I should really attend. I know they didn't mean to be rude but the way Hazel said it came out a bit abruptly even for her. They're very protective of their little village and I have to say, so am I. I've only lived here eight years but most of the locals have been here all their lives so I assured them I'd be at the next meeting and would help to fight the proposals. Though I can't help feeling it's going to be a waste of time. Once the council gets wind that there's going to be lots more money in the council tax pot, I reckon they'll grant the planning permission and tie a red bow around it.

George kindly offered to walk me back to my cottage but it was still light outside so I said I'd be okay. Hazel gave him daggers so it was probably for the best that I declined. (I think he's hoping to walk in on Claire and Melanie at some point as he's been round three times this week while they've been here, offering to help mow the lawn and tidy up the bushes.) I wouldn't put it past him to have a secret camera about his person, probably ready to click 'record' and film them doing stuff they'd rather a dirty bugger like George McGrundy shouldn't be witnessing.

When I got back to the cottage it was my turn at Trivial Pursuits which I was quite pleased about as Claire and Melanie were wiping the floor with me.

Claire won in the end and we all sank in to the sofa and opened another bottle.

Of course, we spent most of the week with hangovers and we shopped till we dropped in Perth, but it was a fabulous week and I was really sad when I said goodbye to them both at the station. As my wedding gift to them I've bought their outfits for the ceremony, as neither of them want to wear a traditional wedding dress which I can understand. They aren't really dressy women, though Claire would look amazing in a beautiful ivory wedding gown. But Melanie is quite well built and definitely suits trousers more. So we had a great time at the shops trying on suitable outfits and being treated to champagne in Joanna's Boutique on the High street. They managed to find what they wanted and I'm glad to say neither outfit was that expensive. Joanna gave me a discount as we bought both outfits from her plus the shoes as well, so I did quite well out of it. I'll get them a gift also, just as something to open on the actual day. They're going to Lanzarote for their honeymoon and staying in a villa with a pool in Playa Blanca. I could do with a holiday abroad myself and joked that I'd carry their suitcases. When Claire's face lit up I had to say I wouldn't dream of encroaching on their romantic holiday, but she said I'm very welcome to join them if I really want to. But as much as I love Claire and Melanie, intruding on their honeymoon would just seem a wee bit odd.

CHAPTER FOUR

The meeting at the pub was very interesting. I was last to arrive and Helen had saved me a seat next to her. There was already a glass of wine waiting for me, on the house as Hazel made sure I knew. I'm starting to wonder if she's got a problem with me because she's hardly spoken to me all week and when I took Claire and Melanie there for tea on Wednesday night, she kept glaring at me from behind the bar.

Apparently, Prenton Homes have applied for planning permission and it looks like it's going to be approved. The local parish council got together, most of them who were at the pub, and have decided to fight the plans to build new homes. They reckon it will most probably bring a Co-operative store to the village and possibly another pub of which neither are needed. Besides, if that were to happen, it would most definitely put Helen out of business and would probably be a slippery slope for The Cornfield Arms. Certainly not what we locals want. So I agreed to support the cause and we all signed a petition that Andy the taxi driver has drawn up with his dad, who's a solicitor in Tewsford. My cottage is situated at the end of the village and as the new houses have been planned for the opposite end to where I am, they probably won't affect me. But the point is, as George pointed out, once they start one phase, they'll probably start another in due course, and then another. It could lead to Cornfield being turned into a miniature town. The tiny school next to the pub only has twenty pupils and most of them come from the neighbouring village of Deeran, but I didn't dare point out that executive homes will probably bring children to the village as well and that will in turn mean the school will have more pupils. Plus, the fact it could help the economy, and Helen, George and Hazel who own the local businesses could maybe turn it around in their favour and profit from it. But I didn't feel qualified or confident enough to put my point across so I just nodded, agreed and signed the petition. I do hope the locals get what they want otherwise it might divide the village and turn my little heavenly home into an awkward and difficult environment in which to while away the rest of my days. I love my little cottage and have even been thinking about extending it. But I'll hang fire for now. If they build the homes, I might even have a look around one. I have to say, a part of me does support the new proposals, but I guess I'll stay loyal to the locals. After all, it's what we villagers do, isn't it?

****

Angela Braithwaite who runs the Cancer Research shop in Tewsford has asked me if I'll do a few more hours for them as Mrs. Turner has gone into hospital. It's doubtful she'll come back to the shop as she's got awful arthritis and her doctor has advised her to get plenty of rest. She did tell me a few weeks ago that she's probably going to move in with her daughter and son-in-law at Christmas as she's finding it hard to cope on her own now. It makes me want to stay young forever. I don't want to be reliant on someone to look after me in my old age and as I haven't got any children and aren't likely to now that I'm in my mid 40's with no man, this does worry me a bit. At least I've got enough money to go into a home if it comes to it. God, I'm feeling morbid today. Angela always does that to me. She can be so depressing and I used to feel sorry for her after both her parents died of cancer, but every time I arrive for work, she cocks her head to one side and asks, 'how are you doing my love, are you managing?'

I think I'd have a problem if I wasn't. I certainly wouldn't be volunteering in the charity shop twice a week. And now she wants me to go in on Wednesday mornings as well, though she has offered to pay me a little. I'm in the fortunate position of telling her I don't help out for the money but simply for something to do, not to mention because I actually enjoy working there. I've met a lot of really nice people who come in regularly, not only to buy stuff but to drop black bin bags off too, and some of the stuff they send could be put back on the rails at Marks & Spencer's. I keep telling Angela to mark items of clothing at higher prices but she insists we shouldn't.

'You need to remember that if we over value an item, Rachel, we won't get people in buying our stock.'

'But surely the shop can't be making a profit, Angela,' I insist, when I pick up a very nicely tailored suit that would have cost a few hundred pounds in Debenhams and she's selling it for twenty quid.

'Admittedly, it doesn't make a huge profit, but we do well on the gifts, dear, and especially at

Christmas, people want a nice bargain as a present to give.'

She does have a point. The new gifts that we get in regularly seem to fly out the door. And Christmas does get busy. I think most people are looking for a bargain these days and where better than a charity shop that sells cut priced brand new gifts together with cheap clothes that have probably only been worn once. So I've agreed to go in on Wednesday mornings as well as Tuesday and Thursday mornings. She mentioned Saturday's as well but I said I'd rather not. I suppose if they get really desperate then I might change my mind, but I like my weekends just to myself, with Helen occasionally, but usually spent pottering in the garden or reading books.

Angela asked me about the new plans for the executive homes in our village as she'd seen the notice in the local paper. I said I didn't agree with them as far as the village was concerned but I could see it being a possibility for a better economy in the area.

'Gregory and I are thinking of moving. We're sick of our pokey two bedroom terraced and now that Gregory's been promoted at work we've been thinking about moving out of the town and into a nearby village. When we saw the planning permission notice in the paper, we both looked at each other and said "Ideal", so who knows, if they get built, we could be neighbours!' She did a little highland jig then sang 'woohoo'. I'm not sure I can imagine her and the gregarious Gregory fitting in to Cornfield. He could be a bit much for the locals, what with his red trousers and soft top sports car, not to mention his extraordinary loud laugh. I don't really know how the likes of Mrs. McCraikie will take him. Though I reckon the Reverend will find him fun. And I guess they could use the little village hall for a regular Ceilidh event and perhaps even organise a few karaoke sessions at The Cornfield Arms.

But no, my loyalties lie with the locals already there so I'm not going to encourage Angela to buy a house in the village if they do decide to build.

After my three hour shift at the shop on Tuesday, I decided to pop into Perth and have a look in Joanna's Boutique for an outfit for me. I didn't get anything for myself when I took Claire and Melanie last week as we spent such a long time getting those two sorted out. Fortunately, I managed to find a gorgeous brown and cream dress with a bolero jacket to match. It won't clash with either Claire or Melanie's outfits and as Joanna pointed out, it makes me look really glamorous. I'm very pleased with it and was even more pleased when she gave me yet another discount for being a loyal customer. I'm sure she makes a substantial profit throughout the year which is why she's able to give discounts to loyal customers, but it really was generous.

But then something really weird happened when I walked out of the shop. There was a tall, grey haired man standing with a shorter woman and they were chatting and glancing around the town at the same time. The man looked straight at me from the opposite side of the road and he stared at me for about fifteen seconds, though at the time it felt like a lot longer. I didn't recognise him at first but then when I looked at the woman a bit more carefully, I knew I'd seen her somewhere before. Both looked in their 60's and even though he did look familiar, the only men I know with a full head of grey hair are George at the pub and Andy, the taxi man, and it definitely wasn't either of them or they'd have come over to say hello. Plus, George is about twenty stone and this guy was much slimmer.

I walked back to my car racking my brain as to who it could be and wondering why the man had stared at me for so long. As I was driving home it suddenly occurred to me where I'd seen the woman before; in one of Steve's holiday photographs. She was Olivia Harris.

CHAPTER FIVE

I f I'm right, I thought, and that woman was indeed Olivia Harris that means the man she was with could have been Steve. He certainly acted as though he recognised me with the way he seemed to freeze and stare. He had a full head of brown hair with sophisticated grey sideburns when we were together but it was seventeen years ago and I guess it's possible that he's gone completely grey by now. But what would he be doing up here? Maybe they're on holiday, or perhaps he's in a golf tournament in the area and she's travelled up with him. I don't believe this. It can't have been Steve. It just can't.

But inside I knew it was him. Olivia hadn't changed much, she still had the lovely blonde curly hair that she had in the photograph. As I remember rightly, she was quite a lot smaller than him as they posed together for one picture that a waiter took in Majorca, and there was a distinct size difference between the two people I saw in Perth. It was too late to ring Claire so I decided to ring Helen instead.

'I'm sure it's him,' I said, and I heard her sigh down the phone.

'Even if it is you'd be better off not knowing. What can you do if he's staying in the area? He's with his wife, Rachel, it's not like he's going to be able to see you.'

'I'm not sure I want to see him really,' I said, though doubted myself as I was saying it because I'd love to see Steve again. 'If it is him and I see him again, do you think I should say hello or just ignore him?'

'If he's with Olivia, I'd just ignore him. You really don't want to start world war three. It's been how long?'

'Seventeen years,' I told Helen, knowing I was probably kidding myself that he'd even want to talk to me anyway.

'It's too long, Rach. There's a lot happened in seventeen years, to both of you I shouldn't wonder. If he did recognise you he'll be just as shocked and he'll probably avoid going into Perth again.' Helen had a point.

'I guess so. But I'm not sure I'm going to be able to sleep tonight. Fancy a night cap?'

Helen arrived before I'd had chance to have a wee and brush my hair.

'What am I going to do?' I asked her, as I poured the last dregs of the bottle of Sauvignon Blanc into our glasses.

'I'll go and get another bottle from the shop. I won't be long.' Helen stood up and reached for her keys.

'I mean about Steve, you muppet.'

She laughed and put the keys back on the table. 'Nothing,' she replied. 'Leave it be. If it is him you'll only end up upsetting yourself when he ignores you which he probably will if he's with his wife, and if it isn't him you'll be all down in the dumps. I'd try and forget about it. Chances are it wasn't him but just someone you've probably seen around, maybe in the charity shop or something, and your subconscious made you think of Steve. It happens, Rach.'

I finished the drop of wine that was hardly worth tilting my head for and went to the fridge to get another bottle. 'How do you fancy coming to Claire and Melanie's wedding with me?'

Helen stared at me and smiled. 'Have they invited me?' she asked.

'Well, not officially, it's just them, me, John and Sarah, but I know for a fact they'll be delighted if you go.'

'I'd love to,' she grinned, and passed me her empty glass for a refill. 'Are you sure they won't mind?'

'They won't mind, I promise. I'll ring Claire tomorrow and tell her you're coming with me. It'll be nice to have some company on the journey plus I can show you round some of my old haunts.'

'Are you intending on seeking out some of these old haunts as well?' Helen asked, rather coyly.

'I might be,' I grinned. 'Besides, I don't know anyone down there anymore so it's not like I'll be able to introduce you to anyone. We'll have a hoot. I'll book us into a nice hotel in the city centre and we can do some Christmas shopping while we're there.'

'Fabulous,' she said, clinking her glass against mine and then taking a massive gulp. 'But I want to be sure that Claire and Melanie don't mind me going. I'd hate to feel like I was intruding.'

I assured Helen that it would be absolutely fine and we finished off the bottle before she staggered back home in the dark. She could have done with George to escort her to the door but she gave me three rings when she got in just to tell me she was home.

****

As I expected, Claire and Melanie were thrilled when I asked about taking Helen to the wedding. They were going to invite her anyway as my plus one, but forgot to mention it. I told Claire about the couple I saw in Perth and that I think it could be Steve and Olivia. I expected her to tell me to stop being silly but she didn't.

'What are you going do?' she asked, much to my surprise.

'I have no idea.'

'Well, what happens if you see them again and he recognises you?'

'I honestly don't know.'

'Rachel, you need to have a back-up plan. If it is them and you bump into them somewhere, or imagine if they go into the shop, what the hell are you going to say? Did Olivia ever see you after she found out about your affair?'

'Not that I know of,' I replied, straining my mind as I thought back to when we were together, wondering if he'd taken any photos of me. 'I don't remember giving him my photo. I was always scared in case Olivia ever found it. So no, she doesn't know what I look like.'

'Well that's something at least. I suppose if you do see them again you can walk the other way and it's doubtful he'll say hello to you because then Olivia will want to know who you are. Shit, Rachel, you really don't need this.'

'When I went in to work this morning, I was on pins wondering if I'd spot them somewhere. If I do see them again I'll make sure whether it is or isn't him. It definitely looked like Olivia. I'll never forget her face.'

'Rachel, can I ask you something?' Claire got serious for a moment.

'Sure.'

'Do you still have feelings for Steve? Even after all these years and being married and moving away? Do you think you might still be in love with him?'

I wanted to say yes. I wanted to tell Claire that I would never stop loving Steve Harris and I would have loved to see him again, but we've been through so much together, especially after Christopher died. She knows my inner most secrets about my marriage to Christopher and I've told her things that I wouldn't dare tell anyone else, not even Helen. But instead I made a stupid noise that sounded like an opera singer with tonsillitis.

'Don't be daft, Claire. I'll always have a soft spot for him but the love went years ago.' I wasn't sure what else to say because I'd already lied to my best friend. And I reckon she knew it, too.

CHAPTER SIX

I was quite nervous about going to work on Thursday and even though I looked around extensively on Wednesday, probably to the point of me resembling a rather crap German spy, and didn't see either Steve or Olivia, I couldn't help envisaging one of them walking past the shop and looking through the window. A huge part of me wanted them to walk into the shop, but then the sensible part of me took over and asked me what the hell I was thinking.

I finished at midday, collected my handbag from the back room and said goodbye to Angela who was serving a customer and making a cock up with the change. Angela isn't great with the till and has to keep asking me over to help. She still uses a calculator and reckons up in her head or on a bit of paper, even though we have a super-duper till that calculates everything up for you, including how much change to give. For someone who's only a few years older than me, she really is quite scatty.

So there I was, walking out of the shop, throwing my bag strap over my shoulder and trying not to walk into the throngs of shoppers, when I saw him again, this time in Tewsford, my home town. He was stood on the opposite side of the road, with the same woman and once again he was staring straight at me. He was holding a Boots plastic carrier bag whilst the woman next to him was talking on her mobile phone and completely oblivious to her husband staring at the woman across the street. I looked at him and nearly fell to the floor.

It was definitely Steve. He smiled at me but quickly turned away. I just stood there and stared at him because I was somehow super-glued to the pavement. The customer that Angela had been serving came out of the shop and asked if I was okay. I nodded and said I was fine then I turned and walked off really quickly towards my car.

Steve is in Perthshire. I need to get my head around that. Steve is in Perthshire. God, no, Steve is in Tewsford. What the hell is he doing in my home town?

****

I was going to pop to Boots myself after work but decided to give it a miss. When I arrived back at my car I couldn't find the keys and stood against the bonnet wondering if I'd just woken from a dream. Not sure if it would have been classed as a nightmare, but I chose to call it a dream. About five minutes after coming out of my day dream, I found the keys buried at the bottom of my bag, where they usually are when I can't find them, and got into the car. I started the engine and began to pull out of the space. It was then that I saw Steve and Olivia again, obviously heading to *their* car. He saw me as I drove slowly past him and he stared into my car, looking straight at me, reminding me of the feelings I still had but thought I had said goodbye to. I realised after I'd got onto the main road that I needed to pull over as I wasn't concentrating on the driving and nearly ran up the back end of a bus. Bewildered passengers that were sat on the back seat turned their heads as I screeched to a halt, probably more worried about the fact they could have been squashed by my Freelander rather than the fact I could have been squashed by the bus.

I sat in a lay-by for about ten minutes, shaking and not knowing what I was going to do. My first thought was to phone Helen but she works in the shop during the day and it would have been unfair to ask her to come and save me from myself. So I opened the window, breathed in some fresh fumes and pulled back onto the main road, this time making sure I wasn't going to hit anything.

The traffic lights ahead turned to red and naturally I ground the car to a halt. It just had to happen didn't it, it really had to happen; if only I hadn't stopped in that lay-by. One glance in my rear-view mirror and there they were, Steve and Olivia in their Volvo behind me, Steve with a look of disbelief etched on his face and Olivia still speaking into the mobile phone. I kept looking in the mirror, realising he would have known it was me, then the lights started to change and I moved on slowly. I turned left into Leighton Road, a little country lane that leads out of Tewsford and towards Cornfield. Steve turned left, too. I approached the roundabout where I would take the third exit, bypassing the industrial estate and an easier way to get into my village. Steve also took the third exit. I looked in my rear-view mirror again and noticed Olivia looking at him, probably asking where they were going. And then she smiled and turned to look out of the passenger window.

Steve followed me into Cornfield village. I couldn't believe it when he drove passed my cottage and pretended he hadn't seen me turn right. He must have seen me though. He had to slow down so I could turn into my driveway without him ramming his car into mine. By the time I stopped outside my front door I was seriously shaking, as though some stalker had just followed me home, not the man I had once wanted to spend the rest of my life with.

I rang Helen as soon as I got in and although she was still in the shop she promised to come round as soon as she'd closed up, taking a detour into Tewsford for a Chinese takeaway. I pointed out that I needed a drink as well and she assured me she'd grab a few bottles off the shelves in the shop. I must owe her a fortune for all the wine she keeps bringing out of her shop; I have no idea if she has to declare it in her accounts.

'It's him,' I screeched, as she arrived at my cottage. She hadn't even put the food down and I was trembling. I'm not sure whether it was excitement that was making me tremble or the fact I'd seen Steve again. Or maybe it was the fact I was scared to death of what might happen now that he'd seen me, but she hugged me and ordered me to sit down while she put the food onto plates.

'Are you absolutely sure?' she asked, as she passed me a knife and fork.

'Positive. He bloody well followed me from Tewsford, Helen. I saw him on the other side of the road when I came out of the charity shop. There he was, standing holding a Boots bag, Olivia talking on a mobile.' I shovelled a fork full of chow mein into my mouth and munched it noisily, impatient to get the rest of what I needed to say out as soon as possible. 'I went to my car and just as I pulled out of the car park he was there again, walking to his car. He saw me and obviously clocked my car because then he followed me all the way here. I thought he was going to stop at one point but he just carried on.'

'Wonder where he was going then?' said Helen, not the brightest button in the box.

'He was following me, you numpty. They must be staying in the area on holiday and when he realised it was me, he decided to take Olivia for a drive in the country, follow me and see where I was going. I wonder if he thinks I'm on holiday, too. Shit, what if he comes here?' Even though I thought I'd be too nervous to eat, the Chinese was delicious and the food was actually making me feel better. 'Pour me another glass will you,' I said to Helen as she was pouring one for herself.

'Does he look the same? I mean, I know he looks the same otherwise you wouldn't have recognised him, but do you think he's changed over the years?'

'He's gone very grey, but it has been seventeen years and maybe a lot's happened in his life in that time. He still has rosy red cheeks and a lovely smile.' I suddenly cast my mind back to the times when he'd come into reception at Winterson's, lean against the wall and just smile at me. I used to ask him what he wanted and he'd say, 'Nothing, I just wanted to look at you.' That would really turn me on.

'Rach, have you thought about what you'll say if he does come here?' Helen, forever practical, brought me back down to earth with a bump when I realised there might be a chance he'd turn up. 'I mean, what happens if he wants to, you know, carry on where you left off?'

'I doubt that very much, Helen,' I scoffed, spitting a piece of chicken onto the carpet. I bent down to pick it up then popped it into the bin by the sofa. 'Even if he does come here he's not likely to want any romance is he. After all, I started going out with Brian and that really pissed him off.'

'But that was revenge. And quite rightly so from what I gather. He treated you like shit, Rach. He used you and you got your own back with Brian.'

I cast my mind back once again, only this time to remind myself about what I'd told Helen. I hadn't told her that I was a bit cut up when Brian decided his ex-girlfriend was a better option than me, nor did I tell her that Brian was incredible in bed. I kind of gave her the impression that Brian was a rebound, which I'm sure, looking back, he was, but he was also very caring and a good friend and certainly didn't deserve me using him. Though saying that, he *was* using me I suppose.

'I guess you're right,' I mused, not wanting to get into a conversation about Brian. 'I just can't believe I've seen Steve again, and on my home territory as well. I always thought if I ever did see him again it would be where he lives or at least in Manchester. I just don't know what to make of it.'

'Are you ex-directory?'

'What?' I asked, scooping up the last of the chow mein.

'Are you in the phone book or not? If he thinks you live here and you're in the phone book then he might find your number and ring you.'

'No, I'm ex-directory,' I said.

'Well that's something. I suppose if he comes here you can always ignore him and pretend you're not in.'

'But my car will be parked in the drive.'

'Everyone in this village walks everywhere don't they; it won't make a difference if your car's there. And besides, I can't imagine he's moved up here to live so chances are he'll only be here for a few days anyway. I bet he'll be gone by next week and you'll never need to worry about seeing him again.'

But that was my problem. And still is. I think I'd like to see him again. In fact, I'm hoping he'll call at the cottage and knock on my front door and I'll open it and we'll make mad passionate love like they do in films when they haven't seen each other for years and suddenly realised they're still in love.

What am I saying? I'm losing it. I'm friggin' losing my mind.

Helen went home at nine as she had a supplier calling in the morning with sweets and crisps. I thanked her for the food and the wine and gave her a big hug as she stood on my door step.

'How much do I owe you for all the food and wine?' I asked, reaching for my purse in my handbag.

'You can buy next time. Just be careful and don't do anything silly. And keep me posted on what happens. If he comes here I want to know straight away.' And she left.

I stood in my lounge for a moment, looking at the low beams and thinking they'll probably be too low for Steve and he'll have to stoop. Then I shook myself off, poured another glass of wine and sat in front of the telly for a couple of hours, wondering if I would ever really get over Steve Harris.

CHAPTER SEVEN

My head was spinning with thoughts of the past. I knew Steve would always be a part of my life in some form or another and I would always think about him, but I just wanted to turn the clock back and sink into his arms. He might have gone grey but he's still the man I fell in love with. What I can't get my head around is the fact that I want to see him and so I got into my car on Saturday afternoon and had a drive into Tewsford just to see if he was there. He wasn't, or at least I didn't see him, but when I got back home there was a car parked a few yards past my house. I knew instinctively that it was him. My heart almost thumped its way out of my chest and I went a bit light headed as I turned into my drive and parked up. I sat behind the wheel for a minute until he walked towards my house. He stood at the gate and watched me as I got out of the car. I wanted to hug him. But instead I invited him in telling him to watch out for the low beams.

He followed me inside, his smile still as I remembered it all those years ago. 'I hope you don't mind me coming here?' he asked.

I smiled. 'I can't believe it's really you,' I said, my eyes glazing over with the surreal events that were beginning to unfold.

'We're here on holiday, staying in Tewsford for a couple of weeks in a guest house. What are you doing here?' His eyes seemed glazed over too, but they still shone like two diamonds in a clear night sky.

'I live here,' I said, turning around in my front room, proud to show Steve my home. 'I moved here eight years ago.'

'You've chosen a beautiful part of the world to live.'

'Would you like a coffee or something? I have some cans in the fridge, or I could open a bottle of wine?' I started to stumble over my words, too many memories of when we used to meet at my flat back in Gadsbury racing to the front of my mind. The first thing I used to do was open a bottle of wine and then we'd snog and make love, either on the sofa or in my bed. I was aware that wasn't on the cards this time, but I really needed a drink.

'I'd love a cup of tea,' he replied. 'No sugar, just milk.'

He followed me into the kitchen and leaned against the worktops. I gestured to him to sit down at the table which he did, moving a pile of papers and magazines so he could rest his elbows. I thought how much his hair suited him, making him look sophisticated. It was a lot shorter, more fashionable for a man of his age. But that beautiful smile and those delicious eyes were still the ones I remembered, the expression that would light up my day as he sauntered into reception at Winterson's and asked me if I wanted a coffee. I half expected him to put his arms around me as I made the tea, just like he used to do in my flat, but he stayed seated at the kitchen table and watched as I sat down opposite him.

'You don't mind if I have a glass of wine, do you?' I asked, before pouring. 'I think I need it!'

It broke the ice. He laughed and said, 'Go ahead, I'd join you but I don't want to go back to Olivia stinking of booze.' And then reality hit me.

'How is Olivia?' I asked, not particularly interested but trying hard to keep the conversation going.

'She's very well, thanks for asking. The holiday was her idea as I retired last year. We haven't managed to get away anywhere for a couple of years.'

'Retired?' I spluttered. 'I didn't think you'd be the retiring type.'

'I was ready to finish, love. I've spent most of my working life at Winterson's and it was time to go. The place expanded such a lot over the years, it wasn't the same. I'd been thinking of leaving for a while but the money was too good to lose.' He took a sip of his tea. 'What about you, love, do you work? Are you married?'

'No to both questions. It's a long story.' I wasn't ready to explain to Steve my complicated marriage to Christopher. 'I work in the Cancer Research shop in Tewsford a few mornings a week, and I'm single, live here on my own.'

'I don't believe you never got married,' he laughed. 'I thought you'd have the pick of the bunch.'

'I did get married but he died.' I noticed Steve flinch and he went to speak but I continued. 'That was one of the reasons why I moved up here, to get away from the memories, start a new life.' I looked down at the table. 'It's complicated.' I took an extra-large gulp of wine. 'I'm happy now though, never been happier in fact.'

'That's good to hear. I always wondered what you'd do with your life after we...'

'...split up?' I interrupted.

'Yes. It wasn't an easy time for either of us was it?'

'It was a shit time for me, I know that much.' I curled my mouth, the smile not quite reaching my eyes, and then I turned away from him.

'I'm sorry I hurt you, Rachel.'

I turned back to face him and glared into his eyes. 'It's a long time ago, Steve. A lot's happened in the last seventeen years.'

'Seventeen years? Is that how long it's been?' He smiled and shook his head then continued to sip his tea. 'It feels like yesterday since I last saw you. You haven't changed. You're still as beautiful as you were back then.'

I laughed at that comment. 'I've changed inside, Steve, probably for the better. I'm not the same woman you knew back then.' I felt I needed to point out how I was no longer that gullible twenty-six year old with a desperate yearning for a married man to love me more than his wife. I think he must have known how desperate I was back then, but I wasn't prepared to have him think that of me now.

'I can see that, love,' he replied with that sweet smile he always gave me when he was just about to tell me he loved me. 'I couldn't believe it when I saw you in Tewsford the other day. I thought I was seeing things.'

'Me too,' I responded. 'Do you remember Claire from Winterson's?' He nodded. 'We became very close friends after I left and stayed in touch. When I saw you that first time in Perth, I rang her to tell her about it.'

'I remember Claire, lovely girl with the blonde hair, turned out to be a lesbian didn't she?'

'Yes, and she's getting married in November to her girlfriend, Melanie.'

'Married?'

'Yes, they're ever so happy. They were up here a couple of weeks ago actually. I'm being a witness at the wedding.'

Steve shook his head. 'Good grief, how times change. I didn't think gay people could get married.'

'Oh yes,' I said excitedly. 'What about Elton John, he got married didn't he? And there have been a few others, too. I think it's wonderful that society's moved on so much. It's about time people were given equal opportunities.' I realised I was getting on my soap box and tried to laugh it off.

'Still feisty,' Steve said, that familiar smile burning into my heart.

I finished my glass of wine and he finished his tea, then he walked over to the sink and put the cup into it. 'Would you like to sit in the lounge?' I asked.

'Sure. I can't stay long I'm afraid. I wasn't going to come but when Olivia said she'd like a few hours on her own this afternoon, it gave me an opportunity to go for a drive. I've told her I'm checking out the local golf course.' My heart sank a little as the lies once again poured from Steve's mouth.

'And didn't she want to go, too?' I asked.

'Nope, she was quite content sitting in the room with her book. She's not been well lately. It's another reason why we came away, to give her a little time to recuperate.'

We sat on the sofa. I made sure we weren't touching as I leaned up against the arm, far enough away from him so he didn't think I was expecting anything other than a chat.

'How long are you staying in Tewsford, did you say?' I hadn't forgotten it was two weeks, but I felt we needed to find something to talk about.

'Two weeks. We've already had one week and go home next Saturday. Though now I know you live up here I'm not going to want to go home.' He laughed after saying that, as though a little embarrassed that he'd said something he perhaps meant to keep to himself. 'This is a lovely cottage.'

He looked around the room, his eyes resting on a photograph of me and Claire before he stood up, walked over to it and picked it up. 'You look good in this picture, so does Claire. Where was it taken?'

'Melanie took it when they came up one time. It was a few years ago now but we spent a weekend in a spa hotel. We'd just had a makeover.'

He replaced the photo and came back to the sofa, sitting a bit closer to me. 'I never thought I'd see you again. I wasn't surprised when it didn't work out between you and Brian, he wasn't your type. I wanted to tell you that but I know I didn't have the right to say anything after what I put you through. I'm sorry, Rachel.'

'Stop apologising.' I smiled at him. I didn't want our time together to be spent apologising to each other and raking up painful memories. 'It's all water under the bridge, happened a long time ago. We've all moved on since then.'

'I know,' he said, 'but there have been a lot of times over the years when I've felt I needed to talk to you. It hasn't been easy, love.'

'What hasn't been easy?' I asked.

He sighed. 'My marriage. Living with Olivia. She made my life hell for a long time after you and I split up.' He must have noticed the shock in my expression. 'I put a brave face on because I knew I wasn't going to leave her and I wanted you to get on with your life. But it's taken her a long time to trust me again. I'm not even sure she does now really, but we stayed together for the sake of Susan and Sonia.'

'I always wondered what happened with Susan. I take it she came round in the end then?'

'Yes, she did. Took a while but at least she never stopped me seeing the kids. She has a son as well, Jake. He's fourteen.' I could see the relief in his expression. I remember how upset he was when Susan wouldn't speak to him and threatened to keep her baby away from him. He might only be her step-father, but he'd always considered Susan to be his own.

'Are you still living in Great Willowby?' I asked.

'Yes, we decided to have an extension on the house rather than move. Olivia decided she wanted a room of her own and as we lost money on the house anyway, we got the builders in and added a little snug onto the side. I'm quite glad we did in the end because there were a lot of times when we needed our own space. I don't blame her, but Olivia was pretty hard to live with for a long time.'

'I guess it's understandable,' I said, trying to muster up a little sympathy in my tone.

'We've been talking about moving recently though as the mortgage is paid off now and we could probably manage to downsize. Not sure I really want to leave Great Willowby but I know Olivia's been looking at some new houses being built at Fire Grove.'

'Is that the town a few miles away from you? It rings a bell.'

'Yes, love, it's a nice area, too. A bit pricey but I suppose that's because it's a nicer place to live. They've recently been redeveloping it so I think when we get back we'll be going to have a look at some of the show homes.'

We both knew we were just making small talk. There were so many questions burning through me that I wanted to ask Steve. And I imagine there were lots he wanted to ask me, too.

'So, you were married?' he enquired, at last breaking the minute's silence.

I stood up. 'Would you like another cup of tea?' I wanted to give myself a little extra time to think about what I would say on the subject of my marriage.

He stood up and followed me into the kitchen. 'I'd love another cup, thanks.'

'I could do with another glass of wine,' I laughed.

'I'm sorry, you don't need to tell me about your marriage, it's none of my business.'

I turned to him. 'Not at all. It's just not a subject I talk about much these days. I haven't really told anyone up here about Christopher, except my friend Helen who owns the village store.' I switched the kettle on then took the bottle of wine out of the fridge. 'We weren't married very long. Four years altogether, then he collapsed with a brain haemorrhage.'

'I'm so sorry, love. That must have been awful for you.'

'It's a long story. We knew he wasn't well but didn't know it was quite that serious. We weren't very close and our marriage was a bit of a farce.' As I was telling him this, I wondered if having another glass of wine was such a good idea.

'You can tell me anything, Rachel. It's not like I'm going to repeat it.' He had a point. I made his tea and passed him the cup then we went back into the lounge where I opened up to the man I used to respect more than anyone in the world. Except mum of course.

'I'm a bit ashamed, I have to admit, but at the time we just went along with each other's plans. He was head of accounts at Campbell & Co., you know, the firm I went to work at after leaving Winterson's?' Steve nodded. 'We went out for about three months. He took me to loads of functions, really high profile events where all the top lawyers and accountants went. I knew I was just a decoration to him and someone he could turn up with and introduce as his girlfriend. I think people kept asking him why he didn't have a woman in his life and I guess me being young, free and single at the time was quite convenient for him. I met a lot of very influential people, most were snobs, but all very well-off. Anyway, one weekend he took me to a conference in London, full of toffs and snooty gits parading around in suits and long dresses, and there was me in a short skirt and high heels. I felt totally out of place but Christopher insisted I looked amazing. After about an hour I told him I was leaving because I felt so uncomfortable and next thing I knew he was standing on the stage and saying "testing, testing" into the microphone. Then the whole room went silent and he said "Rachel Phillips, will you marry me?" I couldn't bloody believe it, talk about embarrassing.'

Steve laughed and shook his head. 'I can imagine. And I take it you said yes?'

'Felt I had no choice. Everyone was looking at me then and I just croaked yes at him as he stood there like a muppet. I hated him for doing that. He knew I wouldn't have been able to say anything other than yes in front of all those people. They thought the world of him and hardly knew me. Anyway, he jumped off the stage and scooped me up like in that scene of An Officer and a Gentleman?' Steve nodded again. 'I felt such a pillock, especially with my skirt being so short. I wanted to slap his face.' I took a gulp of wine. 'Three months later we were married. Just did it at the local register office.'

'I'm taking it you didn't love him?' Steve asked, peering over his cup.

'No, I didn't.' Years ago I would have replied to that question with embarrassment and guilt in my voice. 'After we were married I found out that he was absolutely minted. He had property all over England, mainly in the south east. And not only that, he'd been left with millions in the bank after his father died in a car crash some years back. His mum inherited a lot and she never did approve of me, probably knew that I didn't love him. He got a job in a London accountancy firm a year after the wedding and started commuting every week. Eventually it became every fortnight so I only saw him a couple of times a month.'

'I suppose that was one consolation if you didn't love him. Do you think he loved you?' Steve was more interested in my revelations than I expected him to be.

'No. He never loved me. He just used to throw money at me every so often and tell me to go and have a good spend. He couldn't give a shit about me. Then one day I got a phone call from his colleague telling me that he'd collapsed and had been taken to the hospital. I rung his mother and we both went down to London to see him. He was in a bad way, on a life support machine. His mum was obviously devastated and we had the awful job of giving the doctor permission to switch it off. Even though we didn't love each other, I must admit that was one of the hardest things I've ever had to do. Grace, his mum, was in bits.'

'It can't have been easy for either of you.'

I shook my head in response. 'When we got back to Manchester, I discovered that he'd left most of his fortune to me, including the houses in the south east. Grace didn't seem bothered as she didn't need his money anyway, and so I sold the houses and ended up with a big fat bank account.' Steve stared at me. I suppose it did sound callous when I said it like that.

'Wow, quite a story. And I suppose you were able to move away and buy this place?'

'Yep, after a few months of being hounded by Christopher's colleagues about how sorry they were for me and how much they wanted to do for me, I couldn't take anymore. I felt guilty knowing that I'd never loved him and that I was rolling in his money. I gave quite a lot to charities, just to ease the guilt a bit. Plus, I was fed up with Grace popping round to see if I was okay. She drove me nuts. I just couldn't pretend to be the grieving widow when I wasn't grieving. But every time she came round I had to put on a sad face and act as though I was missing him. So I came up here and bought this place outright. I've never seen Grace since. She died in 2007. Claire saw the obituary in the paper.'

'And I thought my life was complicated.' Steve's eyes opened wide as he finished his cup of tea, naturally quite shocked to hear what I'd been up to. 'And your mum? How's she doing?'

'She died a year after Christopher. I hadn't been up here very long and I never got chance to say goodbye to her.' I knew that if I started talking about mum, I'd probably end up crying on Steve's shoulder.

'Oh hell, I'm so sorry, Rachel. I know how close you were to your mum. It must have been a terrible year for you, losing your husband and your mum so close together.'

'Losing my mum was awful. It took a long time to come to terms with that. The locals have been amazing though and welcomed me into their community with open arms. I do a lot of work for the village church, kind of my way to say thanks. Moving here was the best thing I could have done.'

'You're lucky to have good friends around you. I can't believe you haven't got a man in your life though.' He laughed after saying that.

'I'm not bothered,' I announced, a little too quickly. 'I've had a few boyfriends over the years but none that have compared to...' I stopped myself.

Steve knew what I was going to say and he turned away.

'I guess I must be going.' He got up from the sofa. 'I hope you didn't mind me coming to see you?'

'I had a feeling you might after I noticed you following me home the other day.'

He laughed a little sheepishly. 'I'm sorry about doing that. I was just curious to know where you were going. Forgive me?'

I looked into his deep blue eyes and realised the love I still had for him. 'There's nothing to forgive,' I said. 'It was nice to see you. I wish we could have spent more time together but I know you need to get back.'

'Can I come again?' he blurted out, much to my surprise.

I hesitated for a moment then shrugged. 'If you like. But what about Olivia? Won't she get a bit suspicious if you keep nipping out for a drive?' I think my smile was the thing that made him kiss me.

It was the same kiss that I remember. Tender; loving; affectionate. I felt my whole body being whisked back to 1996, to that first time he kissed me outside the Crown Green pub. He stroked my arm as he pressed his lips against mine, sending shivers up and down my spine and tingles all through my body. Then he drew away, moved his hand up to my face and caressed my lips with his finger.

'I'll manage to get away somehow, let me worry about that.' He turned slowly towards the front door and reached for the handle. 'Can I call you?'

'Yes, of course you can. Here...' I rushed over to the telephone table and wrote my number on a piece of paper then handed it to him. Our fingers overlapped. 'Ring anytime. I work at the shop Tuesday, Wednesday and Thursday mornings.'

'Thanks for the cups of tea, and thanks for not turning me away.' He kissed me again, this time a gentle peck on the cheek, more of a friendly gesture I felt. But I closed my eyes and inhaled his aftershave, a few seconds of living in a past I realised there and then I would never be able to say goodbye to.

CHAPTER EIGHT

I told Helen about my encounter with Steve. She came round and wanted all the juicy details. She wasn't surprised that he'd called to see me and reckoned he'd definitely be back. Since spending time with him I realised that I never got over our affair coming to an end. I'd known for years that he'd always be locked inside my heart, maybe the deepest recesses where no one will ever find him, but after seeing him again it felt like he'd pushed himself to the surface and what we once had, even though could never be the same, would always be a huge part of my life. I can still feel his lips against mine and the way he stroked my arm as he kissed me. Every time I closed my eyes I saw his beautiful smile etching its way across my body, sending tingles through my veins, and his touch emanating all over me like the incredible rush of adrenalin it always was. I longed for him to come back to see me so I could sense his mutual love all over again.

So much has happened in both our lives yet I could hardly remember anything he told me as my mind continued to wander to that kiss. I wanted to ask about the difficulties he spoke of. How his marriage has been strained and how long it took Olivia to start trusting him again. Perhaps I don't have a right to know; after all, we did split up and we both moved on. But he never took a back seat in my life, not in the way I did in his. It's like something stirred within me and woke me from a life I'd been living in a parallel universe. It wasn't going back in time that I wanted; I knew I couldn't have what I had back then and I didn't want to be that other woman again. But just to spend a little more time with him, another hug, maybe another kiss as lingering and gentle as the last one, perhaps would bring me contentment for the rest of my life.

I wasn't prepared to settle as the woman who was second best in Steve's life, I knew that for sure. Having grown up since being that naive and gullible twenty-something I wanted to make sure Steve knew I was still there, albeit not at his beck and call; I wanted him to know that I still loved him.

'Bring him to the shop,' Helen said. 'Pretend you've run out of milk or something and have a walk down with him then I can meet him.'

I laughed. 'If he comes back again I might just do that. But I don't want you interrogating him.'

'I wouldn't dream of it,' she said. But I wasn't convinced.

****

'Hello?' The phone rang quite late, much later than I've known it to ring before.

'Hi, love, it's me, Steve.'

'I didn't think you'd ring quite so soon,' I smiled, the excitement probably creeping through in my voice.

'I couldn't help it. I've really enjoyed spending time with you today. Are you busy on Tuesday afternoon?'

'Well I work in the charity shop till twelve but will be home by half past.'

'Would it be okay if I called to see you again?' Steve spoke quietly.

'Yes, of course you can.' I hesitated. 'Where are you?'

'In the lobby. We don't have a phone in the room so I'm using the main one. If I get to yours for half past one, is that okay?'

'That would be fine. Are you having lunch before you come?' But he'd gone, hung up on me. I suspected he was in danger of being overheard and I replaced the receiver, staring into space for a few moments as I imagined opening the front door on Tuesday to Steve.

****

The next day I rang Claire to tell her what had happened. I thought she sounded a bit unsure at first, especially when she answered with a questionable, 'oh?' But after a minute of me telling her how lovely it was to see Steve again, she sighed.

'You know I'm going to tell you to be careful, Rachel, and you know why. I only hope you don't get in too deep again. Just remember how much he hurt you, and remember he could be capable of doing it again if you let him.'

'I'm not going to let him hurt me, he just wants to be friends.' I was a little disappointed that Claire wasn't happier for me.

'And you kiss all your friends like you kissed him, do you?' She had a point. I stayed silent. 'Have a good time but stay aware that he wouldn't leave Olivia for you back then and he's not likely to now either.'

'Claire, I know you mean well, and I told you because you know everything that went on between us, but please understand that I don't want him to leave Olivia now. It's not like that. It's good to see him again, of course it is, and I can't wait for him to come back on Tuesday, but I'm not going to be the other woman again, absolutely no way. I learned the hard way. You were there, you saw.'

'Yes, I was there, Rachel, and I did see, and what I saw was how much he broke your heart. A lot's happened in both your lives in the last seventeen years and you can't turn back the clock.' Her mother hen approach was starting to annoy me. I wanted Claire to say she was happy for me, thrilled in fact. But instead she was talking sense. As usual.

'I won't let him hurt me, Claire, I promise.' I looked at the ceiling and said a silent prayer in the hope that I wouldn't break that promise, the way Steve had broken my heart.

'Just ring me after he's been and tell me how it went. I'm not going out tomorrow night. Melanie will be at the gym, she's trying to shed a few pounds before the wedding.'

188

I thought about Melanie for a moment and couldn't imagine her working out at a gym. 'Melanie looks fine the way she is,' I pointed out. 'I didn't think she was the type to use a gym.'

'Stop changing the subject,' Claire said, a welcome chuckle in her voice. 'I'll expect your call, girlfriend.'

'Yes, mum.' We said our goodbyes and hung up.

****

It seemed to go really slowly at work, which I guess is typical when you're looking forward to something so much. Angela kept asking me stupid questions as she was putting prices on a bag full of clothes that she'd since washed and ironed. I might have snapped at her at one point but I don't think she realised. As the clock struck midday, I grabbed my bag and almost bolted out of the shop, shouting 'byeee' as I reached for the door handle. I don't remember her saying 'bye' to me, though I'm sure she did.

As usual, there was the lunchtime traffic holding everybody up until I got to the roundabout and was able to zoom off towards Cornfield. Andy flashed his lights at me as I neared the village so I waved. He probably wondered why I was driving much faster than I usually do.

Despite it being the end of August, it was pretty chilly in my little cottage so I lit the fire. It always makes it feel cosy and particularly romantic, though the romantic element has never been something I've thought about too much over the years. I rushed into the bedroom and got changed into jeans and a blouse, making sure my underarms didn't stink and I had adequate perfume on, just enough to smell lush but not enough to drown Steve in if he were to kiss me again. Then I ran a hairbrush through my hair and cleaned my teeth. I felt like a teenager going on a first date. The nerves kicked in and I reached for a whisky glass from the cabinet, pouring about an inch of Southern Comfort into it to calm myself down. Then I cleaned my teeth again.

Steve was on time. He knocked on the door at half past one and after straightening my clothes and glancing at my reflection in the mirror, I opened it.

'Come in,' I said, a huge grin plastered on my face.

'I've parked my car just up the road as I didn't want any of your neighbours asking who your guest is. Is that okay?'

'It doesn't matter, you can move it and put it next to mine if you like. No one will ask. And if anyone does I'll just say you're a friend of mine.' I giggled like a nervous school girl. 'Which of course you are,' I added.

As he entered the house he leaned towards me and planted a kiss softly on my lips. It wasn't as lingering as the last time but it still sent shivers through my whole body. I took his jacket and hung it in the cloakroom, inhaling his scent and stroking my hand down its soft cotton material.

'What can I get you to drink?' I asked as we walked into the kitchen.

'I've got all afternoon so I can have something alcoholic if you've got anything?' He rubbed his hands together then leaned against the work top.

I opened the fridge, leaving the door open wide enough for him to look inside. 'There are a few cans of Budweiser, white wine, or I can get you a Southern Comfort if you like. Failing that, there's tea, coffee, orange juice or water.' I smiled at him and waited for his answer.

'A can of Bud will do nicely, thanks, haven't had that for years.' I took a can out of the fridge and passed it to him.

'Do you want a glass?' I asked.

'No thanks, I'll drink straight from the can, like we used to do in your flat.' He laughed again. 'Do you remember all those cans we used to drink together and then I'd drive home. I must have been over the limit often. I can't believe I used to do that. How stupid.'

'It was stupid, but I guess you always got home safely.' I poured myself a glass of wine then carried the glass and the bottle into the lounge and sat on the sofa where Steve joined me. 'Where are you supposed to be? Out for another drive?'

'Playing golf. There's a club in Abbeygate isn't there, I spotted it the other day on our way back from Perth.' He took a swig of the Budweiser then placed it on the coffee table. 'I felt a bit awful lying to Olivia, but she got a taxi into Tewsford and is spending the afternoon at that spa hotel. I gave her some money to pay for a few treatments.'

'Doesn't it bother her that you've come on holiday together yet you're doing separate things?'

'Not at all. We do very little together these days.' He said that as though it was just the norm.

'So long as you won't get quizzed when you get back; I'd hate to think you were arguing on holiday because of me.'

He picked up the can again then sunk back against the sofa. 'Do you want some fresh air?' he asked.

I looked at him, puzzled.

'A walk. Let's go for a walk like we used to do in the woods. I imagine there are lots of lovely walks around here.'

It was a welcome distraction so I agreed and put my boots and coat on, then grabbed my house keys and locked the door behind me. I noticed Steve had parked his car in the same place as he did the other day. I was glad of the coat as there was a cool breeze and at one point Steve put his arm around me and pulled me into him. Then he pulled away and placed his hands in his pockets as we made our way to Jed's fields.

'The fire will have gone out by the time we get back but I can relight it. It warms the house up really quickly.' I tried to break the ice by making small talk again.

'So does the Bud,' Steve laughed.

'What time are you expected back?'

'I said it'd probably be about six-ish, depending on how busy the golf course is. I've got plenty time.'

I looked at the surrounding countryside, once more drinking it in, always a view I love to admire no matter how many times I see it.

'So we talked mostly about me the other day,' I said. 'Now I want to know about you. What's been going on in your life these past seventeen years?' I looked up at him as we walked along, his cheeks starting to redden in the cool air.

He sighed. 'It hasn't been an easy time.'

'In what way?'

'Oh, you know, with Olivia. She made my life a living hell for about ten years, that sort of thing.'

'I'm sorry, Steve, I shouldn't have asked, and you don't need to tell me if you'd rather not.'

'She gave me what I deserved I suppose; a life of misery.'

'Why did you stay?'

He stopped and looked towards the horizon. 'I owed it to her.' Then he turned to face me. 'I knew it wasn't going to be easy for a while but it was harder than I ever imagined. Naturally she wouldn't trust me and wanted to know where I was going every time I went through the front door. It seemed to get worse after those initial three months of trying to mend the marriage. She really hated me.'

'I'm struggling to understand why you didn't leave. I know it's not something that concerns me now but you know you could have come back to me.'

'I do know that, yes, and I'll always be grateful to you for being so kind, love.'

'Kind?' There was a bit of surprise in my tone. 'I wasn't being kind, Steve. I *wanted* you to come back to me.'

'But then you started seeing Brian and I wasn't sure why.' He carried on walking, unable to look at me. 'There was a time when I would have left Olivia and come to you but I thought it was too late.'

'It was never too late, Steve.'

'I owed Olivia, Rachel. I had to stay, make a go of it.'

'For her sake or Susan's?'

'Both. I couldn't bear the thought of never seeing Susan and my grandchild. And I really did feel as though I owed her a chance at our marriage, at the very least. We'd been married eighteen years and had been through a lot together. I didn't really understand just how devastated she was until about a year after we...'

'Split up?' I finished his sentence again. 'Maybe you did owe her something, but you didn't need to sacrifice your happiness, surely?'

'Maybe not, love, but it was a long time ago and things were different back then. What I did to Olivia was unforgivable, but she did her best to forgive me and get on with living our lives together.

Admittedly, it was hard, bloody hard, but I had to try for her sake as well.' It was obviously a painful recollection for him judging by his expression.

'You always seemed happy and content when you were in work, and even when you came to see me. Why did you hide your unhappiness from me? I was there for you.'

'I couldn't let you see what was going on between me and Olivia. I didn't want you feeling sorry for me. I knew what I was doing with you was wrong, especially after Olivia had found out and thought it was all over between us, but I couldn't stop myself. I loved you so much, Rachel.' He stopped again and turned to look at me. I think he had tears in his eyes, though it could have been the wind.

'But you loved Olivia more.' I said flatly.

'I loved you both. But there was one vital difference.'

'What?'

He held my hand in his. 'I wasn't *in* love with Olivia.'

'I don't understand.' I frowned.

'I was in love with *you*. I might have loved Olivia, but I wasn't *in* love with her. But because of what we'd shared in the past, the fact that she was my wife, I felt I owed it to her. I'd hurt her, more than I could ever have imagined. I know I hurt you too, Rachel, and that made it so bloody hard for me.'

'You broke my heart, Steve.' I paused. 'Twice.'

'I know, and I'm sorry for doing that. I truly am. I was a bastard back then and knew it. I know it now. But I've never been able to stop thinking about you.'

I sighed and looked down at our entwined fingers. 'Like you say, it's in the past. There's a lot of water gone under the bridge over the years and I'm sure your marriage is back to normal now, right?'

He let go of my hand and turned around, once more looking at the scenery, but perhaps not actually taking much notice of it.

'Our marriage will never be like it was before I met you. It wasn't great back then, but I spent almost ten years trying to get Olivia to trust me again. These last seven years have been strained to say the least but she doesn't question my every move anymore. It's as though she doesn't care where I go. I wonder if it's because she thinks at my age I'm past it and no one will want me in that way anymore, or if she just simply doesn't care if I have another affair. I know she doesn't love me. Well, not the way she used to.' I touched his arm. 'It's okay, love, it's understandable. But there have been a lot of times especially in the past five years when I've wished I was somewhere else.' A tear escaped from Steve's eye and he wiped it away quickly, probably hoping I hadn't seen.

I rubbed my hand up and down his arm. 'I'm glad you told me all this. But I'm so sorry that it's been such a mess for you. I honestly thought everything was well between you two and you were getting on with your lives. I even thought you'd have forgotten about me.'

He stroked my face. 'I could never forget about you, love. You were a big part of my life, a part that almost changed my life forever.'

'It seems like our affair *did* change your life forever, as far as being with Olivia is concerned anyway. Are you going to stay with her?' I wasn't sure I wanted to know the answer to that question and as soon as it left my lips, I wished I hadn't asked it.

He sighed again. 'I honestly don't know what the future holds for us. Right now, we're just sailing along, quite content. She's happy enough the way things are and like I say, she doesn't hassle me anymore. But if you asked me where I see myself in five year's time, I really couldn't answer.'

We started walking again, slowly across a stubble barley field.

'Why did you never contact me again after that last phone call when you told me you knew about Brian?' I asked, almost falling over the straw stubble.

'I didn't think there was a point, love. I thought you and Brian were an item and he admitted to me that he was fond of you and he said you were fond of him, so I figured it was best just to let you get on with it. I kind of guessed it wouldn't last with him. Even when he was seeing you he was still talking about his ex-girlfriend, whatever her name was. My memory's getting worse these days.' He laughed.

'Chantelle I think. He got back with her in the end.'

'I know and I couldn't help thinking that you'd have your heart broken again.'

'He didn't break my heart, Steve. I didn't love him. We enjoyed each other's company for a while but there was no real closeness between us.'

'Was it a rebound thing?'

'At first it was to make you jealous, make you see that I wasn't sitting around moping for you to come back to me. But after a while, after your phone call really, it turned into just enjoying each other's company. I was quite sure there wasn't any chance you'd contact me again so I decided to enjoy myself for a while. Brian was available, or so I thought until he announced he was getting back with his ex. And then I discovered he'd been seeing her all along, the bastard. But he didn't break my heart. He set me free. In a roundabout way he made me find myself.' I smiled, realising how corny it sounded. 'I realised I didn't need a man in my life after all. I was quite content on my own, well, until Christopher of course.'

'I spent ten bloody years trying to convince Olivia that I wanted to stay when all along I could have got in contact with you again and done something about my sham of a marriage.' We came to a closed metal gate and leaned against it. 'I regret not getting in touch with you, I really do. But I reckon there's a reason for it. I always remember you telling me everything happens for a reason, and you're right, it does.'

'Even your visit to Scotland now?' I asked.

'Probably. I don't know. Olivia wanted to come up here. I wanted to go abroad but she suggested getting the map out and having a look to see where we haven't been. We went up to Inverness a few years ago and she wanted to see a bit more of Perthshire and Tayside this time. It was when I saw Tewsford on the map that I thought of you.'

'Why did you think of me?'

'I remembered you telling me that you went to Tewsford with your mum and dad when you were little and it was the only holiday you can really remember spending with your dad.'

I couldn't believe he'd remembered that. It made butterflies soar in my stomach as I looked into his eyes and felt the warmth penetrating into mine.

'I thought you said your memory was bad,' I smiled.

'There are certain things I'll never forget about you, love. You told me stuff that I know you never told anyone else. I suppose I kept it locked up all these years because I swore not to tell anyone.'

'So you chose Tewsford because it reminds you of me?'

'Yes, I suppose that was the reason. I imagine it's changed over the years but it's still a beautiful town and I'm glad we came.' Steve had his back leaning on the gate now, his hands fixed in his jacket pocket. 'Olivia got on the internet and chose the guest house and I booked it there and then. I had no idea you would be up here of course, that was just a coincidence.'

'A nice coincidence I hope?'

'Naturally,' he smiled. Then he pressed his lips against mine. His kiss was tender and with meaning.

I was first to pull away. 'Did you have any idea I lived up here?' I asked.

'None whatsoever, honest. When I saw you in Perth last week it was as much of a surprise to me as it was to you. And when I saw you in Tewsford I knew it was you. Your hair's much longer now and I think it's a different colour...' he ran his finger through a few strands. 'But you're still as beautiful.'

This time I kissed him, placing my arms around his neck and making sure he wasn't able to pull away in a hurry. My grip on him was perhaps a little too tight but to be standing there, in the middle of nowhere surrounded by stubble fields, took me right back to our romantic encounters in Nightingale Woods. And it did exactly the same to him, too.

'It feels like all those years ago, doesn't it, the times we walked through the woods and stopped in that little clearing? Do you remember the nightingale?' Steve held me in his arms, my head pressed up against his chest.

'How could I forget the nightingale? We even named the woods after it. Nightingale Woods; the most romantic place in the whole world.'

'I went back you know, a few times after we split up. I always hoped that you'd turn up one day.'

I lifted my head to face him, shocked at what he'd just told me. 'I don't know what to say. I did exactly the same but you never did turn up. I sat in my car one Saturday afternoon for an hour and a half once. I was determined not to leave. I just kept listening to Michael Bolton over and over again. Then I gave up. Maybe if I'd stayed I would have seen you.'

'I haven't listened to Michael Bolton since we finished.' He cupped my face in his hands and kissed me again, then withdrew and said, 'It hurt too much to listen to our song.'

'It hurt me too, but it felt like it was all I had left of you.'

'What was that song called now?' He rubbed his chin and smiled a little mischievously.

'Said I Loved You...But I...'

'Lied,' he finished, and then kissed me again. 'It's a beautiful song; we listened to it over and over again, sat in your car on those cold winter nights.'

'Shall we walk back?' I asked.

'Yes, I could do with finishing that can of Budweiser otherwise I'll not be able to drive back.'

'You could always stay the night; say your car broke down.' I laughed, but meant every word.

'That *would* put me in the bad books.' Steve laughed with me, perhaps not thinking I meant it. 'What time is it anyway?'

I looked at my watch. 'Nearly three. You've still got plenty time.'

CHAPTER NINE

We walked briskly back to the cottage and I was quite pleased when he took off his coat and hung it in the cloakroom, seemingly making himself at home. The fire was almost out so I gathered some logs from the basket in the Inglenook and put them on top, the gentle sounds of crackling flames adding to the atmosphere. Then I sat on the sofa and topped up my wine glass, watching Steve as he reached for his can of Budweiser.

'Shall I get you another?' I indicated to the can with my eyes.

'No, I'd better not. I don't want to be over the limit on these country roads.'

'I'll make you a strong coffee later.' We smiled at each other and a comfortable ambience enveloped the room. It felt like we'd never been apart, like the last seventeen years had been erased from our lives.

'It's certainly a lovely area; I'm not surprised you chose to live here. Was moving from Manchester a big upheaval?'

'Not really,' I answered truthfully. 'There were too many memories for me down there and I knew as long as I lived in Quayside I'd never be free of Christopher. His colleagues became a nuisance in the end. I think they did me a favour by driving me away.'

'Must have been a wrench leaving your mum though?'

'It wasn't easy, but she knew I was desperate to get away. She was very supportive. I think she might have moved up here eventually.' I sighed, sadness once more overwhelming my thoughts as I imagined mum living in Cornfield. 'So,' I began, changing the subject, 'what are your plans for the rest of the week?'

Steve put his can on the table and sat back against the sofa, positioning himself so that his body was at an angle to mine. 'Olivia wants to go to Scone Palace tomorrow then on Thursday we might have a ride into the mountains. And on Friday I'm hoping she'll be happy just chilling out. I don't mind driving round when I go away but she gets a bit obsessed with visiting places. I just want a rest.'

'I guess walking around the golf course is therapeutic for you?' I smirked.

'Of course,' he smiled, realising my attempt at innuendo.

'So how many holes have you done today then?' I took a large gulp of my wine, suddenly wishing I hadn't asked that question.

'None, yet,' he grinned.

A little embarrassed, I shuffled on the sofa, trying to disguise the fact that I hadn't meant to make another innuendo remark. 'Do you want that coffee now?' I asked.

'Not really.' He inched towards me, his hand now resting on my thigh. 'But I know what I do want.'

I looked into his eyes, the soft expression screaming at me to give him what he wanted. Then I leaned towards him and kissed him, a long, drawn-out and very passionate kiss that eventually led to him pushing me down gently against the sofa cushions and lying almost on top of me. I ran my fingers through his hair as he continued to light up my whole body with desire. A few moments later his hand moved down to my breasts and explored their roundness, a new feeling that I noticed left little room in his trousers. I let him carry on, my arms now wrapped around his back.

'Are you comfortable with this?' he whispered, his hand still resting on my breast.

'Very,' I replied, moving my lips to his, our bodies remembering the perfect harmony they had gotten used to all those years ago. 'Would you like to go to my bedroom?'

'Come on then.' He stood up, a little slower than I remembered, and held out his hand to help me up. I led him upstairs and opened the door to my bedroom, the four poster bed inviting us to lower ourselves onto it.

He helped me take off my t-shirt before he started to undo the buttons on his own shirt. I noticed how grey his chest hair had become, almost white compared to the dark silver fox I used to remember.

He looked at my breasts before staring into my eyes, lust washing over him. My heart was racing as his hands continued to fondle me, manoeuvring to my back before he unhooked my bra and helped me take it off. Then he wrapped his mouth around my nipple, stroking it with his tongue, his other hand still caressing my other breast. It was pure ecstasy, like another first time. Steve had always been a breast man; he hadn't changed.

Eventually our jeans were removed and thrown onto the floor, then underwear was ripped off in a desperate frenzy to get on with the love making. His deep penetration almost made me pass out, my body moving in rhythm to his. He hadn't lost his ability to satisfy me and I assumed I hadn't lost mine either, as his rhythm slowed and he rolled over to lie beside me. We lay for a few minutes, panting and getting our breath back before he turned to look at me, a huge grin etched on his face. I was feeling cold after sweat poured down my back and I got off the bed and pulled at the duvet, beckoning for him to get under with me.

We lay in my bed for an hour, my head resting on his chest as I continued to stroke his chest hairs, occasionally bringing my face to his for another kiss. I can't describe how magical it all felt. He lifted my head and stroked my face.

'We're still good together, don't you think?' he said, smiling.

'Always,' I answered. 'It feels like we've just gone back seventeen years.'

He laughed. 'I'm not sure I can keep up like I did seventeen years ago, but I reckon you could.'

'With the right person you can always keep up.' I laughed also, not wanting to turn our romantic moments into a serious discussion.

'Don't expect me to do it again though because I'm knackered after that.'

'I just want to lay here with you for a while; being in your arms is enough. And besides, I'm not getting any younger either, I'm not sure I could manage that again!' I kissed him gently, hoping he didn't think it would disappoint me that he couldn't make love to me a second time.

'I know we shouldn't have done that, Rachel, but I love you. I've always loved you, all these years. I know we could never have what we had before, but it doesn't stop the way I feel.' He was sincere. I'd got the old Steve back, the one who truly loved me, and it was the best feeling in the world.

'Let's not think we shouldn't have done it, Steve, let's just enjoy it. And for what it's worth, I love you, too. I always have and always will. As far as I'm concerned we can have what we had before but on different terms.' He sat up when I said that.

'On your terms?' he asked.

'Yes.' I sat up also and covered myself with the duvet. 'I don't want to be the other woman again, I think I deserve better than that. But I'm not going to turn you away because I've realised now that I can. Part of me wanted to though. I wanted to tell you not to come back. I wanted to be strong enough not to invite you in the other day, but I caved. Seventeen years might have passed but the way I feel for you never will.'

'Does this mean you want to see me again?'

My smile grew broader. 'If you like. When do you go home?'

'Saturday.' He sighed loudly. 'If I can get away on Friday, would it be okay to come back then?'

I didn't need time to think. 'Yes, definitely. I'll stay in all day in case you can come. If you don't manage to, don't worry, I won't make a fuss. I understand the situation.'

'If I can't make it I'll ring you. I don't think Olivia will object if I go for another game of golf, especially if I treat her to another spa afternoon.'

'Doesn't it bother you that you're lying to her again?'

'A bit, I suppose.' He leaned on his elbow and put his hand under the duvet to fondle my breast. 'We're not like a married couple anymore, haven't been for years. Obviously I don't want to hurt her again but I'm not missing an opportunity of spending some more time with you before I go home.'

'Then come round on Friday afternoon. We can just talk if you like, I don't mind.'

'Talk?' he laughed. 'Are you kidding?'

Then he moved his mouth back to my breast and once more threw me into ecstasy. Steve was wrong. He *was* able to make love to me again that afternoon.

CHAPTER TEN

The phone rang that night and it was Claire wanting to know the latest. I filled her in on Steve and me going for a walk in Jed's field, our discussion about how Steve had had a really difficult time but decided to put a brave face on at work in the hope of setting me free.

'It doesn't surprise me she gave him a hard time, Rachel, he had an affair. She was a woman scorned.'

'I know, but he could have left her.'

'But he didn't, Rachel, doesn't that tell you something?'

'He doesn't feel the love for her anymore, not like he used to. He says he often wished he'd walked out but he felt he owed it to her to make a go of their marriage. I told him that I would have had him back.' Was I making excuses for him again, I wondered.

'But he didn't go back to you, sweetheart, and that's something you need to remember.' There was a moment's hesitation. 'I'm really worried that you're going to get hurt again.'

'It won't happen, Claire. I'm stronger now, I'm not going to let him get to me like he did back then. I know he isn't going to leave Olivia and I accept that. I'm just enjoying spending a bit of time with him. It's been amazing today, absolutely amazing.' My mind started wandering back to the love making and the way his hands had discovered my body all over again; his gentle touch and his softly spoken words. 'He told me he still loves me and that he'll never stop. I can't ignore that, Claire, not even if I wanted to.'

'You still love him, don't you.' I don't think it was a question.

'Yes, I really do. More than I thought I did. We might have been apart for seventeen years but today has proved to us both that neither of us has moved on from how we felt back then. I know it'll never be the same as it was, but at least I know he loves me and thinks about me often. I suppose I'll have to settle for that.'

'So are you going to see him again before he leaves on Saturday?'

'He's ringing me on Friday morning to let me know if he can get away.'

'And I take it you want him to?'

'Totally,' I replied, without hesitation.

'I'm here for you, honey, and I want you to know that. But I want you to be careful and try not to get in too deep. He hasn't left Olivia and he's not likely to now, if that's what you're thinking is going to happen.' I didn't want Claire to think I'd been imagining him living in the cottage with me. It would have made her worry for me even more.

I tried to respond with a blasé tone in my voice. 'He's going home on Saturday and I'll probably never see him again. We'll just enjoy each other's company on Friday if he manages to get here and then we'll say our goodbyes.' I sighed. 'I admit it won't be easy watching him walk away again, but this is all I have left of him so I'm making the most of it. Please understand, Claire, I really need your support.'

'Will you ring me over the weekend, just so I know you're okay?' she asked.

'Of course I will. Please don't worry about me. I'm just having a good time with an old flame, that's all.'

When I hung up I thought about those words for a moment; A good time with an old flame. But Steve wasn't an old flame; he was the love of my life and I felt I was perfectly entitled to rekindle the flame that I realised had only ever flickered and never actually gone out.

****

And then there was Helen. She wanted the details also, of which I had to give just to stop her from squealing with excitement. She was adamant that I took him in the shop if he was to turn up on Friday, but I doubted he'd want to. I think Helen assumed we'd got back together and our once-upon-a-time-affair was now a prospective marriage proposal. Too big a part of me hoped she was right.

****

The phone rang on Friday morning and true to his word, it was Steve saying he'd offered to treat Olivia to an afternoon at the spa hotel in Tewsford again whilst he did another eighteen holes on the golf course. She wasn't sure at first but then decided to say yes. I was thrilled when he told me he'd be arriving at the cottage before one. I'd already cleaned and put fresh bedding on, plus I'd been down to Helen's shop and bought a few bottles of wine and four cans of Budweiser just in case he *was* able to come.

Hair brushed and lacquered – tick; makeup applied – tick; an easy-to-open blouse – tick; and some ivory coloured lacy underwear - tick. I went to Bessie's and treated myself to a new matching set. One last glance at myself in the mirror before getting dressed made me feel confident that if we did end up in bed, he would leave with a lasting memory of what he'd been missing over the last seventeen years. I was overwhelmed with excitement. In fact, I felt like a naughty school girl waiting for her pop idol backstage.

At one o'clock I paraded in front of the lounge window that looks onto the roadside. I didn't want to make it obvious that I was standing there waiting for him to arrive, but I couldn't sit still for more than half a minute. It was when I saw Reverend Holdsworthy coming down my drive that I started to panic. I hid in the kitchen hoping to high heaven he wouldn't come round the back and see me crouching behind the table like a rent evader. He knocked on the door a few times but I stood my ground, or rather crouched, my knees going numb. He was quite persistent as there was another knock after what felt like five minutes. Peering round the large wooden beam that separates the kitchen and lounge, a sudden concern ran through me when I thought the second knock could be Steve. There was only one way to find out and that was to open the kitchen door, sneak round the side of the cottage and see if I could see Steve's car parked up the road.

I felt like a cat burglar as I quietly unlocked my own back door. Turning the handle really slowly so as not to alert the Reverend to the noise it always makes, I managed to open it and creep outside. I stood on my tip toes to see over the hedge towards the first of Jed's fields. Steve's car was there, parked in its usual place. I had asked him to park in the drive but he said he didn't want to alert my neighbours as they'd probably start asking questions about him.

Shit, I thought, as I crept back inside, gently closing the back door and turning the key in the lock. I had to take the chance. If it was the Reverend I'd just tell him I was on my way out, and if it was Steve then there would be a good chance the Reverend had seen him, perhaps even spoken to him and told him I wasn't in. I wasn't going to risk Steve thinking I'd gone out when he'd arranged to come at one. That could have been the end of us. So I plucked up the courage and went to the front door, fluffing my hair up a little before turning the handle.

It *was* Steve. Phew. But the Reverend was still within vision as he was just walking past my next door neighbour's house. I ushered Steve in the house quickly, hoping the Reverend wouldn't come back when he realised that the man he saw walking down my drive had been let inside the house.

'What's up?' Steve asked, chuckling at my somewhat spy-like behaviour.

'I didn't want Reverend Holdsworthy knowing I'm in otherwise I'll never get rid of him. He's probably giving out leaflets for a coffee morning or something and if he sees you're here, he'll want to come in and welcome you to Cornfield before insisting you attend the Sunday service and do a reading.'

Steve laughed. 'That'll be hard when I'm in Manchester,' he said, then removed his coat and took it into the cloakroom. 'He saw me walk down your drive; do you think he'll come back?'

'If he does I'm not answering. I'll tell him we went for a walk and apologise for missing him. He won't mind, he's a very easy-going chap.'

'He looks ancient!' Steve pointed out.

'He *is* ancient!' I laughed. 'Do you want a Budweiser, or would you prefer a hot drink?'

'I'll have a Bud, please. I've been looking forward to a can or two as I don't usually have it at home. It's a bit of a treat while I'm here.' He grabbed me as I started walking into the kitchen, and pulled me into him. 'Talking of treats...' He planted his lips on mine and kissed me with every ounce of passion he could probably muster up.

'Drink first,' I laughed, wriggling free. 'We can go for a walk if you like as well.'

'Do you mind if we just stay in? I didn't get much sleep last night and I honestly can't be bothered going for a walk.'

'But you'd have to walk around eighteen holes wouldn't you? And why didn't you get much sleep?' Once again, I asked a question I wasn't sure I wanted to know the answer to. I held my breath as I waited for the reply.

'I couldn't stop thinking about you. I just lay there for hours, thinking about being with you and how fantastic it was all those years ago. It must have been about four o'clock when I finally dozed off and then I was up again at eight for breakfast.'

I should have known. After the other day it was obvious that Steve was just as enamoured at seeing me as I was at seeing him. We'd had a wonderful afternoon together and it was inevitable I'd be on his mind, just like he was on mine. I hugged him before opening the fridge and taking out a can of Budweiser.

'Cheers,' he said. 'To us.'

I thought about his toast as we made our way back to the lounge and sat down on the sofa, our bodies touching. Did he really mean 'to us', or was it just something he said as a kind of 'him and me' thing? We sank against the back of the sofa and he pulled me towards him, wrapping his arms around me before he kissed the top of my head.

'I still can't believe I've found you again,' he said, cupping my face in his hands.

'Would you like me to put some music on,' I asked.

'Sure. What are you into these days?'

'Well, I guess my tastes have changed a little over the years but I think you'll like my new CD.' I went over to the HiFi cabinet and took out the CD that had arrived in yesterday's post. I slotted it into the machine, pressed a few buttons until it arrived at track eight, then went back to the sofa and snuggled back underneath Steve's arm.

As Michael Bolton's beautiful voice starting to ring out, Steve once more lifted my face towards his and gave me the most captivating kiss he's ever given me. It lasted for the whole duration of 'Said I Loved You...But I Lied' as it played in the background. When it finished he held me the way he always used to, as though he never wanted to let me go. His hugs were one of the reasons why I fell in love with him, that gentle but firm grip. And I felt it again, seventeen years after he'd fallen in love with me for the first time, I knew he'd done it again.

'We might have aged, love, but we still have it don't we.' He stroked my cheek with his finger.

'We still have what?' I whispered.

'The most sincere love we've ever felt for anyone.' He kissed me again and I pulled away, half of me wanting him to elaborate on what he'd just said but the other half wanting to take him to my bed. 'What's up?' he asked.

'What you just said. Did you mean it?'

He looked serious for a moment. 'Yes, I meant it. I love you.'

I held out my hand which he took, then we stood up and he walked behind me as we climbed the stairs and went into my bedroom.

CHAPTER ELEVEN

Once more it felt like the first time as the tingles around my body encased me in lust. It was the love as well though, the deep and meaningful adoration that we'd always had for each other, that sent me into a whirlwind of intense pleasure.

I lay against his chest, our eyes staring at the ceiling as thoughts rushed through our minds. I knew what we'd done was wrong, I guess he did too, but it was as though neither of us cared. All that mattered was that moment in time, the comfort we felt as we lay together beneath the duvet. The way he stroked my arm was the way he'd always done. It was such a lot of years ago yet it felt like yesterday since we were embroiled in the affair. The fact he broke my heart didn't seem to matter anymore. I just wanted him in my life, no matter what.

After half an hour of snuggling up and keeping each other wrapped in pleasure, I got up and went to fetch us a drink. I brought two wine glasses and a bottle of Chianti and poured him a glass, passing it to him as he sat up and took it from me.

'It seems more romantic to drink wine after sex,' I smiled. 'A can of Budweiser just doesn't seem right to have by the bed.'

He laughed and tapped his glass against mine. 'To us,' he said, another toast to me and Steve, only this time I was sure he really did mean 'to us'.

'What time do you leave tomorrow?'

'Olivia wants to go about eleven. We have the room till midday but she wants to stop off for a pub lunch on the way home.' I sensed reluctance in his tone. 'You know I don't want to go, don't you?'

'I was hoping you wouldn't want to leave but I know you have no choice.'

'I don't, love, and that's hard. Will you let me ring you?'

'I insist on it,' I replied, refilling my glass.

'I have a mobile phone that Olivia never looks at so I'll give you the number and you can ring me on that if you like. If you ring and I'm with her then I'll just pretend it's a cold-caller. Will that be okay?'

I pondered for a moment. 'I'm not sure, Steve. I mean, what if Olivia *does* look at your phone and decides to ring my number?'

Steve shook his head and put his glass on the bedside table. 'Come here.' I put my glass down, too and lay against his bare chest. 'That won't happen, I promise. She never looks at my phone. And besides...' he paused.

'What?'

'I honestly don't think she'd care if you did ring. We don't have what you'd call a conventional marriage anymore. We're more like friends these days. You're the only person I've told about this but we don't sleep together, we've had separate bedrooms for a while now. We go on holiday together of course and then we do share a bed, but nothing happens. Our marriage is just a companionship. It's been like that for many years.' My first reaction was not to believe him. I couldn't help thinking about Claire's warnings, about how she kept telling me to be careful and how he could hurt me again. But when I sat up and looked into his eyes, I noticed tears forming and sadness etched in his expression. I suspected he had a few regrets about his marriage not being how it should be even if it was something he'd grown to accept.

'I'm sorry to hear that, truly I am. I imagine the two of you being together now is just out of habit after all these years.'

'We've been married thirty-five years, love, and the last seventeen have been so strained it's amazing we've got through. But we have because I know it's my fault that it's been like that. We're friends now and that's important, to both of us. If I'm being honest, I imagine she *would* be hurt if she found out I'd been seeing you again, but I don't think she'd be broken hearted, not like she was back then.' He reached for his wine and finished it off. I lifted the bottle from my side of the bed and offered him some more but he declined. 'Wine goes straight to my head.'

'It goes straight to mine as well,' I joked.

'Will you ring me then?' he asked, a serious expression now covering his piercing blue eyes.

'Yes, I will. If there's a good time to ring then you'd better tell me. You can ring me anytime. I usually go to the pub on a Sunday night with Helen but other than that, I'll be waiting for your call.' I hoped so much that he would ring me. Just to hear his voice was going to have to be enough, and would probably have to last me a very long time, if not forever.

'I was thinking. Did you say Claire and Melanie are getting married in November?'

'Yes, November the 5th.' I laughed. 'Melanie wants fireworks.'

'Then why don't we meet up when you come down?'

I had desperately hoped that he would suggest meeting up because I wasn't sure I should. I'd spent hours wondering if it would have made me look too desperate to see him again, which of course I was. But I really didn't want him to realise just how eager I was after wanting him to believe I was no longer the Rachel he used to know, the one who let him walk all over her for fear of being on her own.

'I'll have to check with Helen, as she's coming with me, but I'm sure she won't mind us going our separate ways for a day, or a night, whatever. Can I let you know?'

'Of course,' he said. 'Though if Helen is going with you, I doubt she's going to be too pleased about you buggering off to meet me.'

'I honestly don't think she'll mind. She knows about you and she knows how I feel. I'll have a word with her and make sure. If she does feel uncomfortable about it then we'll just have to sort something else out. Claire and Melanie are always asking me to go and stay with them and in the eight years since living up here I've never been. I'm sure they'll be happy for me to go down sometime.'

Steve looked at his watch. 'One more for the road?' he asked.

'Yes,' I replied. 'I'll just go and get you another ...'

He lifted my face towards his with one hand and slid the other beneath the duvet to meet between my legs. 'I didn't mean a drink,' he said, kissing me with such gusto that I nearly fell off the bed.

It was another hour until we got up and he had a quick shower. I got dressed and freshened up my makeup, running my fingers through my bed-hair. Clean and fresh and looking like the silver fox I'd always known and loved, he came towards me and hugged me before kissing me lovingly on the lips.

'I need to go,' he said, slowly drawing away and walking towards the bedroom door.

'I know.' It was the moment I'd been dreading.

I followed him downstairs and watched him put his jacket on. After having a quick peek through the window to make sure no one was about, I went to the front door and leaned against it, unwilling to let Steve leave until I'd at least had one more kiss.

He held me again, caressing my back and sighing deeply. 'God, this is hard,' he said. 'I really don't want to go.'

'Then don't,' I whispered. 'Stay. Live with me. Let's make a go of it once and for all.' I'm not sure where the words came from but they just seemed to roll off my tongue. I couldn't stop myself from opening up to him and he smiled with a sad and reluctant shake of his head.

'I'm sorry, I can't do that.' I wanted to ask if he meant 'can't' or 'won't', but I didn't. Instead I kissed him then opened the front door and watched him walk up my drive towards the road and his car.

He didn't look back and the tears poured down my cheeks. Right then and there I didn't care if anyone saw him leaving my little cottage, not even Olivia. I got that familiar feeling that I'd had twice before when he'd walked out of my life; my heart was breaking and there wasn't a thing I could do about it.

CHAPTER TWELVE

Saturday went by in a haze of confusion. I watched the clock more or less all day telling myself at eleven am, he'll be leaving now, then at midday, he'll be in the Borders now, again at two pm he'll probably be nearly home by now, and so it went on. I rang Helen at half past six knowing she would have closed the shop at six. She offered to go into Tewsford for a pizza and then be at mine within the hour. I was glad of her company and even though I was sad about Steve no longer being in the area, Helen and I managed to have a laugh and get drunk on Southern Comfort. We had a tiring game of Trivial Pursuits of which she won, and by the time it got to eleven pm, we were both ready for bed and I insisted she stay the night. Apart from the fact it was raining heavily I really didn't want to be in the cottage on my own and Helen's company was a welcome distraction to missing Steve.

'I really don't mind if you want to spend some time with him when we go to the wedding,' she said kindly, smiling and pouring the last of the whisky into our glasses. 'I know you'll be disappointed if you don't.'

'So long as he calls me and keeps in touch, then I'd love to see him in November. But honestly, if you're just saying that to be kind and you'd rather I didn't leave you alone then I really don't mind. I can go down to Claire's anytime, they're always asking me to go and visit.'

'Seriously, I don't mind. I'll enjoy a mooch in the city centre anyway. It'll be nice to be somewhere different. You go and enjoy yourself. Spend the night with him if you like.'

'I'll see,' I replied, a hopeful expression on my face that I was trying to disguise so as not to make Helen think I'd be completely disappointed if it didn't happen.

'Why don't you ask Claire if they mind him going to their place for the night while they're on honeymoon? And I'll bugger off to a hotel or something. It will work, Rachel, if you really want it to.'

'I do really want it to, but I don't know how Claire and Melanie will feel about it. Claire's happy that *I'm* happy but she doesn't really approve of me seeing Steve again.' I drank the last drop of Southern Comfort and stood up to walk to the kitchen. Helen followed me.

'I reckon Claire will be too pre-occupied to even think about not approving of Steve being there. They're very broad minded and they're good friends, too. Ask them. They can always say no. And if they say yes, you can then ask Steve and I'll book myself into a hotel for a night, give you two some space.' She picked the kettle up. 'Can I make a coffee?'

I nodded and reached for the coffee jar. 'I'll ask them this week, see what they think. But even if they do say yes, I doubt Steve will be able to get away for a whole night.' I spooned coffee into two cups.

Once we'd got our drinks we went back into the lounge and sat down again. 'Do you think I'm mad for being in love with a married man, Helen? And one who broke my heart?'

'Yes,' she answered truthfully. 'But it's got nothing to do with me who you fall in love with. You were with Steve long before we met. It's unlikely he's going to leave his wife for you but that doesn't mean you can turn your feelings on and off. It's a complicated situation to be in, but it's one that you need to work out for yourself.'

Helen was being as sensible as Claire and even though I didn't want to hear her tell me I was mad for loving Steve, I knew she was right.

'If he left Olivia tomorrow I'd let him come and live here with me. I told him as much before he left here yesterday.'

Helen gave me a sympathetic smile. 'What was his reaction to that?' she asked.

'He laughed, said he didn't want to go but had to.' I sipped my coffee then placed the cup on the table. 'I asked him to stay knowing he wouldn't of course, but I just couldn't help myself. The words came from nowhere and before I had chance to realise what I'd said, he was answering me, probably the only way he knew how.'

'It's such a shame how it's turned out. Does a part of you wish you hadn't seen him in Perth last week?'

'Yes.' I sighed. 'But seeing him after all these years was incredible. I've dreamed of it for years and then it came true. I suppose if I hadn't seen him then I wouldn't be feeling like this now. But as I have seen him I've realised that I still love him. My feelings for him have never gone away; they were just buried, waiting to be excavated.'

Helen smiled at me and raised her eyebrows. 'You've had too much to drink,' she said. 'You always get philosophical when you've had too many. Drink your coffee.'

I laughed. 'Sorry, but you know what I mean.' I picked my cup up again and did as I was told.

'I think it's a bit sad that he says his wife doesn't care what he does. I bet she does care. Did you believe him when he said that or do you think he was just doing the 'my wife doesn't understand me' shit?'

'I can't say for sure but I *want* to believe him. I have to admit I thought similar when he first told me, but he explained how his marriage isn't really a marriage anymore. They have separate bedrooms and don't share anything apart from their annual holiday. They're more like friends now.'

'I wish you'd brought him to meet me.'

'He wasn't keen on being shown off!' I laughed. 'And besides, if I'd brought him into the shop you'd have asked him the twenty questions and embarrassed him to death.'

'No, I wouldn't,' she scoffed. 'But I would like to meet him. Married or not, you obviously think the world of him and you make him sound almost perfect, if it wasn't for the wife.'

'He *is* almost perfect. Our relationship is almost perfect. It *was* seventeen years ago and a big part of me wants it to be again.'

'But?'

'Well, I live up here now and we're three hundred miles apart. It's impossible for us to carry on seeing each other. All I have to look forward to is a phone call and I'm not absolutely sure he'll ring yet.'

'But you can see him in November,' she pointed out, nodding and smiling at me. 'Even if Claire and Melanie don't approve of him staying the night, at least you can see him during the day, or even for an evening.'

'I guess. And he's given me his mobile number.'

'There you go then. If he doesn't ring you this week, why don't you ring him?'

I nodded and looked towards the telephone table where the little piece of paper with Steve's number lay next to the phone.

'I will. If he doesn't ring me by next weekend, I'll ring him. One way or another I'm going to at least try to see him again. And if he doesn't want to see me then I suppose I'll just have to accept it and move on with my life.' I thought about that for a few moments, remembering I'd tried that once and failed.

'Exactly. If he gave you his number he must want to talk to you. You've told me he said he's still in love with you. Stay positive. I've known you eight years now, Rachel, and I've never known you to be pessimistic.'

I'm not at all pessimistic. In fact, since I moved the Scotland I'd made a point of always looking at life from a positive angle. As the strong and independent woman I'd become I wasn't going to let anyone knock my confidence. Steve had been the only one to do that and I'd climbed back up again and got on with my life.

It was midnight when we went to bed. The spare bed was already made up and I lent Helen a pair of my pyjamas and a new toothbrush that had been in my cupboard for a while. She laughed at me when I said I didn't want the toothbrush back, then gave me a little peck on the cheek and said goodnight.

CHAPTER THIRTEEN

It was Wednesday night when Steve rang me. I couldn't believe it when I heard his voice on the other end of the phone and just sat there for a moment in a daze, wondering what to say. Stumbling over my words a little, I told him how glad I was that he'd phoned.

'Did you think I wouldn't?' he asked.

'Part of me did, I suppose.'

'I was going to ring you last night but Susan came round and by the time she left it was gone nine so I thought it was a bit late.'

'I've told you, you can ring me anytime, it doesn't matter what time it is.' Right then, I was just glad he'd rung me at all. I had hoped he would have phoned on Saturday night or at least on Sunday. When he hadn't rung by Tuesday I was starting to worry and plan what I would say when I rang him on his mobile at the weekend.

'I've missed you. It feels strange being home again after spending time with you.'

'I've missed you, too. I've thought about you such a lot this week.'

'I'm at the golf club at the moment, sat in the car.'

'The golf club with the driving range where I went a few times?'

'Yes, the very same.' He laughed. 'Have you ever had a go at golf since?'

'No,' I mocked. 'And I never will either. It's definitely not my game!'

'I'm with you there. Thought I was going to get clobbered a few times with you behind the golf club.'

'And ruin your potential?' We both laughed.

'God, I've missed talking to you. I still can't believe we made love last week. You are so beautiful. Still the sexy Rachel I know and love.' I smiled when he said that wondering if it was the lace he liked so much or if it was my mid-forties figure that had long since started to droop.

'I asked Helen about meeting you in November when we go down for Claire's wedding and she doesn't mind. I haven't had chance to speak to Claire and Melanie yet as they never seem to be in when I ring, but Helen suggested we spend the night together and she'll stay in a hotel.' The line went quiet.

I sat for a few moments, cringing at the fact Steve obviously didn't know what to say. Was I being too pushy? Was it too soon? Had I put him in a difficult position? Oh God, I thought, why the hell did I just blurt it out?

'I can try,' he said eventually, 'though it won't be easy. I might not be able to do a full overnight stay but we can definitely meet up, go out for a meal or something. Maybe a walk in the woods?'

'Yes, that would be lovely. I thought about a walk myself, then going back to Claire's house and you staying for the night.' I could hear myself saying 'please' in my head, pleading in silence, trying to get a telepathic message through the phone lines that I was desperate to spend the night with him.

'Okay, I promise to try, but don't build your hopes up, love. It would be great to spend the whole night together but I'll need a bloody good excuse first.'

'I realise that.' I made myself sound like it didn't really matter and a walk or a meal would suffice.

'I bet you've been telling your friend all about what happened last week?' he said with a chuckle.

'Naturally,' I smirked. 'Helen's a good listener. She came round on Saturday night and stayed over, thrashed me at Trivial Pursuits and we got hammered as usual. She knows you almost as well as I do now.'

'You're kidding?'

'She's dying to meet you. She was hoping I'd take you to her shop last week when you were here but I said you'd probably have been embarrassed.'

'It'd get all your neighbours talking wouldn't it?' I noticed he wasn't laughing anymore. 'Maybe I'll meet her when you come down in November.'

'That'd be nice, though she said she'll go into Manchester to give us some space.'

'She sounds like a good friend.'

'She is,' I confirmed. 'She's my best friend up here, that's for sure. Have you told anyone about me?'

'No, love, I haven't. Not really a good idea in case it gets back to Olivia. Mind you, I'm dying to tell Pete, my golfing partner. We talk about everything and he knows I had an affair and the situation with Olivia now, but I'm not going to tell him I've seen you again. He sees Olivia when we go to functions at the golf club. He takes his wife with him and if he knew about you now it might make things awkward between us.'

'I understand, probably best not to say anything to anyone then.' I hoped Steve hadn't detected the little touch of annoyance in my voice. To think he wasn't prepared to tell anyone he'd seen me kind of made me feel like second best again; 'the other woman' that I swore I would never be.

He promised to ring me over the weekend then hung up. I put the receiver down and looked at the phone for a minute, willing it to ring again. Miraculously, it did.

'I forgot to say, I love you.'

'I love you, too, Steve.' I replied before replacing the receiver for a second time.

****

Steve kept to his word and phoned me regularly. When he first went back to Manchester, there was a part of me that really thought I'd never hear from him again, and I admit now there was a tiny part of me that wondered if the number he'd given me was actually false. Cynical, I know, but I had to stay practical and not get too excited about the prospect of him being in my life again. Of course, we couldn't physically spend time with each other which obviously would have been better, but the phone calls made up for it. His wonderful ability to turn me on, even from three hundred miles away, made our phone calls all the more exciting

I managed to get hold of Claire the day following that first phone call with Steve, and at first she was a bit hesitant.

'I'm not sure, Rachel,' she said. 'Do you think it's a good idea? I mean, what if Olivia follows him to my house and assumes he's having an affair with me?'

'Olivia won't follow him and even if she does, you won't be there.'

'But just say she did follow him and came round the week after we got back from our honeymoon. What would I say to her?'

'Claire, if you don't approve then just say. I won't be offended. It's your house and we understand it's a difficult situation. Talk it over with Melanie and let me know what you think.'

'Hang on.' The line went quiet for a moment then I heard her shout, 'Melanie... Come here a minute.' After a few seconds the line went a bit echoey. 'Right, I have you on loud speaker. Melanie, Rachel's asking if it'll be okay for Steve to come and spend the night here while we're on honeymoon.' I couldn't believe Claire had put Melanie on the spot like that.

'It's fine by me,' Melanie said, much to my surprise. 'You two shagging again?'

I cleared my throat at Melanie bluntness. 'Well, err, yeah, I guess we are.'

'It's not a problem for me. Just be careful, that's all I ask.'

'Okay then. It's fine by me too, in that case,' Claire agreed. 'You've got a good friend in Helen you know, are you sure she doesn't mind having to bugger off for the night?'

'She was the one who suggested it. I think she quite likes the idea of spending a night on her own in Manchester.' I suspected Claire and Melanie could hear the excitement in my voice.

'I know I've said it umpteen times, Rachel, but do be careful, for your sake. He's hurt you twice and I don't want to see you go through that again.'

'Claire, you've known me a long time and you know I'm a different person now. I'm not that gullible fool I was back then. I'm just having some fun.'

'A midlife crisis more like,' Melanie chirped in. 'I'll leave you to it; I've got shirts to iron for tomorrow. Speak soon, flower. Love you.'

'Love you too, Melanie, and thanks again.' I waited a few seconds before continuing. 'You sure it's okay?' I asked Claire, once I'd heard the click and realised she'd taken me off loud speaker.

'Yes, I'm sure. I want you to be happy and if this makes you happy then go for it. You know me and Melanie will always be here to pick up the pieces.' I think I heard her sigh but I can't be sure.

'I hope there won't be any pieces to pick up,' I laughed, perhaps a little too confidently.

CHAPTER FOURTEEN

I had a lovely birthday and was delighted when a card came through the post from Steve. It was signed; '*All my love, Steve,*' and that put a huge smile on my face for the whole day. He also sent me £100 in vouchers to use in Debenhams, no doubt with the lingerie department in mind, but it was incredibly generous of him. The locals put on a bit of a do in the pub for me which was fabulous. Helen told me to meet her there at seven for a few drinks before going into Tewsford for a meal at Pucinnos. When I walked through the door they were all there, the locals stood at the bar singing Happy Birthday. I felt a bit daft really but it was a lovely thing to do; a surprise party just for me. We didn't go into Tewsford after all as Hazel and George had supplied a buffet, but Helen took me to the Italian the following night instead, paid for by her which was even better, as her birthday present to me. She says I'm a woman who has everything and a need for nothing, so I had to make do with a meal. I told her she didn't need to get me anything at all, but she hugged me and said I'm her best friend and the most interesting person she's ever known.

Steve rang me on my birthday. He was at the golf club again.

'I wish I was with you today,' he said. 'I hope this phone call will make up for me not being there?'

'Of course it makes up for it. I've told you a million times that I understand the situation.' Perhaps not quite so much as he would have liked but still, I was grateful he'd phoned. 'Thanks for the vouchers and the beautiful card.'

'I know you like Debenhams.'

'They have a great lingerie department.'

'Do they really?' He laughed, and I tutted.

'Don't worry, if we're able to get together in November I'll make sure you examine the clothing that your vouchers bought.'

'Did you manage to speak to Claire and Melanie?'

'Yes,' I answered. 'They're fine about you staying the night if you can manage it. Claire gave me the usual lecture about being careful. I think she just wishes it could be under different circumstances.'

'What do you mean?'

'Well, that you weren't married and we were together properly.'

He went quiet for a moment. 'I know, I wish that too, but for now we just have to carry on like this.'

I wasn't sure whether I sensed a hint of changes-afoot in his tone but I didn't question it. I'd decided not to go building my hopes up about us being an item and was just happy to settle for what we had.

'So do you think you'll be able to manage an overnighter?'

'I honestly don't know, love. I almost told Pete again last night and I suppose I could mention it to him, but I doubt he'll approve. There's not really anyone I could ask to cover for me except him and as he knows Olivia I can't imagine him wanting to lie to her for me.'

It was my birthday and I had no intention of making it gloomy with disappointing thoughts. I shrugged off his doubts and told him what I was wearing instead, which wasn't very much.

'I can't remember what colour your negligee is,' he said.

'It isn't a colour; it's see-through.'

He sighed loudly. 'Have you bought a new one or is it one that I didn't get to see?'

'I bought it last week, just to wear when I'm on the phone with you.'

'You do realise I'm in my car in the golf club car park?'

'Yes, and?'

'You're turning me on and I'm sat here with a rod down my trousers.'

'Then get rid of it.'

'I'm in a bloody car park,' he laughed.

'Then go somewhere else.'

'I'll get rid of it later.'

'Then imagine me there with you, lying on my bed in this see-through negligee, and I'll imagine you here with me, running your tongue over my breasts.' I lifted my legs onto the sofa and ruffled up my hair. 'Are you still there?'

'Just about,' he said in a whisper.

'Are you okay?'

'Just about.'

I laughed. 'Maybe I should let you go. Shall I ring you later?'

'You can if you like; I should be home by tea time. If I don't answer you'll know why.' I hated it when he said that. It always made me feel like the other woman again, but that was something I suppose I should have been used to after all these years.

We said our goodbyes then hung up, and I went into my bedroom to get dressed.

CHAPTER FIFTEEN

It was the first week of October with only four weeks until Claire and Melanie's wedding. After noticing me skipping into work all week, Angela asked me why I was in such a good mood. She and Gregory had been having a few problems and I sensed she wasn't very happy. She told me she was bored with his anti-social ways and sick of always being the one to instigate a night out.

'If ever you want to chat, Angela, you can always come round for coffee,' I said, worried that she was going to start over pricing garments again.

'Do you remember I told you we were interested in the new houses being built in your village? Well, Gregory doesn't want one now. He says they're too expensive and thinks we'll be pushing ourselves. I reckon we should just go for it as it'll be our last move but he's adamant.'

'Does that mean Prenton Homes are going ahead then? Did they get planning permission to build?'

'Yes, didn't you hear?'

I stopped what I was doing and wondered why no one had mentioned it in the village. I'd noticed the meetings about the proposals had stopped being held in the pub but I'd been so pre-occupied with Steve that I hadn't been showing much interest in what was happening with our little community.

'No, I didn't realise that. I wonder if the villagers know.'

She frowned. 'Would it matter to the villagers?'

'I think so; they're against the plans, they've been opposing them since Prenton put the notice in the paper. I personally think it'll be good for the village but I felt I had to go along with the others.'

'You should have mentioned it when I first told you. I'd hate to have moved into a village and not felt welcome. Maybe Gregory's right then, it's probably best we stay where we are for now.' She walked over to the counter and took out some more tags from the drawer.

'I'm sorry, Angela, I should've said something, I know' I panicked a little as she reached for a black marker pen and poised it over the price tags.

'Well that's not going to happen now anyway. Not to worry, pet, I'm sure my miserable bugger of a husband will have his sights set on somewhere else before long.'

I couldn't wait to leave work and stop off at the pub to tell Hazel and George what I knew.

'We heard,' they said in unison. 'It's a bloody disgrace. Our petition meant nothing to the council, not a jot. They couldn't give a toss about the people that already live here and as for the local businesses, well, we might as well kiss goodbye to our livelihoods. It's Helen I feel sorry for,' George said.

I was inclined to disagree. 'I don't think it'll be all that bad. They're only building about six homes so it's unlikely the Co-operative will want to build a store here when they have a big one in Tewsford. And as for the pub, well, it'll just bring in more punters, surely?'

'I hope you're right, Rachel,' Hazel said, pulling a pint for Joe, one of the locals. 'Two pounds thirty, my love,' she said as he passed her the money. 'What worries me is that once they've built their first six homes they'll most likely want to start building more, and that's when the problems will start. Someone will come in and want to open a restaurant and then we'll be buggered.'

'I do agree with you to a certain extent; I'm not too chuffed about a farmer's field being turned into a housing development either but I think, now that it's definitely going ahead, we need to be positive about it and try to turn it around to our benefit. Maybe you could expand the pub and Helen could expand her shop. I'm sure something can be done to stop any more businesses coming into the village.'

'We already serve food, Rachel, I'm not sure expanding will help.' George looked at me with a patronising expression.

'What about bed and breakfast?' I asked.

His eyes looked away for a moment, his head still, and then he turned to Hazel and I noticed a twinkle appear in his eyes. 'The girl's got a point,

Hazel. We've got two spare rooms upstairs that could easily be turned into a bed and breakfast with a bit of building work. They're big enough to put an en-suite in.'

'And who's going to look after the bed and breakfast side of the business?' asked Hazel, scoffing a little.

'We'll do it together and there's always Pat, she's always asking for extra shifts. If we started doing B&B we could afford to give her a few extra shifts and she could run that side of it.' He looked at me. 'This could work,' he said, then went to pull a pint for Andy the taxi man, who'd just walked in.

'What might work?' Andy asked.

'Rachel here has just given us an idea. Since these new homes are being built now, she reckons we should start doing bed and breakfast.' He put the pint of bitter on the counter and took the money from Andy.

'That's a great idea,' Andy agreed. 'The nearest rooms round here are in Tewsford. Every time my mates come down on a bender, I always end up staying with them there and it costs me a fortune. They could start coming here and use your pub.'

'We'll have a think about it, George,' Hazel said quickly, not one to be tempted by someone else's suggestions.

'Of course we will, my love, and I'll give Albert a ring tonight and ask him to pop in and give us a quote on the building work.'

I decided to leave at that point as Hazel had started giving me daggers. I met Mrs. McCraikie on my way out; she was just going in for a chat with Hazel about the church flowers. She smiled at me and asked how I was. I apologised as I really didn't want to hang around talking to her when Hazel was clearly throwing me out with her thunderous looks. I laughed as I got into the car and imagined them both sat at the bar discussing how much of a busy-body I am.

****

Steve rang me that night with some disappointing news.

'I'm sorry, love, I very much doubt I'll be able to stay all night with you. I just can't bring myself to ask Pete to be my alibi. It's not fair on him.'

I sat for a moment, starting to feel totally deflated, yet knowing this was more likely to happen than us spending the night together.

'It's okay,' I lied. 'So long as we get some time during the day, that'll just have to do. Are you sure Pete will object?'

'I'm not sure he'll object, but I'm pretty sure he won't approve. We played nine holes yesterday and he's asked if Olivia and I want to go to Wales next weekend with him and Carol. I couldn't really say no. But if I go and ask him to lie for me that would be really awkward, don't you think?'

I did think it would be awkward and I knew it couldn't happen, so I decided not to push it.

'Helen and I will be down on the Thursday and the wedding's on the Friday. Maybe we could get together on the Saturday, spend the day together. Would that be okay?'

'That would be grand. I'll make sure I'm playing golf, even if it's raining. Don't worry, I won't let you down.'

But he already had. I sat on the sofa after his phone call, crying into my Southern Comfort and realising that so long as he was married, he would always let me down, forever and a day.

CHAPTER SIXTEEN

After that last phone call with Steve I found myself in a depressed state. I put a brave face on for Helen when we went to the pub for supper, but I think she guessed something was up. You can't be friends with someone for eight years and they not know when you're feeling down. George walked us home, much to Hazel's annoyance, and we said goodnight to Helen at her front door. When we got to my house he waited for me to get the keys out of my bag then leaned against the wall next to the door.

'What do you think of Hazel?' he asked, unable to look me in the eyes.

'What do you mean?'

'She seems to be watching me like a hawk for some reason and I'm not doing anything I shouldn't be. Have you noticed how possessive she is?'

I cleared my throat. 'Well, yes I have, but I reckon that's because she loves you, George.' I unlocked the door and pushed it open, unsure whether he was angling for an invite inside.

'I love her, Rachel, I really do, but I'm so sick of this distrust she has for me. It's driving me nuts.'

'Does she have a reason not to trust you?'

'No.' He shuffled nervously. 'She did, I admit that, but it was years ago. But now it seems she's jealous of you and Helen and any other woman I look at. It's getting ridiculous. This bed and breakfast business is a great idea but last night she said if we did go ahead with it, one of the rules would be no young, single women on their own. I mean, how daft would that be?'

'Do you want to come in, George?' I asked, with a very deep sigh. I felt I needed to have a chat with him about the way a woman's mind works.

'Err, better not, my love, otherwise she'll be running down the road shaking a broom at me.'

I smiled at him, feeling a tad sorry for the big strong man who stood in front of me. 'Look, if you need a chat anytime, you know where I am. Maybe the two of you need to sit down and have a good talk about her insecurities. I can see you love her, but I'd hate to think she thought there was something going on with me and you, or you and Helen for that matter. We really appreciate you walking us home, especially me living at this end of the village, but if it's becoming a problem then I can always ask someone else.'

He shook his head. 'No, no, I enjoy walking you home. I like the fresh air after being stuck behind that bar all night. Plus, I dare say I do like your company, Rachel.'

I noticed a leery smile appear on his face. I could imagine him being a 'jack-the-lad' in his younger days but I could never fancy him and I was quite adamant that he wasn't going to take our friendship any further.

'Goodnight, George,' I said, now standing in my lounge and blocking the doorway. 'Thanks for walking me home again.'

'Night, love, and thanks for listening. I might take you up on that chat sometime.' He walked up my drive towards the lane, closing the gate behind him.

Is this how men of a certain age get, I thought; is that what a midlife crisis is? Perhaps that's all Steve had when we had an affair all those years ago. But he still loves me. How can a midlife crisis last so long?

****

I woke up in the middle of the night having a hot flush. I was in a bit of a state worrying about George and feeling sorry for him as, come to think of it, I had noticed Hazel's evil eye on several occasions. I just thought she was insecure and maybe even a bit jealous. Then my thoughts wandered to Steve. When we were together seventeen years ago I knew he was a ladies' man, but I was the one who stole his heart. It gave me a warm glow, along with the hot flush, as I snuggled down under the duvet and went back to sleep.

****

'Hi, Helen, it's just me, I wanted to catch you before you opened the shop.' I rang Helen at half past seven feeling a burning need to tell her about

George's woes. I think it got to me more than I realised.

'You'll have to be quick,' she said, 'I'm expecting a delivery any minute.'

'When we got back to my place last night, George told me he's worried about Hazel and how possessive she is. I thought I'd mention it to you in case you've noticed her giving you daggers as well.'

'She gives everyone daggers. But yes, I know what you mean. She doesn't like it much when he walks us home.'

'Helen, do you think she knows about me and Steve?'

'I don't know how she can. And why should that matter?'

'Well if she knows I'm seeing a married man she might think I'm an easy ride. I have a feeling George has had an affair in his younger days.'

'He did.' Helen said, quietly. 'With me.'

I had to sit down at that point.

'It's okay, Rach, I would have probably told you one day. It wasn't anything like you and Steve had, it was just a daft fling years ago. I knew he'd never leave Hazel and I didn't want him to but he tried it on with me one night and I let him. It sort of went from there really.'

'Fuck a duck, Helen. Do you think Hazel thinks it's you he's seeing, and not me?'

'I wouldn't be surprised. I have to go, Rach, I can hear the van outside. I'll come round tonight and tell you all about it. I'll bring a pizza and some wine. Talk later, honey.'

I couldn't believe Helen hadn't told me about her and George. It obviously didn't mean anything to her but I did feel a bit peeved that she hadn't trusted me enough to tell me, especially when she knew all about Steve. I spent most of that day in a dream, afraid to walk out of my front door in case George was walking past with Bess, his faithful border terrier, and wanted to have the 'chat'. What on earth was I supposed to say to him now that I knew what he'd been up to? And another thought was starting to cross my mind, too. Was I safe with him or would it only be a matter of time before he thought his luck was in with me as well. He'd already tried it on with me and I'd more or less laughed him off, but maybe he'd been deadly serious. Poor Hazel, I thought. Then realised what a hypocrite I was.

****

True to her word, Helen knocked on my front door at seven o'clock that evening with a huge twelve inch Hawaiian and two bottles of Claret. I felt it was going to be a long night. We separated the pizza onto two plates and I opened the wine, pouring it into two very large glasses. Then we went into the lounge and settled ourselves down on the sofa.

'So?' I asked, my mouth full of pizza.

'You're probably wondering why I haven't told you.' I nodded. 'I'm sorry about that, Rachel, but the truth is I was embarrassed, and still am. It was a drunken one night stand at first and we both agreed never to talk about it again. Then he did his usual walking me home bit and we ended up snogging in my hallway. That second time I hadn't had much to drink and he hadn't touched a drop so we kind of thought we might fancy each other after all. He was a lot slimmer back then, about twelve years ago now, and had a lot of charisma. I have to admit I did fancy him and was going through a bit of a lonely spell at the time.'

'What about Derek?' I asked, wondering where Helen's ex-husband came into all this.

'I didn't meet Derek until a few years later. I never told him about George because I didn't want him to think I was a desperate tart.' She took a swig of wine to wash down the pizza that I thought for a moment she was going to choke on. 'Me and George had a few months of good times, you know, sex and all that, but it was never a serious relationship. I knew full well he didn't love me and would never have left Hazel so I decided not to get too involved and just enjoy the sex, which *was* good.' It was my turn to choke.

'Sex with George, good?'

'Oh yes, he was a stallion in bed. I wasn't his first affair though, he's had many over the years and that's probably why Hazel's so insecure. But no one likes her much so it's never a subject for discussion.'

'I can't believe I've lived in this village for eight years and no one has told me this.' I loved a good gossip and felt really disappointed that I didn't know the juicy details of George's infidelities.

'I don't think he's strayed for a long time now. He still likes to think he's a ladies' man but I think he's kidding himself.'

'So why did it end between you?'

'Reverend Holdsworthy caught us snogging one night on my doorstep. George had walked me home after quiz night and the Reverend was putting his bin out and having a crafty fag at his front gate. There we were, eating each other, and the Reverend coughed which made us turn around. He was looking straight at us.'

'Oh my God, Helen, what did you say?'

'We didn't say anything at the time. George just scurried off quick and ran back to the pub. I went inside and locked the door and hoped the Reverend didn't come knocking. Fortunately he didn't. But he came into the shop the next morning and said I should end whatever was going on because it would devastate Hazel. Then he told me he didn't blame me as I was a young, single woman living on my own but he was disgusted with George and wouldn't drink in the pub for a while. I had to tell George obviously and he went round to see the Reverend. They had a good chat and cleared the air and the Reverend promised not to mention it to anyone so long as he got a month's worth of free booze.'

I laughed. 'He's a bit of a one isn't he? Didn't Hazel ask why George was serving him free drinks?'

'No, because George was buying them all so the takings were never down. Our little fling cost him a bloody fortune because the Reverend kept ordering doubles!'

'That's so funny. I reckon the Reverend was pretty chuffed he'd seen you in the end!'

'Yes, I don't doubt that for a second. But it made us realise that we had to stop. I did miss not seeing George for a while and kept going into the pub to try and attract his attention, but then Derek moved into the village and lived in Andy's spare room for a while before he moved in with me. And you know the rest.'

We carried on munching pizza and got through both bottles of wine. I forgave Helen for not telling me about George and could see her reason for it. At least it explained why Hazel was insecure. Maybe having that chat with him won't be so bad after all, I thought.

She left at half past ten and I went to bed realising I had more in common with Helen than I first thought.

CHAPTER SEVENTEEN

With the wedding fast approaching, the thought that I might or might not have been spending a full night with Steve, amazingly enough, wasn't really at the forefront of my mind as Claire had been on the phone nearly every night for the past week with squeals of excitement as she told me about another wedding present they'd received.

'Honestly, Rachel, I can't believe how generous people have been. I feel like I should have invited them all to the ceremony but Melanie really wants it to be a private affair. They'll all be at the reception though and we can thank them all there. You should see what Jane and Scott sent, do you remember me telling you about them, they won three million quid on the lottery a few years ago? Well, they've sent us two tickets for a holiday in Barbados to be taken whenever we like within the next two years. I'm chuffed to bits. It's always been somewhere we've wanted to go and now we can. Oh, and Melanie's cousin has sent us a year's membership to Halter Spa and Country House Hotel, I mean, can you imagine? Those memberships cost a bloody fortune, and for two of us...'

I wanted to tell Claire to stop for a moment and breathe. But I couldn't get a word in.

'Melanie looks amazing in her outfit, she's lost half a stone and had it taken in a bit at the waist. Talk about sex on legs.' I smiled at that. 'She's staying at her cousin's house the night before the wedding so it'll be just you, me and Helen. Will you do my nails for me?'

'Yes,' I answered, grateful to be able to use my vocal chords again. 'Have you chosen the colour?'

'Bright red; I'm going brazen hussy. You can have a look at my undies when you come down as well. They'll blow you away!'

'Think you should keep your undies for Melanie's eyes only, flower, I really don't think she'd approve if you showed your wedding night lingerie to me and Helen.'

'Hmmm, suppose you have a point. It's ivory and very lacy, with silk flowers embroidered into the bra cups. I've gone for stockings and suspenders as they're Melanie's...'

'Claire!' I raised my voice. 'Too much information.'

She laughed. 'Oh shit, what am I like?! I'm sooo excited, can you tell?'

'I'm excited for you and I can't wait to see the two of you making your vows. It's fabulous to see you both so happy and in love.'

'Have you and Steve sorted out what you're doing yet?'

'He still isn't sure he can stay the night but we're definitely meeting up on the Saturday.'

'That'll be nice then, at least you'll get to spend some time with him. Where are you meeting him?'

I smiled to myself and felt that lovely warm glow tingle through my veins. 'Nightingale Woods,' I answered.

'One of these days I'm going to take Melanie there.'

'Preferably not when me and Steve are there,' I laughed.

CHAPTER EIGHTEEN

I pulled up outside Helen's shop at nine am. She was standing in the window watching out for me. Mrs. McCraikie had kindly offered to look after the shop until we got back so Helen was content that it would be left in good hands. As Mrs. McCraikie had helped out in the shop often, it made it easier for Helen to take a few days off. It was a gorgeous crisp November morning and the sun was low in the sky, making driving conditions a little hazardous. I noticed George stood in the pub doorway as we drove past, and he waved with his left hand, a cigarette clenched in his right. Fortunately, by the time we hit the A1, there wasn't quite as much traffic and we managed to get a good run down to the M62. We stopped a couple of times at services; my bladder wasn't going to last all that way, but we finally made it to Claire and Melanie's dockside apartment by half past two, a pretty good journey by all accounts.

Claire had given me simple directions, though I do know the area, but I couldn't believe how much it had changed in the last eight years. Beautiful, plush apartments sprouted up everywhere and designer shops poking out of every street corner. She was stood at the entrance to their building when we drew up in my car and waved like a mad woman to let us know we were in the right place. It wasn't long before she was stood next to the car, hopping about from leg to leg with excitement. I opened the door which meant she had to step back a little, then got out and gave her a huge bear hug.

'Oh my God,' she expressed. 'I can't believe you're finally here!'

'Hi, Claire.' Helen got out of the passenger side, adjusting her jeans and walking around the front of the car with stiff legs. 'It's lovely to see you again.' Claire gave Helen a hug as I opened the boot and reached for our bags.

'Bloody nora, Helen,' I exclaimed. 'What have you got in here?'

'Be careful with it, Rach, it's got ten bottles of Beaujolais in it and a large bottle of Southern Comfort.'

I put the bag down extra carefully on the tarmac and moved away so that Helen could carry it in. We had our wedding outfits in suit bags hung up in the back of the car.

'Here, I'll get those,' Claire reached in to get them. 'Come on, let's get inside, it's a bit chilly isn't it. I've put the heaters on.'

Claire led us to a lift where we all clambered in and she pressed button number 1. It was all very up-market, and very Claire. Once the lift arrived at its destination, we got out and walked a few yards down a hallway until we came to a large oak door with 35 in brass numbers fixed onto it. 'In you come then,' she said, opening the door and standing aside for us to walk through while she stood against it.

My first thought was wow. Very modern colours of beige and deep red borders covered the hallway with white glossed doors leading into what I assumed were bedrooms. A set of white double doors led into the open plan lounge, dining area and kitchen, all very tastefully decorated, contemporary and swish. The apartment was warm and flowed beautifully from area to area. A huge L shaped dark brown sofa dominated one wall and a smaller sofa of the same fabric and colour opposite it, a glass coffee table separating them. A stunning bronze lamp stand with beige fabric shade stood on a corner unit and the biggest plasma screen I've ever seen adorned the wall above the small fireplace. It was an electric fire but an elegant feature of the room, with a marble Adam-style surround and minimalistic appearance. Helen and I put our bags on the floor and stared around us, probably looking like two guppy fish. The kitchen had an island with contemporary units and stainless steel oven. There was even a small utility room with a washing machine and tumble drier.

French doors led out from the lounge onto a large balcony overlooking the modern and newly refurbished docks, and a few pots with greenery were positioned on the balcony along with a wooden table and four wooden chairs. I knew Claire and Melanie were both earning decent wages but this place must have cost them a fortune to buy, especially in its prime location. I thought about my little cottage in Cornfield for a moment, picturing the dust and the cobwebs and the ancient beams. But I wouldn't have swapped it, even though this apartment was pretty spectacular.

'I've made up the twin beds in the spare room. We use the third bedroom as an office so it's got no bed in. Are you two okay sharing a room?'

I nodded and looked at Helen.

'This is a stunning place,' Helen said, still admiring the decor and the ornaments and the complete contrast to her flat above the shop. 'I can see why you like living here.'

'Melanie chose it. I would have bought one of the new properties in Upton Road just around the corner because I'd prefer to have a house, but she really wanted this position overlooking the docks so I gave in.' Claire looked around lovingly. 'I do love it, but if we decide to move in the future, I'm going to try my hardest to talk her round to buying a house. Not sure there'll be any left in Upton Road though, and if there are any for sale when we're ready to move, they'll probably be far too expensive. People were buying them off-plan then we noticed a few went back up for sale a year later with a couple of hundred thousand added onto the price. Crafty buggers.'

'It's the way to do it these days isn't it?' I said. 'But I don't think property is doing too well anymore. Did I tell you about the new houses in Cornfield?'

'Yes, you did. I quite fancy one actually but I doubt Melanie will move to Scotland.'

My heart did a little flip at that because I'd have loved Claire and Melanie to move to the village, but I would doubt they'd settle for long with the only town nearby being Tewsford.

'You go and get yourselves settled, second door on the right, and I'll make us a brew. Or would you prefer I opened a bottle of something?'

'Brew for me,' shouted Helen, already standing at the second door on the right.

'Same here thanks, Claire.' I followed Helen into the spare bedroom, a large, beige coloured room with a beige carpet, beige curtains, brass curtain poles and comfy-looking twin beds adorned with beige duvets and gold sashes. Stylish was an understatement. The whole apartment resembled a show home.

Later, Helen and I settled ourselves onto the L shaped sofa whilst Claire sat on the opposite one and we sipped our tea. Even though the apartment was big and airy it was also cosy, and the electric fire was a welcome addition.

'Are you ready for tomorrow then?' I asked Claire.

'Yes, I think so. Melanie's staying at John and Sarah's tonight so you won't see her till tomorrow. Everything's organised. Everyone we sent invitations to for the reception is coming so that's great. There should be about a hundred people. Then on Saturday morning we fly to Lanzarote for the week.' Claire stared into space for a moment before coming back down to earth and remembering she had guests. 'How long are you staying for?'

'We need to be going on Tuesday,' I replied.

'Yes, I need to get back to the shop really. Vera doesn't mind looking after the place and she does a good job I admit, but it's hard leaving it in someone else's hands for too long. She means well but I've known her give credit to the locals when she's been looking after it, and she even took six boxes of Milk Tray off the shelf once and handed them out at the pub on quiz night, said they were prizes!'

Claire and I laughed. I could just imagine Mrs. McCraikie doing that with her kind heart and big warm smile.

'Thing is, it means my books don't balance properly at the end of the month and I end up making up the difference out of any profit I make. I don't like telling her because she's so kind for helping me out.'

'Oh Helen, what are you like?' I laughed. 'You might have to tell her if she keeps giving your stock away.'

'Nah, she's a kind old bat with nothing else to do. Being in charge of the church flowers is about all she does these days, and taking part in the pub quiz of course.'

'So, what's happening with Steve?' Claire looked at me over her cup, her eyes staring with intrigue.

'Well, we're meeting up on Saturday like I told you and guess we'll take it from there.'

'He's welcome to stay if he were to change his mind.' Claire put her cup down and lifted her legs onto the sofa.

'I don't think he will, Claire. I'd love him to but from the sounds of it, it's just going to be too difficult.'

Helen piped up. 'Are you still okay with me staying at the spa hotel for the night? I can cancel it if you want some company.'

'No, not at all. You go and have a good night out. I know how much you're looking forward to it. I'll be fine here.' I looked up at the plasma. 'I might even hire a porn movie and a bottomless bucket of popcorn.'

In hysterics, we just about managed to drink our tea. 'Do you fancy a takeaway tonight or shall I cook something?' Claire asked.

'Takeaway for me,' I said, looking at Helen again for her opinion.

'Yep, that'll be great. And I'm buying.'

Claire and I tried to object but Helen insisted. She was adamant to treat us as I'd driven and Claire was letting us stay so she felt she had to do her bit. I didn't mention the ten bottles of Beaujolais and the huge bottle of Southern Comfort that she'd so kindly brought and no doubt would be paying for out of next month's profit.

****

The Chinese was delivered at seven pm and we sat at the dining table, Claire with chop sticks, Helen and I with a knife and fork, our skills not quite reaching to a balancing act with knitting needles. After supper I did Claire's nails for her, a gorgeous metallic red that complimented her tanned hands. She blew gently on them as she lifted them up and admired them. Then it was my turn and I placed my hands onto the table cloth while Helen opened the bottle of glittery brown varnish, gently stroking it on with precision.

It couldn't have happened at a worse time. My mobile started to ring and the name 'Steve' flashed on the screen. I asked Helen to answer it for me and tell him I'd ring back shortly. She picked up the phone and pressed the call button.

'Hi, Steve, it's Helen here. Rachel's just having her nails done and she can't hold the phone.' I cringed. 'Sure, will do. She shouldn't be long. Bye.' She pressed the call button again and put it back on the table next to me. 'He said he'll wait for you to ring him back when you're ready but said to tell you he's sat in his car.'

'Thanks, Helen. He'll be at the golf club no doubt. You guys don't mind if I pop into the bedroom to ring him do you?'

Both Helen and Claire shook their heads. 'You don't want us listening to you whispering sweet nothings to each other.' Claire laughed, still blowing on her nails.

Helen finished the job, topped up all our glasses, passed me mine then handed me my mobile phone as well. 'Shall I dial for you?' she asked. I gratefully accepted her offer and then carefully took the phone from her before walking into the bedroom. I sat on the bed and leaned against the headboard as Steve answered.

'Sorry about that,' I said. 'Was in mid varnish.'

'Can't wait for you to run those varnished nails along my chest,' he said, sending the usual shivers up and down my spine. 'You obviously got there okay. Was it a good journey?'

'A great journey, hardly any traffic once we got over the Forth Road Bridge. A build up at Newcastle but that was all really. Where are you?'

'Golf club. I've just come out for an hour to ring you, but I might pop in and do a few rounds at the range. I see Pete's here, I'm parked next to him.'

'Everything still okay for Saturday then?'

'Yes, definitely, love. I'll be at Nightingale Woods in our usual spot at one o'clock. That okay with you?'

'Of course it is. I wonder if it's changed since we were last there.'

'It has, yes,' Steve answered matter of fact. 'They've built some new houses there in the last ten years, and a hotel I think. I haven't been back; well, not after the few times I went after we split up, but I remember seeing it advertised in the Manchester Life. It brought a tear to my eyes at the time.'

'I hope our little lay-by is still there. What should we do if it isn't?'

'We could maybe meet at the Plough and Horses and just go to the woods in one car? Would that be better do you think?'

'I reckon so, then maybe if it's really cold and wet we could have a drink in the pub rather than sit in the car.'

'I can't make love to you in the pub.' I could sense Steve smirking on the other end of the phone.

'You can't make love to me in the car in broad daylight either,' I chuckled. 'I thought you might have time to come back here. I know you can't stay overnight but I was hoping you might manage a couple of hours or something?'

'Let's see what happens on Saturday, love. It might be a gorgeous day and perfect for a walk through the woods. I don't need to be back until evening but let's wait and see.'

I could feel my mood deflating and my heart crying out in disappointment. I still hoped Steve would change his mind about staying the night but it didn't look like he even wanted to come back to Claire's. I'd been telling myself ever since we arranged to meet, that even to spend an hour with him would have been perfect, but after the three large glasses of wine I'd had in the last hour, I was feeling brave and willing myself to say something.

'Steve, I'm really looking forward to seeing you. I'd really hoped that you'd come back here for a while. Can't you do something?'

He went quiet and I imagined him pulling a face and staring out of the car window. Eventually he spoke. 'I promise I'll try my best to get away for as long as possible. I really am looking forward to seeing you.'

I couldn't think of much else to say to him after I once again mulled over that feeling of distrust. He sent his best wishes to Claire and Melanie and told me to have a great time at the wedding. Then we hung up.

The rest of the evening was spent painting Helen's nails, finishing off a second bottle of wine and watching a trashy film on Sky television. I think Claire and Helen knew something was wrong when I went back to join them but neither said anything. I guess they'd got used to me being disappointed by Steve.

CHAPTER NINETEEN

Claire and Melanie's big day arrived. Helen and I got up at eight o'clock to find Claire in the kitchen leaning against the island with her hands cupped around a mug of coffee. She didn't even notice us walk towards her. It was lovely and warm in the apartment and the fire was on full. The curtains at the French windows were still closed.

'Any coffee left or have you drunk it all?' I smiled.

'Bloody hell, I never saw you come in. Good morning, did you sleep well?' Claire put the mug down and poured us both a coffee from the percolator.

'Very well thanks,' I replied. 'How about you?'

She passed us both a mug of coffee and went into the lounge to sit on the L shaped sofa. 'I got to sleep eventually. Didn't think I'd be this nervous. What's wrong with me?' She tried to make light of it by offering us a fake grin.

'You're getting married, love, and it's a big thing. It's not surprising you're nervous.'

'Were you nervous when you were marrying Christopher?'

'Very,' I replied, with complete honesty. 'It was a lovely day but I didn't enjoy the build-up much because I was petrified something would go wrong.' I looked over at Helen who was nursing her mug of coffee. 'What about you, Helen, were you nervous on your wedding day?'

Helen looked through me for a moment then adjusted her vision. 'Not really,' she said. 'I wasn't that bothered about getting married but Derek kept harping on that it wasn't right we lived in sin. He came from a very religious family, though you wouldn't have known it. His mum wasn't keen on us just living together so we did it because we felt it was the right thing to do.'

'You got married abroad didn't you?' I asked.

'Yes, in St. Lucia. It was very romantic but it didn't feel like a proper wedding. Our parents were there but we didn't know the priest or the witnesses and it was just like a day on the beach with us wearing fancy clothes. Bit pointless really when you think we got divorced a few years later because he wanted to move and I didn't.' She seemed to be staring into space again. 'Still, that's all in the past now and I'm quite happy being on my own.'

'I would have got married abroad,' Claire said, much to my surprise. 'When Melanie and I went to the register office to fill in the forms, the woman behind reception was really rude. She stared at us both up and down then said, "you're getting married to each other?" in a nasty, patronising way, stupid old bitch. That made Melanie more determined.'

'But you want to get married as well don't you, Claire?'

'Oh, God yes, more than anything. But I just wish Melanie would have agreed to a beach wedding where we could have just been ourselves and not feel embarrassed about having a good snog after the ceremony. Somewhere like Benidorm would have suited me.'

'Benidorm?' I scoffed. 'I never knew you liked Benidorm. Thought you'd be more a five star paradise island girl.'

'Oh, I am,' Claire confirmed. 'But Benidorm's a fabulous place. It's so liberated. Every time Melanie and I have been there we've felt so included, you know, comfortable walking down the street holding hands and kissing in public. There's the fabulous old town where all the gay bars are and it's bloody awesome. Anything goes in Benidorm.'

I looked at Helen and grinned. 'We'll have to go, flower.'

She laughed at me. 'Tell me when and I'll book the tickets.'

Claire looked at her watch for the hundredth time since we'd been sat down drinking our coffee. 'In six and a half hours, I'll be a married woman,' she pointed out. 'I never thought I'd say that. I wonder how Melanie is. Wish I could ring her.' She looked at the portable phone which sat on a table near the French windows. 'Do you think it would be bad luck if I rang her?'

'Yes,' I said, smiling. 'She'll be fine. She's probably as nervous as you and sat at John's right now on their sofa drinking really strong coffee after a night on the lash.'

'I imagine she got wasted last night. They went into town for an Indian then onto a few clubs. Well, that was the intention. She'd better not turn up with a hangover.'

'Claire, stop panicking. Like you say, in six and a half hours you'll be a married woman, and so will Melanie. Now stop being nervous and let's enjoy the biggest day of your life. Go and get in the bath for an hour, pamper yourself whilst Helen and I make some brekkie.' I stood up, collected our empty mugs and carried them into the kitchen.

'Right, I'm going. If Melanie rings bring me the phone will you. I don't believe in all that superstition bollocks anyway.' Claire made a retreat for the bathroom, a smile etched on her pretty face as she mentioned Melanie's name.

She'd been an absolute godsend to me during the rubbish I went through with Christopher. She'd been the only one person I could truly talk to about how I felt. She understood totally every time I turned up at their little poky flat in Edminbury where they used to live before moving to the docks. Melanie used to give Claire and I space to talk, as though she was the man in the relationship and felt a need to make a quick exit to the pub whenever the girls got together. She'd often dish out advice and was as much of a friend to me as Claire but because Claire and I had known each other for such a long time, plus she'd been through all the heartbreak with me when Steve went back to Olivia, it was always as if we had a very special bond, one that nobody could ever break.

I knew she'd be happy with Melanie, but when she'd told me about being keen on one of the new houses in Cornfield I felt a bit sad for her. Much more of a townie than me, I was sure she'd get used to the different way of life eventually, though I could never imagine Melanie would.

Helen sat and read a magazine whilst I made us some bacon butties. I took one into Claire who was sat emerged in a mass of white bubbles, the mirror completely steamed up along with the little square window. She reached out her hand and took the plate and I left a mug of coffee on the toilet seat.

We spent the rest of the morning chilling out on the sofas, watching daytime television and sipping champagne. We agreed not to drink too much as it was inevitable that none of us would be in any fit state to even get into the limousine when it arrived at half past two, which it did, promptly.

A beautiful white elongated limo sat outside the main entrance to the apartment building whilst the three of us piled into it, trying hard not to spoil our hair or get any marks on our outfits. Claire looked stunning in her ivory suit. I'd forgotten how beautiful she was. Her slim figure together with her tanned skin and delicious eyes could turn any man's head, and she definitely knew it. But 'coming out' had been something Claire had needed to do for a long time, especially after the guy she had an affair with went back to his wife and left her devastated. She'd told me often that she was kidding herself thinking about men in *that* way and she would never fancy another man even if women ceased to exist.

We sat in the back of the limo as the driver took us slowly in to Manchester city centre, drawing up outside the register office. He stopped outside the stone steps then got out and came round to open the back door. Helen got out first, followed by Claire and then me. Melanie and her cousin, John, were standing at the top of the steps near the doorway, Melanie looking particularly glamorous in her ivory trouser suit. Next to Melanie's cousin stood a young woman whom was later introduced to us as Sarah, John's wife.

Helen and I shook hands with them both then gave Melanie a little peck on the cheek. I'd never seen her looking so beautiful and could definitely see why Claire called her 'sex on legs'. The two of them kissed then walked arm in arm towards the foyer where we were all greeted by a middle aged woman with a clipboard looking very official and a little bit too serious considering it was a wedding. We were ushered into a small room with a large desk situated against a wall, a gorgeous bouquet of ivory and red roses displayed on a round table and lots of official looking paperwork, together with an enormous book.

The ceremony didn't take long but it was very personal and Claire and Melanie were given a chance to recite the vows they had written for each other. Rings were exchanged as was a lingering kiss, then they signed the enormous book and a few other pieces of paper before the middle aged woman opened the door and watched us all walk through. Helen and I threw a bit of confetti over Claire and Melanie as we got to the steps and then we took some photographs.

The meal at The Staffordshire Hotel was delicious. They'd pulled out all the stops and really gone to town with everything. My fillet steak was done to perfection as were Helen's chicken fillets. I sat next to Sarah at the restaurant and discovered what a lovely lady she is. Only thirty-three with a great job in the city centre and a desire to start a family, though, as she pointed out, John wasn't that bothered about babies so she was pretty sure if they did have one it would be left to her to do all the childcare and she'd have to give up her fantastic job.

After our amazing meal, full to the brim, we all moved into the Tamworth Suite where the reception was to be held. We had a half hour to kill before everyone started to arrive so took the opportunity to refresh our makeup and have a nosy at Claire and Melanie's honeymoon suite which was absolutely out of this world. A giant four poster bed was pushed up against one wall, beautiful sash windows overlooked the lush garden where a fountain bellowed out water into a small pond. The bathroom was a suite in itself with a huge, double corner Jacuzzi bath, separate shower and tons of really expensive-looking toiletries. Melanie had already hung Claire's going-away outfit in the wardrobe after taking it with her when she stayed at John and Sarah's house. They'd all been to the hotel prior to meeting us at the register office, had a large bouquet of flowers put in the room together with pink champagne and Claire's favourite bottle of perfume, J'Adore. It was all very romantic.

I couldn't help thinking about Steve when I walked into their suite, wondering that if we ever did get together and marry one day, I'd want just the same as this. It made me miss him. I hadn't thought about him much during the day which actually surprised me as I'd been half expecting to start crying over him during the ceremony, wishing it had been him and me getting married. But I was just so happy for Claire and Melanie that I hadn't given Steve much thought. Now however, I remembered our arranged rendezvous for the following day at Nightingale Woods and could feel tears pricking the backs of my eyes. I wished he could have come to the wedding, or at least the reception. There would be no one there he knew but I couldn't have asked Claire and Melanie, I wasn't going to put them on the spot like that.

People started filtering into the Tamworth Suite at half past seven and all the food arrived at half past eight with six waitresses setting it out on the buffet table whilst another three waitresses walked around the room with glasses of champagne on silver trays, offering them to the guests. The disco was excellent, playing mostly 80's music which we all loved. I was overwhelmed to see so many lovely people in one room, a lot of them being Claire and Melanie's work colleagues and lots of their gay friends who they'd met over the years in the gay community. By midnight, we all joined hands and made a tunnel for Claire and Melanie to run through before turning back to us, waving, blowing kisses and running out of the room. Their luxurious suite and Jacuzzi bath awaited them.

CHAPTER TWENTY

Helen and I were exhausted the next day. We woke up at ten am and almost screamed when we looked at the clock. My head was a bit delicate and I'd gone to bed without taking my makeup off but I had a day with my lover to look forward to and didn't have time to be hung-over. Helen made us some toast and coffee while I was in the shower, scrubbing the panda eyes and getting rid of all the hairspray from the previous day. I wolfed down the toast before cleaning my teeth and applying fresh makeup then dried my hair. Helen had a little overnight bag packed ready for her stay at the spa hotel. After a sit down and a recap about the wedding, recollecting Claire and Melanie's wonderfully camp friends, not to mention the two lesbians who thought Helen and I were on the pull, we set off for the hotel where Helen was going to spend the night.

'Have a lovely time,' she said to me, leaning against the car. 'Do be careful, Rachel. Ring me if you need me. I'll get a taxi and come straight back if anything goes wrong.'

'You have a lovely time, too. I'll pick you up tomorrow morning at about eleven.'

She turned on her heels and walked up the elegant steps towards the main entrance and I drove back down the drive towards the main road that would eventually lead me to The Plough and Horses.

It was just after one when I arrived at the pub. Steve's car was parked up under some trees in the corner and he got out when he saw me driving towards him. He wore a grey shirt underneath a black jumper, with black trousers. He looked every bit as handsome as I'd always known him to be, and he looked thrilled to see me. I pulled up in the space next to his car and he came round to open my door for me.

'Hi,' he said, a broad smile etched on his face. Then he bent down and kissed me. I melted in the seat.

'Shall we go to the woods in my car?' I asked. It was a beautiful day and I looked forward to a stroll.

He nodded and walked around to the passenger side then got in and put his seatbelt on. 'I can't believe we're back here. It's like we've gone back in time.' It wasn't a question, just a statement that I agreed with, nodding as I reversed out of the space. 'How was the wedding?'

'It was fantastic. They looked beautiful; I've never seen Melanie look so glam before. She and Claire make the perfect couple.' I pulled onto the main road and drove the hundred yards to the entrance which led to Nightingale Woods.

The sight before me found me in shock as I tried hard to remember how it used to look yet was now inundated with large houses and people out washing their cars. It had totally changed.

'It's different isn't it?' Steve said, as I turned down the little lane that led into the woods. 'I know there's a hotel down here somewhere so it's not going to be as private as it used to be.'

'It sure is different. I can't believe it. What have they done to our beautiful love nest?'

Steve laughed a shallow laugh. 'Not much of a love nest now I reckon.'

I drove further down the lane and was grateful when the houses seemed to stop and the woods finally came into view. Our lay-by now had a post box erected and there wasn't anywhere to stop the car so I drove on a little and pulled up in a small clearing that seemed to have evolved, probably by courting couples. I put the handbrake on and turned off the engine then looked at Steve.

'Shall we have a walk or don't you want to stay?'

There was pure love in his eyes. 'Let's have a little walk,' he said. 'I have something to tell you.'

I hated it when he said those words to me, they usually ended with me crying into a Southern Comfort on my own and him walking away for seventeen years. We got out of the car and pressed the central locking system on the key fob then he reached for my hand, held it and kissed the back of it for what felt like a very long time.

'It hasn't changed much in this part,' he said, still holding my hand, his other hand keeping warm in his pocket. 'I reckon they haven't touched this part of the woods. If we're lucky our little clearing might still be there.'

We *were* lucky. It was still there which I thought was a bloody miracle after seeing all those newly built houses. Fortunately, it was dry and we sat on the ground, leaves crunching under us. He put his arm around my shoulder and pulled me into him, kissing the top of my head before I pulled away and looked into his eyes. Then he kissed me again; a long, romantic and very passionate kiss that would quite easily have led to us making love if we'd been in my cottage.

'What is it you need to tell me?' I asked, half wishing I hadn't.

'It's big.'

'How big?'

'Very big. Or at least it could be.'

I sighed heavily then moved away from him a little, giving him a chance to tell me what he needed to without being distracted by our bodies touching.

'It's Olivia,' he said. I thought as much.

'What about Olivia?'

'She wants to move away. She wants to emigrate.' I raised my eyebrows and he continued. 'Susan and Keith are moving to Spain. They've been talking about it for a while now and have decided that Sonia and Jake are at a good age to make the move. Anyway, Olivia thinks it'll be a good idea if we move as well. They've bought a plot of land and are having a villa with a pool built on it. There's another plot of land next door to theirs for sale and Olivia's really keen to sell up and buy it.'

He was right, it was big.

'And is that what you want?' It was another question I dreaded hearing the answer to.

'No, it's not. I don't want to live in Spain, love. I'm happy in this country. I've lived in Great Willowby for more than forty years now and I wouldn't mind moving, but not out of the UK.'

'Have you told Olivia how you feel?'

'Not really. She's only just started talking about it. I didn't want to tell you over the phone. She first mentioned it when we went out a few weeks ago with Susan and Keith. I nearly choked on my pint.'

'So what are you going to do?' Either this would mean him and Olivia would go their separate ways or she'd just have to accept that he didn't want to move and stay over here. Either way, I wasn't sure how it affected me.

'I don't know yet, love. It depends on how keen Olivia is to move.'

'If you move to Spain it'll mean the end of us.' I wasn't annoyed, but I was a bit frustrated at his indecision.

'I'm not moving to Spain.' He sounded pretty adamant.

'And what if Olivia insists?'

'Then we'll separate. She can move to Spain on her own. She'll be with Susan and the grandchildren so it's not like she'll be completely on her own.'

'And if that happens, if she moves without you, what will you do?'

'What would *you* like me to do?'

I stared at him. What was he asking me? My heart was beating so loudly I'm sure he would have heard it. I wasn't prepared to let him break my heart again, even though I was fully prepared for the fact that he might try.

'I think you know the answer to that,' I replied.

'Then I'll come and live with you, in Cornfield. I honestly don't think Olivia will care if I didn't go with her anyway, in fact a part of me thinks this could be an excuse for her to be rid of me. She doesn't love me, Rachel, not like she used to. And she knows I don't love her in that way either. Our marriage was over when you and I split up; she knows that as well as I do. It's never mended and it never will and I think Susan moving to Spain is the excuse Olivia needs to leave.'

'I don't know what to say, Steve. You know how I feel about you and you also know that I'd let you come and live with me tomorrow. But I'm not letting you make false promises and I won't build my hopes up again about us getting together.' I tried to stay calm whilst feeling like my head was going to explode. 'You need to sort this out and quick.'

Steve lifted my face to his and stared lovingly into my eyes. 'I will sort it out, and that's a solemn promise.'

'What happens if Olivia says she won't move and will stay here so you can stay together?'

'She's got her heart pretty much set on moving, but if she does decide not to then I can't answer that question right now.'

It was happening all over again. Claire had said he was capable of breaking my heart again and she was right.

'I love you, Steve, I always will. But I'm not that girl I used to be. I've grown up. I've been through a lot over the years and I'm not prepared to waste my life away on a married man anymore with a slim chance he'll leave his wife. It just isn't going to happen.' I shuffled in my place. The leaves once more crunched beneath me. 'It's my turn to give the ultimatum. Two weeks. I need to know in two weeks what you're planning to do. It's either Olivia or me. I can't be the other woman again, Steve, no matter how much I love you. I won't settle for being second best in your life, not when I love you as much as I do.'

He pulled me back into him, caressing my hair and kissing the top of my head. 'I understand, love, and I promise you, one way or another, this will be sorted out in two weeks, if not sooner.'

'When do you have to get back?' I asked.

'I don't,' was his reply. 'I've told Olivia I'm at the golf club for the day then having a few drinks with the men as one of them is leaving, which isn't a lie because he's moving down south. I said if I have too much to drink I'll hire a room for the night at the hotel and will be back tomorrow morning.'

I sat up, elation overwhelming my expression no doubt. 'So are you staying for the night with me then?'

'It looks like it,' he said, smiling at me like the cat that'd got the cream.

'Well, I never imagined the day would come. I'm thrilled. Will you have to ring her and tell her you're not going home?'

'No.' He held my hands in his. 'Rachel, you don't seem to be getting it. Olivia doesn't care where I am. Our marriage is a farce, a habit that's kept us together all these years. I don't doubt she'll be hurt if she knows I'm with you but I honestly believe she's just waiting for the excuse to leave me.'

'Are you hoping she'll find out about us again?'

'If she does then our marriage will definitely be over anyway. But the way things are now, with her wanting to move to Spain and all, one way or another we need to do something drastic. I don't want to hurt her, I do care about her, love, and in my own way I still love her.' He sighed loudly and held me a little tighter. 'But tonight I'm going to be with you and I can't wait to make love to you.'

I couldn't believe what I was hearing. Determined not to build my hopes up about him living in Cornfield with me, I decided to start enjoying the day we had laid out before us, and was determined to make the night truly magical.

CHAPTER TWENTY-ONE

We had a meal at the Plough and Horses. Even if there had been people in there I knew, I'm sure they wouldn't have recognised me after seventeen years, and Steve didn't know anyone in that area so we felt quite safe. It was a pleasant change to be able to sit anywhere in the pub rather than huddling ourselves into a discreet corner, and Steve made a point of holding my hand above the table, which I thought was particularly brave. He'd changed somehow. He wasn't the secretive Steve anymore; the man I felt was constantly on edge. He seemed more comfortable with me in a public place.

The waiter brought our meals to us, smiling broadly as he placed them on the table. My chicken in mushroom sauce was delicious as was Steve's gammon and pineapple.

'Did you want to go out somewhere tonight?' Steve asked, just before putting a large piece of gammon into his mouth.

'Not really, we may as well make the most of having Claire and Melanie's place to ourselves.'

'That's good then. I'll stop off at an off licence and get a bottle of something nice.'

'There's no need. Helen brought plenty of wine down with us and Claire said we could help ourselves to anything in the cabinet. It's like a bar, you should see it.'

'It's really good of them to let us stay there together isn't it?' He took a swig of his bitter.

'They're happy for me, Steve. They know how I feel about you and they're both just glad that I'm enjoying myself.'

'I thought they'd have been warning you off me. I know Claire wasn't too fond of me when we worked at Winterson's.'

I was surprised at his revelation. 'I always thought you got on well with Claire?'

'We did, to an extent. But I always got the impression she thought you were far too good for me. Well, you were.' He lifted his eyebrows. 'You still are,' he added.

'Don't be daft. I'm sure she didn't think that. She just cares about me and she doesn't want me to get hurt. But she knows I'm a different person now, not that young and gullible woman I used to be.'

'I've no intention of hurting you, Rachel.' Steve put his knife and fork down and reached for my hand again. 'You do believe that, don't you?'

I wanted to believe it.

'Yes, I guess so. But neither of us can know what's going to happen can we? I mean, with what you've told me today, how do I know whether you're going to change your mind and move to Spain?' I put my knife and fork down too and let Steve caress my hand. 'Surely you'll miss Susan and the kids? You might not think you'll miss Olivia but I bet you will if she moves abroad. Have you really thought this through?'

I had a terrible habit of asking questions I really didn't want to know the answer to. But this one was important. There was a part of me that doubted Steve, for some reason. And I couldn't help but think he'd cave in to Olivia once again, only this time before moving a few thousand miles away to another country.

'That's why we need to talk about it, love. I'm not going to stop Olivia if she really wants to go, but she needs to understand that I don't. I'm not happy being with her and I'm not prepared to spend the rest of my life living in a country I don't want to live in, with a woman I don't want to be with. I've spent too long now being pulled along and it's time it stopped.'

I stared at him. Being assertive had never been his strong point but his little statement made me realise that it wasn't just me who'd changed over the years.

'And if she decides not to go and stay here with you?'

'We'll cross that bridge when *and if* we come to it.' He took his hand away from mine and carried on eating. I got the impression it was my cue to change the subject.

****

We got back to the apartment at five o'clock. It was already dark and the dockside was beautifully lit up. I led Steve to the first floor and opened the door, watching him gasp at the contemporary style of the apartment. He took off his coat and hung it up in the hallway before following me into the living area. I placed my handbag on the kitchen island then went over to the L shaped sofa to join him. He was already sat down staring at the plasma TV like a kid in a sweetshop.

'How long have they lived here?' he asked.

'I think it's about four years now. Gorgeous isn't it?'

'I'm not sure I'd use the word gorgeous, but it's certainly got appeal. Not really my kind of pad if I'm honest, I prefer something more, err, well, like your cottage.'

'What? Old, musty and poky?' I laughed.

'It's not poky, it's beautiful. It'd probably be a squeeze if there was a family of four living in it but just for you it's perfect.'

I imagined for a few seconds Steve and I living in the cottage, but it wasn't a thought that I relished for too long. I'd promised myself I wouldn't build my hopes up and that was exactly what I was doing. I banished the little scene from my mind, stood up and went to open a bottle of wine.

'Is red okay?' I asked, standing with a bottle of Beaujolais in one hand and a corkscrew in the other.

'Perfect,' he replied. 'Can I switch this television on?'

'Sure. The remote's on the coffee ...' but he'd already found it and was examining the buttons.

'I haven't brought my glasses. Is that the right button?' He pointed to it.

'You wear glasses now?'

'Yes, been wearing them for about ten years. Just for reading.'

'Here.' I took the remote off him and pointed to the correct buttons.

For the next hour we sat on the sofa, snuggled up to each other, while Steve flicked through the channels to see which one would give the best 'plasma effect' as he called it. He eventually settled on a football match but I quickly grabbed the remote and switched it off.

'You can get lost,' I said, putting the remote back on the table. 'There's no way I'm sitting watching football on our special night together!'

'What do you want to do instead?' He asked, a mischievous sparkle in his eyes

'How about a game of scrabble?' I suggested.

'How about I show you how much I've missed you?'

'I reckon you've got a deal.' I kissed him softly, noticing the bulge in his pants as I leaned against him. 'Shall I close the curtains?'

****

I'd already pushed the twin beds together in the spare room and made them up with fresh bedding that Claire had left out; king size bottom sheets and duvet that made the bed look like a double. Steve laughed when he first realised they were twin beds and joked about one of us falling into the middle and landing on the floor. But I was too concentrated on the pleasure that was going to happen; the way he put his arms around my neck and kissed me, gently forcing me onto the beds before he placed his hand underneath my jumper. He slid the jumper over my head, admiring my black lacy bra with excited eyes, before turning his attention to my jeans, undoing the belt, the button and the zip. My whole body was alight. How many first times can one couple have?

'Do you like what I bought with your birthday vouchers?' I ran my hand over the bra.

'It's incredible.' They were the only words he could speak before he unhooked it and threw it onto the floor.

Making love felt so pure, a little mixture of lust stirred in, but a desperate portion of absolute, unconditional love. When he rolled over and lay beside me, I don't think I'd ever felt so happy. If he wasn't going to leave Olivia after that, I resigned myself to believing that he never would and I should go back to being Rachel Phillips, mid-forties, single and living alone. It would have been hard to go back to the old Rachel, but I knew I had no choice if it came to it. Even the intensity that I felt for Steve right there and then wasn't going to allow me to have my heart broken should he decide we couldn't work. I knew my future held in the balance, but I had more confidence within me that I would bring to the surface if our relationship once more failed. Maybe it was the stronger Rachel that was turning Steve on so much, for within ten minutes he wanted me again, still erect and burning with desire as he caressed my breasts with his tongue and separated my legs with his hand.

****

It was half past ten when we woke up, still clinging to each other and feeling pretty knackered after the couple of hours we'd spent pleasing one another. I lifted myself from underneath Steve's arm and looked at the clock before turning back to see him open his eyes.

'Shall I make some coffee?' I asked.

'What time is it?'

'Half past ten.'

'Is that all, I thought it was the middle of the night!' He sat up and kissed me softly on my forehead. 'I'd love a coffee.'

'We can sit on the sofa if you like. Seeing you satisfied me so much I think I'll let you watch Match of the Day, it should be coming on about now.' I got up and reached for the dressing gown that Claire had left hanging on the door. It wasn't very flattering but I couldn't be bothered getting dressed again.

'That sounds just the ticket.' Steve got up and put his boxer shorts on. 'Is there a spare dressing gown?'

I opened a few wardrobes but couldn't find anything so he put his clothes back on.

'Right, coffee then. I'll leave you to play with the telly.' He followed me into the lounge and settled himself down on the sofa, reaching for the remote and turning the television on.

I made some coffee and went to join him, tucking myself underneath his arm. I couldn't help asking, 'Are you going to ring Olivia?'

He shook his head. 'No, I'll leave it. She'll assume I'm staying over at the hotel. She won't ask questions.'

But I needed to ask a question that was eating away at me and I knew I wouldn't be able to settle until I knew the answer for definite.

'Steve, are you hoping Olivia will find out about us? Is that why you're not bothering to ring her?'

He turned to me and stroked my face. 'I've already told you, love. I'm not sure it'll matter if she does find out now, it'll give her the excuse to end our marriage.'

'Would you feel better if *she* ended it and not you?'

He sighed and turned back to the telly. 'Do we have to talk about Olivia tonight? Let's enjoy the time we have.'

I decided not to pursue the questioning anymore and snuggled underneath his arm again. He was right; there was no point in wasting the time we had together talking about his wife. She was, after all, a subject I'd much rather didn't exist.

CHAPTER TWENTY-TWO

W e went to bed just after midnight as I was struggling to keep my eyes open though the thought of sleeping next to Steve was starting to turn me on again as we made our way to the bedroom. I cleaned my teeth then snuggled under the duvet and waited for him to finish in the bathroom. He came into the bedroom and stripped down to his boxer shorts. I'd already put my new nightie on, a knee length, half see through negligee type with lots of lace and a little bit of detail near the cleavage. He admired it as I lay in bed before putting his hand up it and satisfying me once more. Then we held each other, had a long lingering kiss and went to sleep.

The alarm clock went off at half past seven and I turned over to see the bed empty on Steve's side. A little panic rose within me as I suddenly thought he might have gone. I looked on the pillow and the dressing table for a possible note but couldn't see one. I shot out of bed, grabbed the dressing gown and bolted into the open plan living area.

'Good morning!' he said cheerfully, comfortably entertaining himself on the sofa as he watched the television. My heart slowed down and I went over to him, sat in just his boxer shorts with a blanket thrown over this shoulders. 'I didn't want to wake you, you looked so peaceful.'

'I thought you'd left,' I said, a smile trying hard to find its way to my lips. 'Would you like some breakfast? There's bacon and eggs, or I can make bacon butties?'

'Bacon butties sound perfect. And some of that coffee as well, please.'

We ate the butties and drank the coffee whilst Steve kept flicking through the channels again. An hour later he stood up and took my hands.

'Fancy having a shower with me?' he asked, a huge grin on his face.

I loved this new easy-going side of Steve that I hadn't really experienced before, not to its full potential like this. He didn't even seem in a hurry to get home, in fact I half expected him to say he'd come home with me when I went back on Tuesday. It was of course rather disappointing when he finally got dressed and jangled his car keys whilst standing in the hallway.

'I'll miss that plasma,' he joked. 'One of those is definitely on my Christmas list.'

I couldn't laugh at his joke because if he were to get a plasma TV for Christmas it would most likely mean he'd decided to stay with Olivia in Great Willowby. It would have been a struggle to have a television quite so big fixed to the wall in my low ceilinged living room. I pretended I wasn't really listening.

'Are you going straight home?' I asked, looking up into his beautiful blue eyes.

'Yes, I suppose so. What time are you leaving on Tuesday?'

'We'll be setting off early I think, probably about nine. Helen wants to get back mid-afternoon to relieve Mrs. McCraikie.'

'I'm going to miss you, love.' I don't think he could have said it with more sadness in his tone.

I held him, tighter than I've ever held him before and I noticed he did the same. That awful feeling was washing over me; the one that makes me dread the next moment. I wanted to beg him to stay, to move back to Scotland with me, leave Olivia and be mine. But I couldn't. I wasn't going to throw my dignity out of the window after all I'd promised myself. And I don't think he would have respected me anymore should I have flung myself at him.

'Ring me,' I said, through tears that were fighting to fall. 'Let me know what happens re the Spain thing. I need to know, Steve. Please don't leave me hanging.'

He looked into my eyes. 'I'll never leave you hanging, Rachel. This isn't like it was before. We're both different people now and I've realised these past few months that I can't have it both ways. You've been patient with me and I love you for that, but I'm not going to take advantage of you.' He kissed me. 'I'll ring you as soon as Olivia and I have talked about it. And I want you to ring me on Tuesday so I know you got home safe.'

'I will. I love you, Steve Harris, no matter what happens. I'll always love you.'

He turned and opened the front door without looking back. I closed it gently after him then sunk to the floor and sobbed like a child who'd just lost everything.

CHAPTER TWENTY-THREE

When I eventually got off the floor, I managed to drag myself into the lounge to grab my bag and car keys before going to pick Helen up from the hotel. I didn't want her to see that I'd been crying, it would only have led to the twenty questions and the lecture about me not allowing Steve to hurt me again. She was waiting in the foyer when I arrived and tottered down the steps to the car. I got out and took her overnight bag from her hand, placing it on the back seat.

She'd had an amazing time, was completely revitalised and did look incredibly healthy. Her hair was perfect, her makeup was perfect. In fact, everything about her looked radiant. I decided I'd be going to a spa hotel when we got back to Scotland.

'Well, how was it with Steve? Did he stay over?'

I drove along the main road back towards the docks. 'Yes,' I smiled. 'It was incredible. I've never enjoyed myself as much in my life.'

'Wow, sounds like you've had the best time. What's happening with him and his wife?'

'Let's get back and I'll tell you everything,' I said, revving the car a little, eager to get back to Claire's and make some lunch.

Helen nodded and smiled. 'Shall we stop off for lunch?

'Why don't we go out for a meal tonight instead? I'm completely knackered.'

Helen laughed. 'I thought you looked tired. That good, eh?!'

'Better,' I corrected her.

****

I spent the next few days trying hard not to let Helen see how crushed I was that Steve hadn't phoned me. I'm not sure why I expected him to ring that Saturday after he'd gone home, but I couldn't help feeling deflated after the wonderful time we'd just spent together. If Helen had picked up on my disappointment, she certainly didn't mention it. We went to Salford Quays on the Monday and had a great time looking around the shops and going to the cinema, then set off at nine o'clock on the Tuesday morning. We cleaned the apartment before we left and put some chocolates and wine in the fridge for Claire and Melanie.

That night, I did as Steve asked and rang his mobile but it went straight through to voice mail. I decided to send him a short text message instead; *'Got home at 3. Really miss u & wish u were here. Thx for a wonderful time on Saturday. Ring me when u can. Love u always, R x'*

I was sure once he'd got the message he'd ring me back but I wasn't going to sit next to the phone wishing for it to ring. He'll ring me when he can, I thought. But it was hard to concentrate on anything other than wanting him to ring me so at half past nine I went to bed. I was pretty tired anyway after the long drive and I'd promised Angela I'd be in work at nine o'clock the following morning.

****

'Good morning!' Angela chirped as I walked through the door. 'Did you have a lovely time at the wedding?'

'Hi, Angela. It was wonderful, absolutely amazing. It's been a fabulous weekend all round.' I put my bag in the back room then went back into the shop to have a root behind the counter and see what had been happening in my absence. 'How are things with you?'

'Oh Rachel, I've been dying to tell you. Gregory changed his mind about moving and we've put a deposit down on one of the new houses in Cornfield. We went down on Friday afternoon and he had the money transferred there and then. I can't believe it. We've bought one of the four bedroom ones.' Angela was beside herself with excitement.

'I'm thrilled for you,' I smiled, and I was. She worked so hard in the shop and deserved to have a nice home. 'So when will it be ready to move in to?'

'They're hoping they'll have all six ready by Easter next year. The show home will be open to the public as from February but it'll be left as a show home until the last one's sold. They're building six altogether but they said if they prove popular, Prenton will probably build a few more and might even build some three beds as well.'

'Well I for one am really chuffed that you'll be living in the village. It'll be good to welcome you to our little community.' I picked up some labels that needed attaching to a box of clothing items.

'I'm so excited. I've already started packing!'

'Angela, you're not moving for another four months at least,' I laughed, picking up a hideous looking skirt that was destined for the back of the rails.

'I'm not bothered. If Gregory sees how excited I am, there's no chance he'll change his mind again.' She busied herself by putting ornaments on a shelf until an elderly couple walked in and started browsing some hats. 'Good morning, if there's anything I can do to help, just ask,' came Angela's voice in full-on X-Factor style. They nodded a polite thank you and turned quickly back to the hats.

I left my mobile switched on in my handbag but it didn't ring. In fact, it didn't ring for ten days. I didn't even get a text message in reply to the one I'd sent Steve, though every time I got a text from Helen and Claire I braced myself, hoping it was from him and he was telling me he was moving in with me.

Claire rang me the day after they got back from Lanzarote. As was expected, they'd had a wonderful time in their five star villa and hadn't wanted to come home. They'd spent most of the week lounging about by the pool and trying out the clubs in town and I reckon were pretty knackered on their return.

It was the end of November and I have to admit I was nervous. I was also getting fed up of looking at my mobile phone to see if Steve had texted or phoned and I'd missed his call. Nothing. It was horrid and I was struggling to keep up the pretence in front of Helen. Even George noticed that I wasn't my usual self when we went to the Sunday night pub quiz.

'You offered me a chat, Rachel,' he said, as we got to my front door after he'd walked me home. 'Now I'm offering you one. You seem sad about something.'

I looked at his big brown eyes and his kind face. 'I'm lonely, George,' I said, not really sure why I'd suddenly blurted it out. Unfortunately, he got the wrong impression and put his arms around me, leaning in for a kiss. 'George!' I exclaimed, yanking myself away from his clutches. 'I'm not lonely for a man.'

'Oh shit, Rachel.' He was flushed with embarrassment. 'I'm so sorry. You know I find you attractive. I just thought you were, you know, asking me to come on to you, in a, sort of...'

'It's okay, George, forget it.' I smiled at him and felt awful that he was so embarrassed. 'Really. There's someone in my life that I can't stop thinking about and it's driving me crazy. I just don't know what to do about him.'

'Is this the guy who came to see you and you went for a walk in Jed's fields with?'

I stared at him.

'This is a small community, Rachel, people gossip.'

'Oh God, how stupid do I feel. Have people been talking about him behind my back?'

'Kind of. Reverend Holdsworthy mentioned he'd seen a tall, good looking man going into your cottage, oooh, way back in August I think it was. Hazel asked Vera McCraikie if I'd heard you were courting and she asked Andy. Obviously, no one knew and we didn't like asking Helen because by then we assumed you wanted to keep it secret and we'd only put her in a difficult position by asking.' I knew he meant well but I so wished they hadn't been gossiping about me. It made my relationship with Steve seem cheap somehow, and now they would be wondering why he'd never been back.

'He's called Steve. I've known him since the mid 90's. We had a very intense relationship back then but it didn't work out. Anyway, he came up to Tewsford for a holiday in August and we bumped into each other so I invited him back here a couple of times.' I fumbled with my key ring, trying to find the front door key and get away from a conversation I really wasn't sure I wanted to have.

'Is he married?'

Once more I stared at George, this time open mouthed.

'It's okay, love, I'm a man of the world. I've been around the block a few times though you probably know that already.'

'Yes, he is, and before you say anything, I haven't heard from him for nearly two weeks now when he said he'd call me, so I'm assuming the worst.'

'That he's not leaving his wife?'

I looked at the floor. 'Yes.'

'They rarely do, Rachel. I've had a few flings in my time but I'd never leave Hazel. She's been unfaithful too you know.'

I lifted my eyes to meet his. 'Hazel? Unfaithful? Bloody hell, George, I find that hard to believe. I always thought Hazel was prim and proper, a bit of a righteous cow sometimes. Hope you don't mind me saying that?'

'No, you can say anything to me. We love each other very much but we both have our faults. We keep the pub running and have a good life together and really, at our time of life, that's all we can ask for.'

'And what about Helen?' I asked. Now it was George's turn to look gobsmacked.

'Helen? Oh, she told you did she? Hazel was cut up about that but we got through it. Our marriage is healthy now and that's important to both of us.'

I wanted to invite George in for coffee as I was intrigued to learn more about this huge frame of a man whom I didn't find attractive at all yet was proving to be a good listener. But instead I put the key in the lock and opened the door, then turned to him and gave him a little peck on the cheek.

'Thanks for walking me home again, George. Why don't you come in for coffee sometime so that we can continue this chat? It's good to be able to talk to someone else about Steve, someone who doesn't know him and someone who isn't going to judge me for being the gullible idiot that I am.'

'You're not gullible. You're in love. You can't help your feelings for someone. If your Steve's got any sense, he'll be living here with you before Christmas. And if he's not, then you should say goodbye and move on with your life. You're still a young woman, Rachel, and a very beautiful one at that. You shouldn't let a man weigh you down with his indecisiveness.'

I closed the door and sat on the sofa for a while, thinking about everything George had just said. He spoke a lot of sense.

CHAPTER TWENTY-FOUR

I put my Christmas decorations up the first week of December after Helen said I should start forgetting about Steve Harris. The fact he hadn't rung me had made me angry and the sadness I felt was quickly subsiding. The tree looked stunning in my lounge, its multi-coloured fairy lights twinkling as the open fire crackled and spat in the grate. The weather was pretty dire and as usual we'd had several snow flurries that meant Helen was unable to restock the shop. Jed kindly took orders from everyone and he and his wife went into Tewsford in their Land Rover to pick up supplies for us all. Fortunately, the wagon was still able to get through to replenish supplies in the pub which meant we could still have our annual Christmas day get-together where we all took our own food and mucked in to make the perfect Christmas dinner. George and Hazel always supplied the booze and the three gigantic turkeys whilst the rest of the village did the rest.

It was the week before Christmas when my mobile phone rang and the name '*Steve*' flashed up on the screen. I was outside at the time, scooping snow from my driveway. My hands were freezing and I fumbled about with it, trying not to press the wrong button and cut him off. I was still a bit angry at the fact he hadn't rung me but I was starting to come to terms with the prospect of never seeing him or hearing from him again.

'Hello,' I said, making my way back to the house.

An angry yet somewhat controlled voice drifted into my ear. 'I know who you are and I know you've been having an affair with my husband. I just wanted to say that you're welcome to him.'

I stopped dead and almost dropped the phone. My heart leapt through my chest and I had to sit down on the cold step.

'I'm sorry?'

'My name is Olivia Harris and my husband is Steve. The fact that I hate the bastard and have done for many years is beside the point. He's all yours now. Though knowing Steve, now that the danger of me not knowing about you is over, he probably won't want you anymore. But personally, I couldn't give a toss.'

I struggled for the right words to reach the surface. 'What do you expect me to say?' Shock was penetrating through my body as I stuttered my words.

'You don't need to say anything. I've known all along that he's in love with you. All these years. I spent a long time thinking we might be able to make a go of it again but Steve's heart has never been in our marriage since he finished with you. I should have set him free years ago but I'm not leaving without what's rightfully mine.' She sighed. 'I don't want an argument with you and I don't want to meet you. I just wanted to say that I've set him free. I only hope he doesn't do to you what he did to me. Oh, and one other thing, he's got piles.'

My backside was numb as I sat on that stone step, staring at the phone when it went dead. I needed to speak to him, ask him what the hell was going on and why Olivia had rung from the phone he told me she never touched, trying to trick me into thinking it was him. I finally lifted myself up and went inside, taking off my snow-covered jacket and hat, and pulled off my wellies. What had just happened there? Why hadn't Steve told me that Olivia knew about us? And where the hell was he?

CHAPTER TWENTY-FIVE

I waited until Helen had closed the quickly diminishing shop then rang her and insisted she come over and bring some wine. She was on my doorstep within ten minutes, shaking her coat under the porch.

'Are you okay?' she asked, as I opened the door and moved aside to let her in.

'Not really. I've had the most bizarre phone call.'

'With Steve? Has he rung you at long last?'

'Well, it was Steve's phone, but it was Olivia on the other end.'

Helen glared at me and sank to the nearest chair. 'Oh, Rachel, are you okay? What did she want?'

'That's the weird thing, Helen. She says she knows about me and Steve and I'm welcome to him. She says she's set him free but she wasn't going to do that until she got what was rightfully hers.'

'And what do you think she meant by that?'

I sat and pondered for a moment. 'Well, I suppose she means the house, maybe his pension. I don't know. He isn't particularly well-off but I know they're comfortable. She said she hates him and has done for years.'

Helen stood up and went into the kitchen to get the corkscrew and a couple of glasses, then came back and poured the wine, handing me a glass.

'Drink,' she said. 'You need it. Sounds like she's spent the last seventeen years exacting some sort of revenge and now I guess she's found out he's been in contact with you again, she's decided enough's enough. Plus, he's probably told her he doesn't want to go to Spain and she's put two and two together.'

'She said she's set him free, Helen. But where is he?'

Helen smiled sympathetically. 'I don't know. Maybe he's decided he doesn't want to come up here and is staying in Great Willowby instead. Who knows what's been going on in that head of his? I know you love him and I'm glad for you but if he really wanted you, don't you think he'd be here now and not still at home with a wife who doesn't want him anymore?'

I gulped back the wine and reached for the bottle to pour another.

'I don't believe he never loved me, Helen. I really don't believe that. We've shared so much together and all those things he said to me at Claire's. He was so sincere. He meant every word, I know he did.' I could feel tears in my eyes and a large drop escaped onto my knee. Helen came and sat next to me, putting her arms around my shoulders.

'Listen, you don't know where he is and why he's not here with you but what you do know is that Olivia's found out about the two of you and you have a choice now. If he wants you and comes up to Scotland it's up to you whether you make a go of it. If he doesn't come up here then you need to start moving on and forget about him. You can't let him cause you all this misery. I didn't know you the first time he broke your heart but I can imagine what you went through. You know I'm here for you whatever happens, but don't be foolish, Rachel, remember how much he hurt you back then. You mustn't let him do that to you again'

As usual, Helen had a point and whilst I sobbed on her shoulder I could only think that once again, a few days before Christmas, my life had been thrown into turmoil by a man I loved with all my heart.

****

She went home at half past ten when I'd calmed down and she was sure she could leave me alone. I was tired out and decided to get into bed. I knew sleep wouldn't come easy but just resting in my warm cosy bed would have to do. Naturally I couldn't stop thinking about the phone call from Olivia, remembering her voice and recollecting how she sounded the same as when I answered her calls at Winterson's.

I knew she hadn't deserved what we'd done back in the 90's, our affair was wrong and we'd both known it from the start yet neither of us had stopped it happening. I wasn't going to end it because I was enjoying myself too much, having spent a few years living on my own and only ever having dates with

311

losers. Steve was a thrill. He excited me more than anyone ever had and I loved the adventure our relationship brought into my life. I liked the thought of people knowing about us at work and how Brian kept winking at me every time he saw Steve in reception. I loved all those meetings at Nightingale Woods and how Steve would sometimes come back to my flat. How he'd built some flat pack furniture for me and helped me fix the tap in the kitchen sink; how he'd surprised me with the lovely gold heart-shaped earrings for my birthday, ones I still wear today. I loved everything about him, but I'd always known at the back of my mind that someone was going to get hurt, and that proved in the end to be all three of us. I'm not sure who came off worse but if Olivia felt half as much devastation as I had back then, I couldn't help but empathise with the woman.

CHAPTER TWENTY-SIX

I wanted desperately to talk to Steve and find out where he was but my pride was too strong. Should I have rung his mobile and had Olivia answer it would probably have made me look more desperate than I really felt. He hadn't left her and moved to Cornfield and I knew one day I'd come to terms with that, but I spent many months after Olivia's phone call wondering what did happen to him.

I imagined him following Olivia to Spain and living a lie. And then I'd imagine him turning up on my doorstep with a suitcase and his tail between his legs. But the more time that passed, the stronger I became until I reached the decision that no matter what happened, I was not going to take Steve back again. His chances had run out, along with his excuses. I needed to move on with my life because I'd spent far too long living in a bubble, watching my self-esteem drown in murky water.

Claire and Melanie came to stay a few times in the New Year, concerned that I would cave in again and end up driving round to Steve's house, demanding answers. 'He's not worth it,' they kept telling me, as I finished off another bottle of Southern Comfort and cried myself to sleep. But underneath I knew they were right. He had broken my heart three times and I'd let him do it. My problem was I could never have hated him because I loved him too much.

I would leave the charity shop each lunch time and look around, up and down the street, for months afterwards, partly hoping he'd be there, waiting for me to finish work. Then I'd get home and realise it was my empty cottage that was waiting for me, and Steve never would.

I can never believe that he didn't love me. The time we spent together in the nineties was too intense, and then again the night we shared at Claire's apartment felt like all the confirmation I needed to be sure he wanted me. But looking back on our relationship, it's obvious he never loved me as much as I loved him. I would always have been second best in his life, and maybe one day I could have lived like that. But not now.

My name is Rachel Phillips; I'm free and single, though perhaps not quite so young anymore.

Acknowledgements:

Thanks go to my good friends and colleagues at Famous Five Plus, a wonderful bunch of talented authors, book reviewers and readers who have supported me immensely and been so patient with me. You have been there for me so often and especially during the formatting of this book. In particular, I want to thank Michelle Betham for helping me make the decision to 'get on with it'. Pauline Barclay, founder of Famous Five Plus, has been an incredible support and continuously there whenever I've needed advice. I also want to say a special thank you to Kim Nash, Jonty and Nikki Bywater, three very special people in my life who have also helped me to find the confidence to publish this book.

Thank you to Cathy Helms at Avalon Graphics for creating the beautiful cover design. Working with you has been an honour.

A very special mention goes to readers and loyal friends of my Blog, Crystal Jigsaw. You have all played your part in inspiring me to carry on writing; your support and encouragement has been phenomenal and many of you have stuck by me over the years, reading my drivel and my rants, laughing with me, crying with me and just being there for me. You are all appreciated, more than you know.

You can find my blog at:
www.crystaljigsaw.blogspot.co.uk

Famous Five Plus can be found at:
http://www.famousfiveplus.com

Printed in Great Britain
by Amazon.co.uk, Ltd.,
Marston Gate.